DRUID JUSTICE

A NEW ADULT URBAN FANTASY NOVEL

M.D. MASSEY

MODERN DIGITAL PUBLISHING

ONE

I sprinted between two cars, doing my best to stay ahead of the thundering footsteps behind me. The source of those footsteps was an enormous ogre, one who took great delight in tossing large objects at me as I zig-zagged through rows of wrecked vehicles. With speed born from a desire to avoid death by angry ogre, I ran for my life while keeping an eye out for O.F.O.s—ogre-impelled flying objects.

And just why was I being chased by an ogre, in the dead of night, through my Uncle Ed's glorious yard of junk? Because Finnegas the Seer, druid extraordinaire and my mentor in all things mystic and arcane, had thought it would be the perfect training exercise for yours truly.

This entire demented exercise was about forcing me to use the magic Finnegas had taught me in the months since I'd returned from Underhill. While I normally preferred to fight my way out of trouble, we'd recently concluded that I needed to develop other options. So, I had to end this Finn's way—the druid way.

Well, at least there are plenty of places to hide around here, I thought. *Too bad the environment also makes for excellent ogre ammunition.*

Junkyards were great locations for playing hide and seek, and my uncle's salvage yard was no exception. When wrecked cars arrived, we left them in the front lot while we sold parts off each car, a little at a time. Once they'd been stripped clean, those vehicles would be added to the stacks in back, where they waited to be crushed into neat cubes of scrap for recycling. But for now, those junkers would serve as cover for my retreat—and hopefully prevent my pursuer from smashing me like an empty beer can before I figured out a way to stop him.

As I scampered between cars, the ogre ran on top of them, giving him a distinct advantage in the speed department. I'd have done the same, but I was in my human form, so even a glancing hit from a flying engine block would ruin my day. Yet I knew I couldn't keep this up forever, and shifting into my Hyde-side wasn't an option. I'd been having... *issues* with it of late, which made me hesitant to let that side of me loose.

Suddenly, the booming cadence of cars being crushed by size twenty feet stopped. A quick glance over my shoulder revealed that the ogre's foot was stuck in the moon roof of an old Datsun 240Z. Sensing an opportunity for a peaceful resolution, I turned around to try to reason with him while I had the chance.

Once I got a good hard look at my pursuer, I couldn't help but question the wisdom of that decision.

The ogre was around eight feet tall and had shoulders half as wide, but he was mostly human-looking despite his size. His head was topped by a wild rat's nest of shoulder-length chestnut hair above a ruddy, almost boyish face. His brown, soulful eyes glowered beneath a thick, protruding forehead, and his crooked yellow teeth were on full display as he roared, struggling to free his foot from the Datsun's roof. Contrary to the rest of his appearance, the ogre wore a ratty Elmo t-shirt that stretched across his prodigious chest and belly, and a filthy canvas tarp that he'd wrapped around his loins like the world's largest diaper.

Honestly, he'd have been kind of cute, if he wasn't trying to kill me.

"Now, now, big guy—let's take a moment to sort this out. There's no need for this to get ugly..."

The ogre freed his foot while I was talking, then cut me off mid-sentence by flinging the detached bed of an '82 Chevy truck at me like a frisbee. I spun out of the way and watched as the projectile hit a stack of cars in the distance, causing them to sway precariously as they absorbed the impact. Worried that they might cut off my escape if they fell, I kept one eye on the stack and the other on the ogre as I did my best to calm him down.

"Seriously, dude, we can talk this out. I know Finnegas told you something about me that really pissed you off—but believe me, the old man is lying." I ducked a driver-side door that the ogre had torn off a Plymouth Duster, noting that his aim was getting better.

"C'mon, man—that car's a classic!" I yelled. The ogre paused from reaching for the rear door of the Duster. "Yeah, that one! If you have to keep throwing things, tear up that Hyundai over there."

The huge creature's brow furrowed as he pointed at a late

eighties Honda Prelude that still had some decent sheet metal on it. "No, that's a Honda. Try the ugly little silver car behind it." He pointed at the Hyundai I'd been referring to, and I nodded. "Yeah, that's the one. It's a worthless piece of junk, so feel free to tear pieces off it to your heart's content."

The ogre shrugged, then began pulling on the Hyundai's front bumper.

"Now, as I was saying, I'm sure we can sort this out..."

The beast yanked the bumper off with a metallic pop and a crunch. Realizing it was mostly plastic and hardly a worthy projectile, he tossed it to the side and smashed the passenger side window so he could pull the door off instead.

"... like a couple of civilized individuals. Maybe we could discuss our differences over dinner? I'm sure I could rustle up a couple of goats for you to eat, or maybe a nice healthy cow might be more to your liking?"

The ogre roared even louder than before as he yanked on the door again. *Just my luck to be chased by a vegan ogre*, I thought.

"Alright already—forget that I mentioned farm animals, okay? We can just do some salad and bread. I know this awesome little Greek place that makes the most amazing tzatziki sauce. Lots of vegetarian options there."

The ogre cocked his head, again pausing in his efforts to remove the Hyundai's door. *Now, time to reel him in.*

"You like that idea, huh? So, how about I go pick us up some feta salad, a little falafel—with some sides of baba ghanouj, tabouli, and hummus? Then, we can sit down and enjoy a nice meal and work this whole thing out. Heck, I'll even skip ordering chicken for myself... whaddaya say, big guy?"

As soon as I mentioned eating chicken, the ogre tore the door from the Hyundai with a single mighty pull. He turned those baby browns on me, glowering as he huffed and puffed; whether that was in anger or exertion, I couldn't be certain. With a snort and a grunt, he crushed the car door between his hands, forming it into a roughly basketball-sized sphere of jagged metal.

Nope, that's definitely anger. Here we go...

"What, was it the chicken comment?" I asked, hoping against hope that I might salvage the situation.

He compressed the car door down to the size of a volleyball, scuffing the dirt with his feet like a bull ready to charge.

"Well, I guess that answers my question. And just when we were starting to make progress."

The ogre opened that huge mouth of his and roared. Despite the twenty feet or so between us, I could smell the stench of his breath, which reeked of wild garlic and canned beans. He bounced the ball of metal once in his right hand, then palmed the sphere in both of his ginormous mitts.

I backed up on the balls of my feet, preparing to dive out of the way at the very last instant. "So, I guess this means no Greek food?"

The ogre exhaled in a long growl as he wound up in a running start, like a high school jock preparing to smash the class nerd at dodgeball. Then, he released the ball of metal with a loud grunt, throwing the damned thing like Pedro Martinez walking Reggie Sanders with a mean fastball.

I'd say that means no, I thought, narrowly avoiding getting my head taken off by eighty pounds of cheap Korean metal. I didn't even bother looking back as I bolted for the relative safety of the stacks at the back of the yard.

THANKS FOR THE AWESOME LESSON, Finn, I thought as the ogre roared somewhere behind me. I dashed between two rows of stacked, stripped cars and reflected on my recent life choices.

I'd been at odds with Finnegas since my girlfriend Jesse had died a few years back, mostly because I'd blamed him for her death, but also because he'd become an alcoholic and drug addict shortly thereafter. But he'd eventually cleaned himself up, and events of late had caused me to reassess our relationship and patch things up with him. We'd recently resumed my druid apprenticeship, and since then he'd been coming up with ever more devious and demented "lessons" by which to teach me the ways of druidry.

Tonight's lesson apparently involved a lot of running, ducking, diving, and rolling to avoid being turned into a hamburger by a seven-hundred-pound ogre named Elmo. Earlier, Finnegas had told me the name had been pinned on the ogre because he was a fan of the public television character. My mentor had also mentioned that Elmo kept quite an extensive collection of memorabilia featuring his eponymous idol, in his burrow beneath a trash dump near Rocko the red cap's trailer park.

Obviously, he'd fed me that info so I'd feel sorry for the ogre—and it had worked. Ogres were normally gentle, sedate creatures, and not at all prone to violence or anger. They just wanted to be left alone for the most part, and most of the other supernaturals were more than happy to give them a wide berth. The creatures were considered by many to be the outcasts of the fae world, more than lower-order fae like the red caps or other half-fae supernaturals like Finnegas' assistant, Maureen, or my friend Sabine.

Unfortunately for them, ogres were not a unique race of their own, but instead the product of a union between a higher fae and a human who carried latent giant DNA. Mixing one supernatural race with human DNA usually turned out okay... but throw another species into the mix and the outcome could be unpredictable, to say the least. Typically, the offspring ended up being almost giant-sized, which was the first strike against them. Adding insult to injury, such offspring were often deformed in some manner, and no higher fae would ever accept a physical defect in one of their children.

Fae were not the most tolerant creatures, and their caste system was based on physical beauty as well as magical power. Higher fae were typically supernaturally attractive, lithe, and graceful. They lorded over the lower-order fae, which included the dwarven folk like the red caps, anthropomorphs and hybrids like kelpies and fuaths, and monsters like nuckelavees and oilliphéists. At the bottom of the heap you had outcasts like ogres, who got shit on by everyone in the fae world.

Finnegas was well aware of how I loved to root for the underdog, and that's why he'd chosen an ogre as my sparring partner for tonight's lesson. He knew I wasn't about to treat this ogre like the rest of his kind had, because I hated bullies and I hated fae bullies even more. Besides that, ogres tended to be simple creatures, and I suspected Elmo thought this was all just a game. Which meant I needed to find other than violent means of dealing with him... and that would require relying on my somewhat anemic magic-wielding skills.

Though the ogre was an impressive specimen—basically a larger-than-life version of a He-Man action figure—he wasn't very nimble or bright. So, after reasoning with him had failed, I led him into the depths of the junkyard through the narrow, twisting labyrinth of stacked junked cars, twelve to fifteen feet high. I'd hoped to lose him in the stacks, but Elmo had proven to be hellaciously fast in the straightaway. And he'd displayed a peculiar knack for sniffing out my hiding spots.

I ducked around a corner and squeezed through a narrow gap between two rows of stacked cars. After turning a few more corners, I crouched behind the bed of a '66 Ranchero, gasping for air like a fish at a skydiving convention. Once the wheezing in my chest and the rushing in my ears settled down, I cocked an ear to determine Elmo's position.

Silence—I must have ditched him. I leaned back against the cars behind me, resting my hands on top of my head to make it easier to breathe. I'd barely gathered my thoughts when I heard the ogre's plodding footsteps headed my way, followed by a resounding *crunch* as seven hundred pounds of ogre collided with the other side of the stack I'd been leaning on.

The impact transferred through the Ranchero, throwing me across the aisle and into the opposite stack. As I landed, my head bounced off the B-post of an eighties-era Taurus. I was still seeing stars and shaking it off when I heard the distinct creaking and groaning sound that every junkyard employee dreads. I didn't need to look to know that I was about to be buried under several tons of American, European, and Japanese steel.

Without a thought, I instinctively dove to the side. As I

did, my pants snagged on a piece of jagged metal, making me hit the ground at an awkward angle. On impact, there was a loud *crack* accompanied by a sharp pain between my neck and shoulder. I tried using my left arm to help me stand, wincing as I felt and heard the grinding agony of broken bones rubbing together in my shoulder. Ignoring the pain, I left the arm dangling and braced my other hand on my knee as I stood up.

I had little time to assess my injuries. With a tremendous crash, three cars fell into the space I'd just occupied, and I knew Elmo would be close behind. Cursing my stupidity, I cradled my injured arm as I sprinted off into the dark. Hopefully, I could lose the ogre long enough to figure out a humane way to stop him from accidentally killing me *on purpose*.

I MANAGED to flee to a corner of the junkyard where Elmo couldn't easily go, a tight little mouse's maze made of cars being prepped for the crusher. I'd enjoyed playing in this area of the junkyard as a kid, taking every opportunity to lose myself for hours on end. Mom and I had visited the junkyard whenever she needed my uncle's auto repair skills, and there were always nooks and crannies back behind the cars where adults wouldn't dare venture. The crusher stacks were continually being replaced with new cars, which meant every time I returned there were new areas to explore. For a chubby, bullied kid, it was like having my own private fortress of solitude.

Today, I'd lucked out by finding a gap between the stacks

big enough for an adult to squeeze through. Holding my injured arm close to my side, I shimmied and squirmed deeper and deeper into the stacks, until several dozen tons of metal stood between me and the ogre.

I moved my arm experimentally to determine the nature of my injury, only to be met with more grinding agony and pain. No doubt about it; I'd broken my collarbone. It was an injury I was familiar with, only because I'd done the same thing as a kid after attempting to emulate my favorite superhero's powers of flight by jumping off my neighbor's picnic table. I also remembered well how much it had hurt to get the break set by our family doctor. Doc Simmons was a retired military physician, and since my dad was killed-in-action he'd always waived our co-pay. But damn, was that guy hardcore. He'd set my shoulder without any anesthetic, and hell if I was looking forward to doing it again as an adult.

But right now, I had bigger problems. Elmo's earth-shaking footsteps reverberated just beyond the relative safety of the cars and trucks between us. Every so often, he'd bellow and bang on the first row of cars protecting me, just to let me know he knew where I was hiding. At first it wasn't a big deal, but after a few hits, the cars started to shift inward. Considering the rate he was going, it wouldn't be long before I'd be crushed between the cars or trapped deep within the stacks.

"I am going to give Finnegas a fucking earful when I get out of here," I muttered.

Elmo must have heard me, because he began hammering at the cars with increased enthusiasm. I slithered farther into the stacks, until I came to a tiny little clearing with the dark summer sky visible above. There, I found an intact 1971

Corolla coupe, all by its lonesome with the seats left inside and decent rubber on the rims.

Leaving the seats and tires on a car you were sending to the crusher was a big no-no, so I figured an employee had hidden it back here while they saved money to buy it from Ed —also a no-no and grounds for termination if he figured out what they'd done. Fortunately, their screw-up worked to my favor, because it gave me an idea.

Druidic magic wasn't like other types of magic, because druids preferred to work with the elements rather than against them. Our magic was subtle, involving more finesse than brute strength. And while it wasn't always as powerful as other types of magic, druids could work spells on the fly and get immediate results, a big plus when you were under a time crunch. Not only that, but our magic didn't require us to use magical power sinks or foci, which was also quite the advantage in a pinch.

Finesse was exactly what I needed right now, because I didn't want to kill Elmo—I just needed to stop him from causing me further harm. I'd thought about calling up a strong wind to nudge a stack of cars on top of him, but that would definitely injure him, possibly mortally. I also considered using a burst of heat and light to frighten him away, but I had no open flames nearby and little light to work with, so there was nothing from which I might create such a spell. If I'd had some water handy I might have been able to submerge him in it and freeze it—but again, there was nothing around that would suffice.

There was, however, one thing I had a great deal of around me: metal. And what was metal good for? *Conduction.* If I could store up enough electricity in the chassis of the Corolla and release it into Elmo all at once—without electrocuting myself—it could act like a sort of supernatural stun-gun, knocking him out. It was a gamble, but I was out of options. The ogre was still banging away on the cars outside, inching them closer and closer to the one I was in, so I had to work fast if I was going to stop him.

After I clambered through the window, I made sure I wasn't touching any metal inside the car by pulling my arms in and my feet up in the seat. Then, I cleared my mind and extended my awareness to the air and metal surrounding me, sensing as the mixture of elemental gasses, water vapor, and dust flowed around the little vintage Corolla. I concentrated on the atoms and molecules in the air itself, willing them to become positive- and negative-charged particles around the metal frame and body of the vehicle. As I did, I coaxed the static charges I'd created so they'd leap from the air into the metal, which was thankfully not grounded at all.

Soon, little sparks of electricity were jumping and arcing all over the surface of the Toyota. Satisfied that I'd stored enough magical electricity in the car's metal, I focused on the nearby stack of cars inching its way toward the Corolla. Finally, they were almost in contact. I grunted as I waited for the next blow, straining against the electrical charge I'd built up, my force of will a dam that held the magical energy in place.

BOOM! Elmo hit the stack one more time, causing the cars to move the final few centimeters needed to make contact with the Toyota. I released the spell, sending all that pent up electrical energy into the cars around me and channeling it toward the ogre. My efforts were rewarded by a loud *zap!*, followed by an earth-shaking thud.

The smell of ozone and burned hair met me as I crawled out of the stacks. Elmo was laid out nearby, snoring like a fat man sleeping off his Thanksgiving dinner. Finnegas was there too, leaning against the crusher as he puffed on a hand-rolled cigarette.

"Took you long enough," he quipped.

Cradling my arm, I took a seat in the dirt against the nearest car and laid my head back against the cool surface of the fender with a frustrated sigh.

"I honestly and truly hate your guts right now, you know that?"

Finn grinned and spit a fleck of tobacco off his lip. "So, I guess that means no Greek food?"

TWO

A few hours later at sunup, I sat nursing a cup of coffee with Finn while we watched Elmo chase dragonflies nearby. After setting my collarbone by hand, Finn had spent the last few hours healing me via magical means. Finn's bone-setting skills were adequate if not expert, and if I'd screamed and cussed a little as he pushed and pulled the ends of my collarbone into place, it'd been a small price to pay to avoid a huge emergency room bill.

"Our ogre friend over there doesn't exactly seem like the smash and bash type," I said as I watched Elmo use the utmost care to cradle an iridescent, green and blue dragonfly in his paving-stone-sized hands. "How'd you get him mad enough to attack me, anyway?"

Finn puffed on his cigarette, exhaling smoke through his nostrils. "I promised him ice cream to get him over here. Then I told him you were another ogre in disguise, and that you'd stolen our ice cream money."

"That's pretty flipping devious."

"But effective," the old man replied. "Once I had him convinced you could take whatever he could dish out, he was more than willing to give chase. Which reminds me..."

Finn reached into a nearby ice chest, waving away a cloud of dry ice fog to retrieve five gallons of Neapolitan ice cream. He whistled to get the ogre's attention before tossing the cartons at Elmo one by one. The ogre's face lit up as he snatched the cartons from the air, squeezing them until huge glops of ice cream oozed into his mouth and dribbled down his chin. He didn't seem to mind the mess, and I couldn't help but chuckle at the expression of sheer delight plastered across his face as he enjoyed his prize.

I took another sip of coffee, enjoying the early morning air. The sharp aroma of fresh-brewed coffee and the acrid tang of tobacco smoke combined with the heady odors of gasoline and engine oil proved to be a strangely comforting combination. I'd been living in my uncle's junkyard way too long, if these were the scents and smells that put me in my comfort zone.

"How'd you know I wouldn't hulk out on the poor guy?" I asked.

Finnegas scratched his nose and flicked ash off his cigarette. "For one, you've gained better control since training with the alpha. And besides that, I know what a bleeding heart you are when it comes to the downtrodden."

The alpha in question was Samson, head of the local werewolf pack. He'd helped me learn how to control my ability to shift, a process I wouldn't care to repeat under any circumstances. Having your guts ripped out and being bled within an inch of your life, then being healed only to do it all over again... well, it wasn't on my list of all-time favorite experiences.

Not that I wasn't grateful for Samson's tutelage, though. It was just too bad that it could have been all for naught.

"The magic's changed, since I got back from Underhill," I stated as I stared into the distance. "I get... urges, when I shift now. And it feels like something is *missing* inside me when I shift, too."

Finnegas raised an eyebrow. "Something like empathy?" I nodded once, and the old man exhaled forcefully. "Cú Chulainn experienced the same when the ríastrad came over him, although as time went on he was able to retain more and more of his humanity as he changed. Strange that the process should be happening in reverse for you, so soon after you've managed to gain control over it."

"You think it might have something to do with being exposed to the magic of Underhill, or the Treasures?"

Finn rubbed his chin. "Maybe—or it could be another kind of fae magic. They've been throwing curses at you nonstop since you got back, you know."

"Oh, I'm well aware. And if it wasn't for the lot of them being cut off from Underhill, I'm sure one of their spells would've gotten through already."

Months before, I'd used the Four Treasures of the Tuatha Dé Danann to close off the portals between the magical realm of Underhill and earth, effectively cutting off all the earthbound fae from the bulk of their magic. This had weakened the higher fae considerably, placing even their most powerful magic-users on par with human mages. And it had caused minor, but annoying, complications for some of the lower-order fae as well. Most of them still hadn't forgiven me, and probably wouldn't for centuries to come.

"But...?"

"But they haven't, and I've been diligent in reinforcing my wards and charms each morning and night. Trust me, I'd know if one of their curses snuck through. No, I don't think that has anything to do with what's happening to me."

The old man drummed his fingers on his thigh. "Still, I don't like it. Best that you don't use your ability to shift, unless it's absolutely necessary. At least, not until we get a handle on what's going on."

I nodded. "Way ahead of you, old man."

"Hah! That'll be the day." Finnegas wheezed a chuckle that turned into a coughing fit. I narrowed my eyes and sat up slightly, but he waved me off as he recovered. "Just the after-effects of healing you earlier. Forces me to feel my age, which isn't necessarily a bad thing. Never hurts to be reminded that you're mortal... especially when you're well past your expiration date." He glanced sideways at me. "Time's short, you know."

"So you keep telling me."

Finnegas had broached this conversation several times since I'd been back from Underhill. The gist of it was that his magic wasn't as strong as it once was, he was getting old, and he needed to pass on everything he could to me while he was able. The subtext was that, if I applied everything he could teach me, I might be in his shoes many centuries hence. Frankly, it all freaked me out a bit, so I tended to avoid delving into the topic whenever it came around.

Finnegas clapped his hands on his knees and stood up. "Fine then, we'll discuss it later. I'm going to take our ogre-friend back to his burrow, before the morning crew shows up. Give that shoulder another hour or so, and it should be good as new."

"Good as something," I muttered as Finnegas walked off and lit up yet another cigarette. "You really should quit smoking, you know!" I yelled after him.

He waved my words off absently while casting a spell that altered the appearance of the ogre. Now, Elmo merely looked like a too-tall human instead of the hulking behemoth he really was. For a moment, I wondered how Finnegas was going to get the big fella back to his trash dump, then I saw him leading Elmo to one of the flatbed tow trucks.

The ogre hopped on the back of the truck, latching on to the light bar over the cab with a huge smile. Finnegas cast a "look away" spell on him, and they were off. I hoped Elmo wouldn't smash his face into an overpass on the way home. Austin had enough problems with road maintenance as it was.

As I watched them drive away, I took another sip of coffee, grimacing when I realized it had grown cold. I said a few words in ancient Gaelic as I rubbed the mug, relying on friction for the energy to fuel the spell. The cup warmed in my hands as the magic amplified the small amount of heat I'd created, and seconds later my next sip was piping hot.

Magic does have its uses, I thought. *When it's not turning you into a cold-blooded killer, that is.*

A FEW HOURS LATER, a call from Sal the red cap roused me from a much-needed nap. Red caps, or *fear dearg*, were a type of lower-order fae once known for waylaying human travelers, brutally torturing and killing them so they could soak their hats in their victims' blood. These days, modern red caps ran low-level cons, protection rackets, and vice schemes, working in organized groups patterned after the mob. They mostly preyed on the dregs of fae society, although they weren't against victimizing the odd human as well.

"Colin—izzat you, paisan?" Sal, his boss Rocko, and their entire crew all dressed and spoke like east coast mobsters. Being around them was like being in an episode of *The Sopranos*, but in miniature. Since coming to somewhat friendly terms with the *fear dearg*, I'd learned to ignore it.

Besides, they were one of the few fae groups who didn't currently have a major beef with me. As it turned out, when I'd cut the fae off from most of their magic it had opened up a world of profitable opportunities for Rocko and his crew. Of late, they'd been doing a significant amount of business dealing in black market glamours and "look away, go away" charms, for those fae who now lacked the ability to cast illusory magic themselves.

I cleared my throat as I put the phone on speaker. "Who else would it be, Sal? The pope?"

"Har, har, very funny. I just thought it might be that hunter girlfriend of yours, answering your phone behind your back. You know how these dames can be. Far be it from me to open my trap and say somethin' that'd get you in hot water with your woman."

"Um, we don't exactly have that sort of relationship. I'm

relatively certain she trusts me enough to respect my privacy."

The dwarf chuckled. "Yeah, you keep telling yourself that. Anyway, 'dis is a business call. We got a lead on whoever's been knocking off fae."

Sal—rather, Rocko by way of Sal—had recently hired me to look into several suspicious deaths of fae in the area. The killings had started occurring not long after I'd cut the fae off from Underhill, while I was still laying low in the aftermath. At first, it had just been low-level fae, the sort of nameless nobodies who comprised the bottom echelons of fae society. But over the last few weeks, the killings had escalated to include prominent fae—including a few who were close to Queen Maeve.

Ah, Maeve. Once my benefactor, she'd long been fond of pulling my strings and making me dance to her tune. I'd finally grown tired of being her errand boy, thus my decision to level the magical playing field between fae and humans. And despite the fact she was my very, very distant ancestor, that single act of defiance had made me persona non grata with Maeve's court... or what remained of it after my trip to Underhill.

A nervous cough from Sal brought my mind back to the present. "So, what's up, Sal? Did another corpse pop up?"

"Bingo, druid. Plus, this time they caught the killer red-handed—literally."

I greatly doubted that the killer had been caught at the scene. After personally investigating half a dozen fae deaths, I knew only one thing for certain; the killer was no dummy or stooge. They had access to magical means of covering their tracks and were very good at doing so. It was highly unlikely they'd slip up at this stage in the game.

But whoever this scapegoat was, they might have witnessed something that could lead me to the killer. It was definitely worth following up on.

"Who's the suspect, Sal?"

"Some ogre who lives in the trash dump behind the trailer park. Elwood, Elmer, Elmore... some shit like that."

"Elmo? You mean to tell me that the fae are trying to pin these deaths on *Elmo*?"

Sal inhaled sharply. "Sheesh, druid, what do you expect us to think? They caught the mook covered in blood, huddled over the body—which incidentally happened to be found at the very trash dump where the ogre lives. Besides, you know ogres and fae don't get along. Seems cut and dry if you ask me. All we need is for you to verify the evidence so the fae can sleep easy at night again."

"Sal, Elmo wouldn't hurt a fly—at least not intentionally. He's the poster child for the gentle giant type, and hardly smart enough to mastermind all those deaths."

Sal tsked. "I guess maybe I could see that. He's never been the sharpest knife in the drawer, that's for sure. And to be honest, he's never caused us any trouble either—he just mostly sticks to himself. You think maybe someone framed him up?"

"I can't really say without being at the scene." I rubbed sleep out of my eyes and looked at the time. "Can you just keep everyone calm until I get there?"

"Hmm..."

"What Sal?"

"Well, about that... the fair folk are pretty riled around

here, and it looked to me like they were working themselves up to do something bad to that ogre."

"Shit." I ran my fingers through my hair. "I'm headed over now. Try to make sure no one hurts Elmo, and if necessary tell them anyone who does will answer to me."

Sal remained silent for the span of a few heartbeats. "You sure that's a good idea, druid? You're not exactly popular around here, you know."

"I'm well aware, Sal. But as Machiavelli said, 'It's better to be feared than loved.'"

"Sounds like my kind of guy. Did he write books or something?"

"Or something. Just make sure we don't end up with two deaths today, alright?"

"Alright, druid. I'll spread the word."

"You do that," I growled, pulling on a t-shirt and some Van's before grabbing my keys and heading out the door.

I GOT to Rocko's trailer park in record time—and if I broke a few traffic laws on the way over, that was between me and the Gremlin's speedometer. Since garnering the hatred of most of the fae population, I'd increased the runes and wards on my vehicle, including some "look away and forget I was here" spells that also helped me avoid speeding tickets. Now, whenever a traffic cop saw me speeding by, their eyes just sort of passed right over my car. It wasn't as good as invisibility, and it wouldn't fool anyone with more than an inkling of power, but it had helped me lose a few tails and escape some fines. I called that a win.

I drove to a small playground in the very back of the trailer park, where the local kids had loosened some boards in the fence to allow them access to the empty lot around back. My friend Hemi and I had discovered their hangout several months ago while investigating the abduction of Sal's son. Despite being fae, the local teens were typical kids, and they preferred to smoke and drink away from the prying eyes of their parents.

A crowd of angry fae had gathered at the playground. More were crowding the hole in the fence, and beyond from what I could tell. The locals hissed and spat as I shoved my way through the crowd, but they all gave me a wide berth as soon as they recognized me. I was lucky these fae were lower order, because their lives hadn't been affected all that much when I'd closed the gateways to Underhill.

In fact, many run-of-the-mill fae didn't seem to be affected by it at all. The lower fae mostly possessed small magics, innate talents that didn't require them to draw on Underhill's power. And those who'd relied on spells to mask their physical anomalies from the human world, well... they'd simply purchased charms from Rocko and his gang that served the same purpose.

Of course, that didn't keep the lower fae from despising me for what I'd done. For one, the fae hated it when mortals pulled one over on them. That made me persona non grata on principle alone. Plus, they resented having to pay for spells that had been child's play to cast before I'd shut the gates down. Yet to them, the level of enmity they felt toward me only merited casting minor curses and the like. For example, making my milk spoil faster, or affecting my luck so I couldn't find a decent parking space—small annoyances that my wards easily intercepted.

But the higher-order fae? If this crowd had been made up of higher fae, I'd have already sprouted a knife in my back.

A world-weary female fae in rollers, a ratty terrycloth robe, and house shoes gave me a look that was equal parts languor and contempt as I ducked through the gap in the fence. She might have been pretty with a little makeup or the right glamour, but without any magic to hide her age she looked like a thirty-something with way too many miles on the odometer.

She took a drag on a long, thin cigarette as she regarded me with a sneer. "Why don't you go back to your own kind, druid? Ain't nobody got any use for you around here."

I adjusted the strap on my Craneskin Bag, ignoring her as I moved past. She spat at my feet and made a few arcane gestures, muttering under her breath. The weak curse slid off my wards like water off a duck's back, and not for the first time I considered adding a reflection spell to my wards. But that'd just be pouring salt in an open wound. I dismissed the thought as I continued to push my way through the crowd.

None present wanted anything to do with me, so the crowd instantly parted to allow me access to the object of their fury. Voices died down as more and more fae recognized my face. As I took in the scene, their angry shouts turned to muttered curses and thinly veiled threats of violence. At least now their anger was directed at me, instead of the bloody, cowering form at the center of the crowd.

Small victories, and all that.

Elmo crouched just a few feet in front of me, cowering over a prone form that I could just barely make out around his bulk. Deep horizontal gashes ran across his back, with dried blood clearly visible where his t-shirt had been sliced open. He'd also been stoned, and an assortment of bloody bricks, rocks, bottles, and chunks of asphalt littered the ground nearby.

I walked around so I could get a better look. Elmo's face was swollen and purple on one side, his lip had been split wide open, and he had more defensive cuts on his forearms and the back of his hands. Like the wounds across his shoulders, these weren't as fresh as the cuts and scrapes he'd sustained from the projectiles the crowd had thrown at him.

Fools. One glance at his injuries should have told anyone with half a lick of sense that he wasn't the killer.

"Elmo," I whispered. The ogre started at the sound of my voice. I reached out a hand, gently touching him on the shoulder. He flinched away with a whining growl. "Hey, it's okay, big guy. I'm going to get you out of here, alright?"

Elmo looked up at me, tilting his head and furrowing his brow all at once. I caught a spark of recognition in those baby brown eyes, and he seemed to calm down a bit. I handed him a candy bar from my bottomless, enchanted Craneskin Bag, then stood up to address the crowd.

"He's not your killer. Go home."

For a second no one spoke, then a male fae piped up from the back. "Damned ogre killed Jeretta!" the man shouted. "He's gotta' pay!"

A chorus of shouts and muttered agreements followed the man's outburst, which I ignored. I glanced down, and for the first time I recognized the lifeless form beneath the ogre. Pink-tipped, dirty-blonde hair framing a too-thin face, and hazel eyes fixed in a permanent stare. Jeretta was a mute seer who'd been a witness in the abduction of Sal's child months before.

Damn it. Why'd it have to be a kid?

I closed my eyes and shook my head, then opened them and leveled my gaze at the crowd. "Have some sense. The only wounds I see on Elmo are defensive wounds on his back and forearms. He's covered in blood, sure—but most of it's his. And none of it is on his hands or under his nails, which is where it would be if he'd had anything to do with this poor girl's death. If anything, Elmo was trying to protect her from her killer, but I suspect he arrived too late to do her much good."

"The druid lies!" some harridan shouted. "He's in on it!"

I rubbed my face as I sucked air through my teeth. "Really? You think that I came down here, directed the ogre to kill the girl, covered my tracks, drove away, and then turned right back around so I could get caught?"

"You've killed fae before!" a nameless male voice shouted.

I sighed. "Go home, people. The killer isn't here"—that I knew of—"and you're trampling any evidence that might reveal who did this. The best thing you can all do is to head back to your homes, so I can figure out who killed poor Jeretta."

"You heard him—go home!" Rocko and two of his crew forced their way through the crowd, using two-by-fours and baseball bats for leverage. "I said, go home!" the dwarf bellowed as he and his boys took up positions between the crowd and Elmo, Jeretta, and me.

With no small amount of grumbling, the crowd dispersed. Once they'd all gone, Rocko turned and squatted next to us.

He brushed some hair from Jeretta's pale face, scratching his nose with a heavy sigh.

"Damn it, druid—she was just a girl, a damned silly kid who never hurt nobody or nuthin'. And now I gotta tell her parents their daughter is dead. Fuck!"

Elmo shied away from Rocko's angry outburst, although the ogre continued to shield Jeretta's body with his own. I laid a hand on the ogre's shoulder. "Elmo—Elmo! It's okay, you don't have to protect her anymore. Rocko and his boys can take it from here."

The ogre looked at me, then down at the girl. A single tear rolled down his cheek, falling to land on Jeretta's blood-stained shirt. I took him by the hand and led him off to the side, where I left him with more candy bars.

"Any idea who did this?" Rocko asked, and I shook my head. He pointed a thumb in Elmo's direction. "He won't last an hour, after my boys and I leave. You got someplace safe for him to go?"

I sniffed and nodded. "Yeah. I'll get him out of here, just as soon as I finish examining the murder scene for evidence." My eyes searched the trampled ground in vain. "Although I doubt there's much left after your tenants tromped all over the place."

"Can you blame them? This makes seven bodies since summer started. Nobody knows who the fuck is doing it, and Maeve and her people... never mind." Rocko knuckled his forehead and squeezed his eyes shut. "Just please tell me you'll catch this fucker, druid."

I glanced down at Jeretta's mangled torso. While her face was untouched, her body was a jigsaw of physical insults. She'd been stabbed dozens of times and from multiple angles, as if once hadn't been enough for the killer—or killers. Her wounds were gruesome, forcing me to swallow a bit of coffee and bile before looking away.

What was going through my mind was, *How in the hell did I let myself get dragged into this?* But what came out of my mouth was, "Sure, Rocko. I'll do my best."

THREE

After Rocko and his men chased the crowd away, they wrapped Jeretta's body in blankets, showing quite a bit more care than I would have expected from a bunch of bloodthirsty *fear dearg*. They carried the body off on a makeshift litter they'd hobbled together from discarded lumber and a dirty, paint-stained tarp. The shifty red cap claimed that his "business" required him to be elsewhere, but I suspected the real reason for Rocko's speedy retreat was simply that he didn't want to clash too hard with his customers.

I'd just gotten Elmo settled in with some candy and a fidget-spinner when three mangy-looking individuals came walking out of the weeds opposite the trailer park fence. They carried an assortment of two-by-fours and roofing hatchets, and something told me they weren't there to replace the shingles. As they came into view, each of them spread out to flank me, indicating they'd attack in a pincher formation if things got ugly.

I hung my head and sighed before taking stock of my

aggressors. The leader wore a dirty wife beater over a dusty pair of gray Dickies, and faded leather work boots that looked a few decades old. He was of average height, but based on the breadth of his shoulders and the swell of his arms, he was no stranger to hard labor. His face was pasty-white and pockmarked, with blemishes here and there that spoke of unclean living and a general lack of physical hygiene. A greasy combover topped off the ensemble nicely.

About ten feet to my right stood a larger and younger version of the leader, wearing grease-stained blue coveralls tucked into unlaced combat boots. Of course, his coveralls were unzipped to his navel, revealing hairy man-boobs and a gut that would have indicated pregnancy in someone of the opposite sex.

On my other side stood a smaller version of both. He was dressed similarly in a wife beater, dirty jeans, and a scuffed pair of leather work shoes, just with more hair and a pair of wire-rimmed spectacles perched on the end of his nose. The guy reminded me of a skinny John Denver. That is, if the singer had stopped performing in Muppets specials and started cooking and smoking meth in his early twenties.

A quick glance at each of them in the magical spectrum clued me in on what I was dealing with. They were hobgoblins, minor fae who'd once inhabited rural homes, doing odd jobs and household chores at night in exchange for saucers of milk and crusts of bread left by the owners each morning. They were nasty creatures, easily offended and prone to spitefulness. Many a farmer and housemaid had experienced soured milk, broken looms, and blighted crops at the hands of their kind.

Naturally, I assumed this confrontation was unlikely to have a peaceful resolution.

"Fellas," I said as I looked at each of them in turn. My eyes settled back on the leader, but I kept track of the others in my peripheral vision. "You guys lost, or just here to sell Girl Scout cookies? If it's the latter, I'll take two boxes of Thin Mints and a box of Do-si-dos."

"'Ark at he, dad," the larger of the two goons said. "Thinks he's funny, this'un does."

The leader spat and shook his head. "Ya know why we're here, druid. Just let us have the ogre, and no one gets hurt."

The two of them spoke with what I thought might have been a West Country English accent, although there was a bit of Texas twang mixed in as well. I couldn't decide if their accents were annoying or charming, but based on the fact they were here to do Elmo harm, I settled on annoying.

"Oh, you know, I can't do that. I have a doubles match later at the country club, and I need a partner." I jerked a thumb at the ogre over my shoulder. "You wouldn't know it by looking at him, but Elmo has a wicked top spin serve."

"The hard way it is, then," the leader replied. "Make it hurt, boys."

The smaller one cackled as they both closed in on me. "Lucky for us, that's our specialty."

I'd been expecting this, so I already had my hand inside my Craneskin Bag when they made their move. "I really don't have time for this shit, so let me make myself clear," I said as I drew two-and-a-half feet of flaming steel from my bag. "The ogre stays."

The two younger hobgoblins shied away from the flaming sword, but their father seemed unimpressed. "It's just druid tricks, just some flaming pitch on a blade. He can't fight all three of us at once. We jump him on the count of three, boys."

I shook my head. "I wouldn't do that, if I were you."

The older hobgoblin began his countdown. "One..."

The two boys' eyes darted back and forth between their dad and my sword. The bigger one gulped audibly as he tightened his grip on his two-by-four. "You sure that's a good idea, Dad? Sword looks real enough to me."

Their father scowled. "Ain't no real flaming swords been seen in centuries! Reach down and grab a pair, boys, so we can kill this ogre and be done with it." He spun his hatchet in tight circles. "Two..."

I held the sword loosely out at my side, keeping my eyes on the dad while I made sure the others were visible peripherally. "I'm telling you guys, this is a really bad idea. Last warning."

"He's bluffing!" the smallest of them screeched. "Right, Dad?"

"S'right, so be ready." Their father took a deep breath, ready to give his sons the final command to attack. Nobody ever said hobgoblins were smart.

"Three," I said, raising the sword as I spun it in a broad, blinding arc. With a single smooth cut, I sheared each of their weapons off neatly, just above their hands. The heads of their hatchets and lengths of lumber clattered to the ground. I spun the sword in a flourish, ending with the tip resting in the dirt, where it sizzled and spat as the flames melted tiny pebbles and burned off organic matter.

"Sword looks real enough to me," I said as I looked the leader in the eye. "Now, are we through here?"

He dropped the smoldering stump of a hatchet handle from his hand, and backed away from me. "Aye, we're done. My apologies, druid."

"Apology accepted. Now, shoo."

They ran, and I watched to make sure they were gone before I put the sword back in my Bag.

AFTER I'D SENT the hobgoblins on their way, I spent a few minutes going over the scene, trying to glean even the smallest bit of information that might point to the real killer. My primary witness, who'd most certainly seen the killer or killers, was unfortunately either unable or unwilling to communicate verbally. Elmo sat quietly off to the side while I completed my search, completely withdrawn.

The crime scene had been utterly destroyed by the crowd of angry fae, but I knew that whoever had killed Jeretta had approached the scene on foot. There were no roads leading back here, so unless they'd flown in they must have left some trace of their passing. I widened my search pattern, looking for footprints, bent stalks of grass, or the telltale scent of magic that might have been used to cover such evidence.

I worked in concentric circles, ranging farther and farther from where Jeretta's body had been found. Ultimately, it wasn't any physical evidence that alerted me to someone's passing, but the lack of said evidence. I missed it on my first pass, but the second time around I sensed an *absence* that faintly tickled my Spidey-senses.

I closed my eyes, extending my awareness the way Finnegas had been teaching me to do recently. I knelt and touched the earth, feeling the natural thrum and rhythm of the land through my fingertips. Slowing my breathing, I allowed the background noises to take center stage in my mind, where I separated them into their individual components. Then I focused on the warm, muggy morning air, taking time to identify each scent that drifted on the lazy breeze. Finally, I opened my eyes, expanding my focus to take in the entire scene all at once, including the sights on the periphery of my vision.

After repeating the process over and over again, I'd come full circle back to the area that had initially piqued my interest.

Every other vector approaching the crime scene appeared completely normal. For three-hundred-fifty-nine degrees around, I detected the passing of various small animals and insects, as well as the effects of the wind and precipitation on the earth and vegetation. But along this line, it was like someone had wiped it clean of every single odor and trail.

Magic, for sure... tricky, tricky magic.

There was an empty wrongness to the area, not unlike what might be left by necromancy. But instead of pure death, it was as if nature had merely been erased. I tried to place the sensation, and the closest I could recall was when I'd visited a friend at their office job at some random tech company, in a high-rise office building off the Mopac Expressway.

Everything inside that building had just felt *dead*, because it was. Modern, synthetic, man-made things had that feel about them. People normally didn't notice it because they were used to it. But to someone who'd spent significant time in nature, it was akin to the total absence of sound. I could practically feel the lack of life sucking the energy out of everyone in that building. That day, I'd swore I'd never work in a place like that, no matter what.

The question was, what kind of magic would cause an absence of nature's rhythms and energy? And in an empty field no less, where nature practically reigned free? It was puzzling, to say the least.

I followed the trail of nothingness, which led me on a beeline to the nearest road, a little two-lane strip of asphalt running from nowhere to nowhere. There was no trace of anyone's passing there, either—not a single tire track, footprint, discarded cigarette butt, nothing. Any evidence had been erased and replaced by that eerie absence of life and sense of emptiness.

I heard a rustling behind me and spun, drawing my Glock in a smooth motion from the small of my back. Elmo stood there with his lower lip stuck out, eyes red from crying and a trail of snot running down his lip. He took a shuddering breath, the kind you make when you're just on the edge of losing it, but you're trying to hold it together.

"Sorry, Elmo—I didn't mean to be so jumpy. I suppose it's just as well that you followed me. It's long past time I got you out of here."

His only response was to grunt and point back to the trash dump.

I holstered my pistol and approached him slowly with my hand extended, like a cowboy approaching a nervous foal. "I bet you want to get some of your things, eh? Maybe a toy, or something to keep you company?" I gently took the ogre's hand, and he responded in kind.

The trash dump was nothing to look at, just a small open area in the middle of a field of weeds full of rubbish and junk.

It looked as though the locals had been dumping their unwanted shit here for decades, as the place was littered with ancient washing machines, busted bathroom sinks, tattered mattresses, bald car tires, and the like. The ogre lifted the tail end of a rusted-out truck with no rims, using it like a trap door to gain entrance to his lair. I sat and waited patiently for him to return.

Minutes later, Elmo the ogre came clambering back out of his burrow with a dirty Tickle Me Elmo doll in one hand and a threadbare quilt in the other. He set the truck bed back down, staring at the entrance to his burrow with a sigh. Then, he wiped his nose with the blanket and slowly walked over to me with his shoulders slumped and head hung low.

"I know it's rough, big guy. But it's just not safe for you around here right now."

Elmo exhaled heavily, plopping down on the ground clutching his binkie and his doll. For lack of any more appropriate response, I patted his head gently with one hand as I dialed Maureen's cell phone with the other. Finnegas rarely used technology, but his assistant would know how to track him down.

"Yeah, Maureen? Can you get Finnegas to borrow one of the flatbeds from Ed, and send him out to the corner of East Yager Lane and Cameron Road? Yeah, I know it's out in the middle of nowhere, but he knows where it is. Tell him I'll explain when he gets here. Uh-huh, thanks, Maureen. I owe you one."

WITH THE LIBERAL application of druid magic to disguise

the ogre's appearance, Finnegas and I got Elmo back to the junkyard without causing a scene. Once there, we dressed his wounds and hid him in the depths of the yard, near the rusted van where Finn had camped out before he got clean and sober.

The old man shook his head as he checked the ogre's wounds for the third time. "If I'd known what he'd be walking into, I'd have just let him stay here at the junkyard," he muttered. "Damned fae are so stupid sometimes. They're a danger to their own existence. As if an ogre would attack a defenseless teenage girl!"

I yawned and stretched where I sat in the open side door of the van. "Way I figure it, Elmo must've seen the murder going down on his way back to his burrow, right after you dropped him off. Then he stepped in, trying to save her. I think the girl was probably already dying or dead at that point, but he got some nasty cuts for his trouble just the same. Killer probably didn't have time to finish Elmo off before the commotion drew the attention of the local residents. So, the perp split and covered his or her tracks, leaving Elmo to take the rap."

I grabbed a beer from the cooler Finn kept in his van and popped the tab with a hiss. The old man didn't sleep here anymore, so the beers were warm. I didn't mind. It was a little early to start drinking, but it had been an eventful twenty-four hours. I needed something to calm my nerves and settle my gut.

Or, rather, something to make me forget Jeretta's mangled corpse.

Shit.

Finn finished fussing with the ogre and took a seat on an

upturned plastic bucket cater-corner to me. "What do you know about the girl who was killed?"

I sniffed and scratched my nose with a knuckle. "Not much. She was clairvoyant, to an extent. Couldn't control it, but from what I understand she occasionally received visions."

Finnegas nodded slowly. "That could be significant. If her gift had revealed something about the killers, well... that could speak to a motive for her death."

"I thought the same thing. I'll need to ask around the trailer park to see if Jeretta spoke to anyone." I thought back to the evidence, or lack of it I'd found in the field. "Finn, what kind of magic do you think they used to hide their tracks?"

"Meh, it's hard to say. Something modern, more than likely. New magic."

"You mean technomancy?"

The old man pulled out his tobacco pouch and started rolling one up. "Yup." He licked the paper and finished rolling the cigarette, pointing it at me for emphasis. "So, you be sure to be on your guard. Whoever's behind these killings, they probably won't take it kindly if you start getting too close to exposing them."

"Fat chance of that. I've been at this case for weeks, and I'm still no closer to finding a killer." I glanced over at the ogre, who had his nose in the dirt, watching a dung beetle push piece of dog turd across the yard. "If only I could get Elmo to finger the killers. Too bad he doesn't talk."

Finn stroked his beard, allowing the ash from his cigarette to lengthen as he considered the situation. "Well, we could teach him sign language."

"Who, Elmo? That's..."

"Crazy?" Finn interjected with a wry grin. "You're just upset because you didn't think of it first."

I scratched my head as I considered his suggestion. "You're right, I do wish I'd thought of it. If scientists can teach gorillas, chimps, and orangutans sign language, then I suppose we can teach Elmo here how to do it. There's just one problem—I don't know how to sign."

Finnegas took a long drag on his cigarette, blowing it out through his nostrils. "Meh, don't worry, I'll take care of it. You don't live on this earth for two millennia without picking up the odd language or two. I'll start working on it, and I'll weave a more permanent glamour to hide his appearance from Ed and the yard crew."

"That sounds like a plan. In the meantime, I'll head back to the trailer park to see if Jeretta knew something that might have gotten her killed. Let me know if you make any headway with Elmo." I poured out the dregs of my beer and started walking back to the main building to clean up before heading out.

"You're welcome!" Finnegas shouted at my back sarcastically.

"I'd have thought of it eventually!" I yelled over my shoulder, just to get his goat.

FOUR

I spent the afternoon canvassing the trailer park without much to show for it. Most of the fae wouldn't speak to me, and those who did were none too friendly. I had several doors slammed in my face, got spat on twice, and an old spriggan tried to run me over with his riding lawnmower.

Overall, I'd say it was quite a productive afternoon.

After I'd knocked on every door in the neighborhood, I decided to drive by a few of the other murder scenes, just to see if there might be some bit of evidence or a pattern I'd missed. Thus far, there'd been over a dozen killings, all fae, but each murder had followed a different MO.

One had been strangled, another drowned, another over-dosed on heroin... the way the victims had died read like a script from that T.V. show, *1,000 Ways to Die*. Pedestrian-motor vehicle accidents, falling off buildings, electrocution, fire—heck, one poor shmuck had even fallen into a vat of lye at a wild game processing facility. And in every single instance, the killer or killers had left nothing behind to indicate who was responsible.

At first, nobody had put the killings together, and they were written off as accidents. But as more and more fae kept dying, everyone had started getting scared.

And that's when Sal had tracked me down, while I'd still been recovering from Maeve leaving me to starve to death. She hadn't taken kindly to being double-crossed, and if frying me on the spot wouldn't have meant that she'd have been trapped herself, I doubted I'd be alive today. Instead, she'd left me for dead in a cavern deep underground, where I'd languished for weeks on end until Finnegas had finally found me.

Understandably, I had mixed emotions about catching this killer. Truth was, I really hadn't put much effort into catching the persons responsible for the killings. There were damned few fae I could stand, and even fewer I'd call friends. Maeve's punishment for my betrayal was just one in a long list of insults my friends and I had suffered at the hands of the fae. In my experience, the faery folk were a cruel and heartless people who completely lacked empathy, at least where humans were concerned.

We were like some mundane species of wildlife to them— often intriguing, sometimes amusing, on rare occasions useful, but ultimately expendable. For millennia, the *aes sídhe* had treated humans like playthings, using their superior skill in and knowledge of magic to meddle in our affairs and cause all manner of havoc. Once, humans had even worshipped them as gods—capricious, callous, malevolent deities who were just as likely to curse you as they were to answer your prayers.

Thus, my current moral dilemma. It wasn't just for shits and giggles that I'd decided to cut the earthbound fae off from that vast pool of magic called Underhill. Naw, those fuckers had it coming.

In fact, a couple of the *Tuatha Dé Danann*, the most ancient and powerful of the fae, had conspired with me to make that happen. And yes, they'd been trying to save Underhill from its eventual destruction, more than they were trying to lend me a hand in getting out from under Maeve's thumb. But far be it from me to look a gift horse in the mouth. They'd offered me the opportunity to knock the earthbound fae down a peg, and who was I to refuse?

So, if the fae wanted to kill each other off, or if some third party had taken it on themselves to pare down their numbers, why should I be the one to stop them?

But seeing Jeretta all cut up in a pool of her own blood, well... that had shaken me up a bit. Not that I'd known her all that well, and I doubted if any of those trailer park kids would piss on me to put me out if I was on fire. Still, she was just a kid, and even if she belonged to a race of sociopaths, it didn't make it right that somebody had sliced her up like a paper snowflake.

Despite my sympathy for Jeretta, I still wasn't feeling particularly enthused about working this case. And as I drove from murder site to murder site, I couldn't help but think that I was helping the fox instead of the farmer by tracking down this killer. Fae had been killing humans indiscriminately since time immemorial, and honestly, I had better things to do than save the fae from a fate they deserved.

Shit, have I really become that damned cynical?

The answer was yes, yes I had. The fae had made me

kill the love of my life, leaving her spirit to haunt me until we fulfilled some cosmic destiny together. Or, at least, that's what she'd told me not long ago. Plus, they'd tried killing me, more times than I cared to count. And during my career as a hunter, I'd seen their gruesome handiwork firsthand.

Sure, most fae were just trying to blend into human society and survive, but their fundamental nature was to take what they wanted from us by any means necessary. And if that meant cheating, lying, stealing, raping, or killing, well... there were always going to be fae willing to cross that line.

Maybe I was just feeling cross because I was bone tired and my shoulder was aching like a motherfucker, or maybe I just didn't give a shit because deep down I would always hate the fae. Regardless of my reasons, I decided I'd call Sal when I got home and tell him I was being stonewalled by his people, so it was pointless to continue the investigation. I didn't feel right about reneging on our deal, but I figured it was high time I stayed away from the fae, for good.

Fuck 'em if they can't take a joke.

SAL WAS DISAPPOINTED at the news, but he said he didn't blame me—which made me feel like even more of a heel for quitting on him. But I *had* rescued his son from a fae sex trafficking ring, so I didn't allow myself to feel too bad. I spent the rest of the afternoon running through the work my uncle had left me, which mostly consisted of diagnosing cars he wanted to flip and pulling parts in the yard. That helped me get my mind off my conversation with Sal, and the knowledge that none of the fae could bother me inside the junkyard helped cheer my mood considerably.

Part of the reason I'd decided to live in my uncle's junkyard was because iron was anathema to the fae. I'd moved to Austin from my hometown after my girlfriend Jesse's death, because everything back home had reminded me of her. This was supposed to be a new start, and the junkyard provided me with the perfect way to isolate myself from the fae. All that iron and steel, combined with the extensive network of wards and spells I'd placed on the metal fence around the yard, served to make the junkyard a fae-free zone.

And that was exactly how I liked it. In the few years since I'd taken up residence here, I'd spent considerable time and effort shoring up the wards so nothing supernatural could enter unless I wanted it to. The junkyard was like my own private island, a place where I could let my guard down and escape all my worries.

Some people liked to golf, some liked to hang out at the park, and others liked to go to the lake to relax. Me? I preferred to wrench on old junked cars, in the only place where I knew I didn't have to watch my back.

I was up to my elbows in grease, pulling the heads off an engine from a VW Bug, when I heard someone clear their throat behind me.

"Are those heads OEM or aftermarket?"

I grabbed a rag and stood up, wiping my hands as I turned around to match the voice with a face. I didn't like being interrupted when I was working, which was why I did a lot of my work deep in the bowels of the yard. Still, it kind of went with the territory.

A lot of gearheads liked to pull their own parts from the

yard to save money. Ed charged less for those parts since he didn't have to pay an employee to remove them, so occasionally I'd have to help our DIY customers find what they were looking for in the yard. I didn't make anything off it, but it helped Ed keep the doors open, which was all that mattered.

What freaked me out about this guy was that he'd managed to sneak up on me. Had I been so caught up in my work that I just hadn't noticed?

I did my best to plaster a smile on my face, my efforts at good humor stalling when I saw the guy. He definitely wasn't dressed to go diving under the hood of some junker, that was for sure. For one, he didn't have any tools with him. Second, he wore neatly-pressed tan slacks, a blue polo shirt, and a black casual jacket that said he probably spent his spare time on the links, and not working on a project car in his home garage.

The guy had aviators on, so I couldn't see his eyes, but his too-friendly smile set me off immediately. That, and his hundred-dollar haircut. Nope, this guy definitely didn't belong here, that was for damned sure.

I finished, wiping my hands off just as I made up my mind about liking the guy—I didn't. Still, he might have been a legit customer, so I couldn't be outright rude to him either.

"They're oversized heads, aftermarket—designed to fit ninety-four-millimeter pistons. This engine came out of a souped-up Bug that some kid wrecked in a street race. His loss, your gain, if you're interested in them."

I could tell the guy's eyes were darting around the yard, even though he kept his head level and fixed on me. "I might be, I might at that. I actually came out here looking for parts for a '67 Stingray."

"Three-twenty-seven, or three-ninety-six?" I asked. It was a trick question, because Chevy didn't offer either of those engines in the Corvette that year.

"Oh, you'll have to ask my mechanic that," the man said as he scratched his nose with his thumb. "I'm just the money man, you know."

Dodged that bullet, didn't you? The guy was cagey, that was for sure.

"Yeah, I get it," I responded noncommittally. "You just want to enjoy the end product. Nothing wrong with that... if you don't want to get your hands dirty."

The man's smile turned cold. "Well, if you have people to do those things for you..." He paused in mid-sentence, doing a double-take at something or someone behind me. "My goodness, but he's a big fella!"

I turned to see Elmo, glamoured to look like a very tall human and dressed in coveralls that were three sizes too small, carrying another VW engine over his shoulder. Finnegas had put him to work in the yard—with Ed's consent, of course. Ed was always taking in strays, so it wasn't that big a deal, and we'd been keeping Elmo busy in the far reaches of the yard where he couldn't get into too much trouble.

"Just set it down over there, Elmo," I said as I pointed to a wooden pallet close by.

The man was a bit too interested in the ogre, which made me nervous. Though it was rare, some mundane humans possessed magical gifts of which they were unaware. Sometimes that meant they'd see glimpses of the world beneath, even through a decent glamour. The last thing I needed was some yuppie freaking out in my uncle's junkyard, so I sent Elmo on his way.

"Strange name, Elmo. Don't hear that much these days."

"Yeah, it's a nickname," I replied, wishing I could get back to my work.

"Does he talk much?"

I sighed internally. "No, not at all. Although he is learning sign language. Anyway, sir, is there anything I can help you with?"

The man stared after Elmo, then shook his head. "No, as it turns out that was all I needed." He turned and walked off without so much as a "have a good day" or wave goodbye.

Fucking entitled yuppies.

I cracked my neck as I watched him leave. Something about the guy was just familiar, but hell if I could figure it out. I put the strange conversation out of my mind, and went back to losing myself in my work.

A FEW NIGHTS LATER, a tremendous roar that came from the depths of the yard woke me from a deep sleep. Since Finnegas had gone back to Éire Imports for the night, the only people left in the junkyard were me and Elmo.

Shit.

I pulled on some jeans, grabbed my Craneskin Bag, and sprinted barefoot through the yard, casting a minor cantrip to protect the soles of my feet along the way. It was past midnight and the sky was overcast, so I drew the flaming sword from my Bag, both for a source of light and as a "just in case" measure.

As I ran, the ogre's roar grew louder and more intense. I also heard a lot of banging and crashing—obviously Elmo was putting up a fight. The hairs on my arms and the back of my neck were standing up, which told me someone was working some major magical juju nearby.

Several thoughts ran through my mind, starting with, *Who the fuck is mucking around with magic—in my junkyard, no less—at this ungodly hour?* And, more importantly, *Why are they attacking Elmo?* I put on more speed as I raced toward the commotion.

I was still running when Elmo's roars turned into a cry of pain, which then morphed into a high-pitched whine. I turned the corner around a stack of cars at top speed, only to find the ogre pinned to another stack of cars by several large lengths of pipe and scrap metal piercing his chest.

As I ran up to the gentle giant, I looked left and right for any sign of his attacker or attackers. I spotted a fleeting shadow, just as it ducked around a corner fifteen yards away. I pivoted on heel to give chase, but the ogre's labored breathing and soft whines stopped me in my tracks. Kicking myself for not having a projectile weapon or suitable long-distance spell handy, I thrust the sword into the dirt and focused my attention on helping Elmo.

Unfortunately, the mage who'd attacked the ogre had done a thorough job on him. Similar to the manner in which Jeretta had been killed, the ogre's torso had been pierced by multiple projectiles from a dozen different angles. Considering the severity of his injuries, I was surprised he was still breathing at all. It was clear that he didn't have long, and I knew there was little I could do to save him.

Cursing myself for leaving him alone this evening, I grabbed one of his huge hands, holding it in my own.

"I'm here, big guy. I'm here."

The ogre's eyes fluttered open, and he pulled his hand from mine. He locked eyes with me, then he made the same gesture with both hands, over and over again.

"I don't understand what you're trying to tell me. Just... just relax and save your energy. I'm going to call Finnegas, and he'll know what to do."

The ogre's eyes softened as he looked at me, and he made the gesture one last time. Then, with a soft whine, he closed his eyes and breathed his last.

"Fuuuuck!" I screamed as I slammed my fist into a nearby car door, splitting my knuckles in the process. Immediately realizing how stupid that display of anger was, I shook my hand out to make sure I hadn't broken it—thankfully, it still worked. I snatched the sword from the dirt and ran in the same direction I'd seen Elmo's assailant fleeing moments before.

I switched my vision to the magical spectrum for a moment, just in case there might be some residual presence of magic that might indicate where he'd gone. It wasn't much, but it was there—fading wisps of power that had peeled off the murderer as he fled. I followed the trail, and it led straight to the junkyard fence. I climbed atop a stack of cars, but there was nothing on the other side but a dark, empty street. Elmo's killer was long gone.

Frustration and anger roiled in my gut as I walked back to the scene of the crime. I only had a few hours to piece together any evidence the killer might have left behind; despite the boiling cauldron of rage inside me, I needed to get to work. I called Finnegas and told him what had happened, then started going over the scene.

I grabbed a few portable spotlights and a generator from the workshop and set them up to illuminate the area. Seeing Elmo lit up like Christmas, hanging like a puppet from a dozen different pieces of scrap and junk... well... it turned my stomach a bit. But as grisly as it was, my inability to save him was more responsible for the pit in my gut than the sight of Elmo's body.

I put all those thoughts out of my mind and focused on doing what I did best, which was deciphering clues and catching supernatural killers. I'd done the same thing at every other murder scene I'd investigated over the last few weeks, but I knew this time it'd be different.

Because this time, I'd chased the killer off before he could cover his tracks. That meant I finally had a chance at catching this piece of shit... and the sight of poor Elmo's broken corpse gave me every motivation to do exactly that.

FIVE

I was still working the scene when the sun came up, searching for every last clue I could find. So far, I'd turned up damned little; a shoe print that indicated the murderer had been of average height and build, a poisoned arrow that had been used to slow the ogre down, and a few torn shreds of clothing where the killer had gotten hung up on some barbed wire clearing the fence.

Since he or she had made it past my wards, I assumed the killer was human or damned good at bypassing supernatural security measures. And based on the mechanism of injury, the killer was adept at casting telekinetic magic.

That last bit was the most telling piece of information I'd gleaned over the last several hours. Telekinesis was a rather uncommon magical skill that fell within the category of spell craft commonly known as psionics. Although psionic spells did in fact have some parallel to the "mind powers" found in popular culture and role-playing games, real psionic practitioners used magic to control and amplify the electromagnetic energy found in nature. This allowed the practitioner of psionics to move metallic objects with their mind, to communicate with others by thought alone, to "read" the thoughts of others, and to mentally manipulate simple electronics.

What was even more intriguing was that psionicists typically mingled technology and magic in order to increase their power. Similar to the way in which alchemists combined magic and chemistry, psionicists used electronic devices to help them amplify and channel their mental energies at a level impossible to achieve through natural means alone.

In short, psionicists were technomancers, and that was an obscure branch of magic indeed. I'd personally never run across anyone who practiced technomancy, simply because it was such an expensive field of magic to pursue. In order to become a practitioner of technomancy of any consequence, a magician would need vast financial resources in order to design, build, and experiment on their own technomagical devices. Such devices weren't something you could just buy at the local Radio Shack—they were almost always expensive, custom tech.

Knowing that our killer practiced technomancy allowed me to narrow our field of suspects down to a very small community of practitioners. And the fact that the killer was likely wealthy immediately made me think of the strange visitor I'd spoken with a few days before. That man's attitude had smacked of entitlement and privilege, and he'd damned sure showed more interest in Elmo than might have been warranted.

Yeah, I was pretty sure that he was either the killer, or somehow connected to the culprit. I just wished I had paid more attention to the guy, but of course hindsight was always

20/20. At least I knew what he looked like. There couldn't be that many people in Austin with access to the sort of money and technology necessary to do technomancy at such a high level.

Could there?

I collected my thoughts as I sipped a cup of coffee, waiting for Finnegas to finish his current task. After I'd gone over the scene again, we finally used a cutting torch to get Elmo's body down. A pressure washer got rid of the blood, and Finnegas used an earth-moving spell to bury the big guy right where he fell. It seemed like we owed him more than just an unmarked grave in junkyard, but the logistics of the situation dictated that we handled it as we did.

At least Ed and the rest of the workers would be none the wiser, so that was something. Ed would wonder where Elmo had gone, but workers came and went all the time around the junkyard. It was nothing unusual for someone to get hired, work a few days, and then quit when they got their first paycheck. No, Elmo would not be missed—at least, not by anyone but me and Finnegas.

"It's done," the old man said as he approached, snapping me out of my thoughts and back to the present.

"Wish I could have been more help with that," I said, noting how slowly Finnegas was moving, and the dark circles that had appeared under his eyes. Spell craft took a lot out of him these days. He used to blame it on the aftereffects of his addiction, but lately he'd revealed—in classic Detective Murtaugh style—that he was simply "getting too old for this shit."

I was pretty sure he was using his age to guilt me into

working overtime to learn druidry from him—but to be honest, it was working.

Finnegas grunted in response to my polite overture. We both knew that he was ten times the druid I was, even on my best day, and that I couldn't work a spell of that enormity if my life depended on it. I could toss a little lightning around, or start a fire, or amplify a small explosion, but that mostly involved redirecting existing energy to where I wanted it to go.

Moving several tons of dirt, on the other hand... that was serious magic, and it'd be some time before I possessed that kind of mojo.

The old man sat heavily on the tailgate of a rusted-out truck. I handed him a warm thermos of coffee, and he poured himself a cup in the cap.

"I'm gonna miss that big dummy," Finnegas said with a sniffle as he wiped his nose with the back of his hand.

"Me too, even though he tried to kill me once." I raised my mug in the air. "To Elmo."

Finnegas copied the gesture. "To Elmo. May he roam forever in Mag Mell, chasing dragonflies and playing with furry red dolls to his heart's content."

Several minutes passed in uncomfortable silence. Finnegas was old-school, and I was a bit too much of a dude to start talking about the feels with another guy. So, I ignored the few tears he shed while keeping my own to a bare minimum as well. Once I felt that I could speak without choking up, I broke the silence.

"I'm going to catch this fucker, you know," I said in a low growl. "And I'm going to start by going through that fae trailer park door to door, to find out why the killer chose Jeretta..."

A PLEASANT TENOR voice with a peculiar brogue cut me off mid-sentence. "No need, my boy, no need. I took the liberty of doing so me self."

There stood Click, one of the teens from the trailer park. Or, at least, that's what he wanted everyone to believe. During my investigation into the disappearance of Sal's son, I'd discovered that Click was much more than he appeared. At the very least, he was a powerful magic user, and probably very old as well.

Finnegas hissed slightly, crossing his arms with a scowl at the sight of the strange youth. Apparently, there was some history there that I was unaware of. Not wanting to be rude, I greeted the object of Finnegas' discontent.

"Click. I guess I don't need to ask what brings you here. My condolences on the loss of your friend." Click had known Jeretta well, and I had no doubt that was why he was here.

The mysterious youth acknowledged me and Finnegas, each in turn. "Druid. Seer." Finn's scowl deepened, but Click ignored his reaction as he regarded me. "I thank you for that, Colin, I surely do. And that'd indeed be what brings me to your home on this otherwise fine day. Sad that it should be marred by the loss of such a gentle soul. As such, I came to beseech you to find the killer or killers, so that justice might be served."

Finnegas pursed his lips, exhaling with a *pfft* and an eye roll. He laid a hand gently on my arm and stood. "Be wary around this one, kid." He tilted his head at Click. "He's a wolf in sow's clothing, if ever there was one."

I watched Finnegas walk away from us as he ignored Click entirely. "Well, that was interesting. What'd you do to get the old man in such a tissy?"

Click's mouth twitched side to side. "Old prejudices die hard, I suppose. But, what's done is done. I'm more concerned about events in the present, than a grudge held long past its due."

I sipped my coffee as I regarded Click through narrowed eyes. There was a story there, I was sure of it, but now wasn't the appropriate time to tease it out of him. I pointed at the tailgate Finnegas had just vacated.

"Have a seat, Click. Care to tell me how you skirted my wards?"

He sat, fixing me with an inscrutable stare. "Yes."

I waited for several moments, then sighed and shook my head. "Fine then, don't tell me. What'd you learn from the folks in the trailer park? Did Jeretta reveal anything that might indicate she knew something about her killer?"

Click leaned in, crossing an ankle over his knee. "Indeed. But as you're well aware, our Jeretta wasn't given over to communicating via the spoken word—much the same as our enormous friend, the ogre." He glanced around, obviously looking for Elmo. "Where is he, by the way?"

My voice trembled slightly as I shared the news. "Someone snuck in here and killed him last night."

Click's expression grew even more serious. "That's a damned shame, it is. The poor oaf never bothered a soul, and we both know he nearly died trying to save fair Jeretta. I should've seen this coming and offered my help sooner, druid. For that, I am sorry."

I coughed and took another swig of coffee, trying to avoid an inadvertent display of emotion. "Well, what's done is done. Getting back to Jeretta, did she communicate anything of interest lately? Like maybe a vision or viewing that seemed out of place?"

Click tsked. "Well that's just the thing, isn't it? Of late, she'd clammed up, so to speak. The girl had stopped interacting with her friends, and instead took to spending hours on end wandering the area alone. She seemed quite melancholy, she did, which was unusual for her."

"Something must've happened recently to cause such an abrupt change in her personality," I said.

"I agree. And while no one could tell me a thing about what sort of visions Jeretta had been experiencing recently, I believe I have a fairly good idea of what her last revelation was."

"Okay. And...?"

Click spread his arms wide, stretching the tight white t-shirt he wore across his model-thin chest. "Well, isn't it obvious, lad? She saw a vision of her own death!"

"That would explain her sudden change," I said. "But this helps us how, exactly?"

Click drew himself up imperiously. "I'm not the sleuth—how am I supposed to know where that bit of information might lead? I'm merely the messenger, druid, not the *justiciar*. That responsibility falls to you, does it not? For who else might serve as judge, jury, and executioner, but one with ties to no faction but his own?"

"Right," I said. "Well, I'd already been hired by the red

caps to figure out who's behind these killings. But I sort of quit on them a few days ago. That being said, Elmo's death changes things—I just can't let something like that stand. Rest assured, I'm on the case."

"Yes, but what will you do once you find the killers, hmm? Arrest them?" Click leaned forward, hands on his knees, eyes hooded and glowering. "Blood cries for blood, lad! Promise me that if it's within your power, you'll see that the scales are balanced. Promise!"

I sighed. "Click, I can't promise something like that, because I don't know the whole story yet. And if you're so invested in seeing justice done, why don't you do it yourself? You're certainly capable, from what I've seen."

Click shook his head with a sigh. "My hands are tied, druid—conditions of presiding in Maeve's demesne, you see. Although she's hardly in a position to enforce those stipulations these days. But manners maketh the man, so I'll stick to my word regardless. Thus, it falls to you to right these wrongs, and to see the killer or killers brought to justice."

He looked at me, twitching his nose like the White Rabbit. I set my coffee down, returning his stare. There was more coming, and I'd learned when dealing with the fae that the less you spoke, the better.

"Plus, I'll make it worth your while."

"There it is," I said as I crossed my arms, stroking my chin while I considered the implications of entering an agreement with Click. For one, I might be able to call on him for back up, if things got nasty. And from what I'd seen, Click was no pushover. On the down side, though, making deals with the fae never did quite turn out the way you expected.

"Fine. I mean, I was going to do it anyway," I said. "But

since you're offering to hire me, I suppose we need to discuss the manner and terms of compensation."

"Payment will be in the way of knowledge—magical knowledge, in fact, of a sort you covet. My magic."

"You're going to teach me your magic? In exchange for hunting Jeretta's killer down?"

"I will and I am, and I suppose there's no better time than the present to begin." Then, with a snap of his fingers, he disappeared.

"I'd like to know how you do that," I muttered.

"And you will, eventually," Click's disembodied voice replied from nearby. "But we must walk before we run. So, here's your first lesson: the tactical offensive use of temporal fields, and methods of escaping said constructs."

I stood up quickly, spilling my coffee. "Huh? Wait, I never—"

My protest came too late. I heard Click snap his fingers, and suddenly I was paralyzed, frozen in place like a fly in amber.

WHAT THE HELL *has he done to me?* I wondered. I could see things moving around me, but I couldn't move a muscle. I watched as a dragonfly flew toward me.

Obviously, this spell isn't affecting anything else in my vicinity. Or so I thought. As the dragonfly sped closer to me, it suddenly froze like it had hit a wall of peanut butter. No more than eighteen inches in front of my face, the dragonfly was suspended in midair.

But on closer inspection, I noticed something peculiar.

The dragonfly's wings were still beating, albeit in slow motion.

Temporal fields—of course. He told me what he was doing before he did it. Obviously, Click had locked me in some sort of temporal stasis field—the dragonfly was evidence of that. And if it could still move, so could I.

I observed the dragonfly for a few moments, doing some rough calculations in my head. Dragonflies beat their wings about thirty times a second, and it was taking about three seconds per wing beat... so, time was moving approximately one hundred times slower inside Click's stasis field.

Funny that I should be able to think at normal speed. I supposed it must have something to do with the metaphysical nature of the mind-body-spirit connection. Perhaps the spirit interacted with the mind and body to process thought, and that precluded the influence of time manipulation on thought patterns. Or maybe the brain processed information so quickly that a stasis field barely affected its functions.

I decided that I could think about it all day and still be no closer to an answer, so I turned my thoughts toward finding a way to escape the spell. Obviously, I possessed a means or method of doing so, else Click wouldn't have cast the spell on me. I supposed I should've been upset about it, but after years of training with Finnegas, I'd gotten used to shitty surprises like this one.

So, how do I escape this spell?

First off, I had to assume that it was a stationary spell. I also had to assume that it had a limited radius, based on how the dragonfly had been caught within it. So, all I needed to do was figure out a way to move out of the spell. Walking out of the spell would take forever—and besides, that wasn't the point. For all I knew, Click was watching somewhere close by, and if I cheated he'd just trap me again.

That meant I needed to think like a magic user to escape. I considered calling up a strong wind, but the air molecules would simply slow down the second they hit the stasis field. What I needed was something to push me out of the field—something large enough so that most of its mass would reside outside the field's influence.

I couldn't move my eyeballs—at least, not very fast—so I used Finnegas' druid trick to relax, allowing my mind to take in everything in my field of vision. *Up there.* A truck hood was resting atop some junked cars nearby. It'd have to do.

I tried to think of a spell or cantrip that required few words and minimal gestures. Truth be told, the phrases and gestures that I used when doing spell work were merely devices to help me focus, like training wheels for beginners. Advanced practitioners of druidry could cast simple spells with a thought, a single word, or a twitch of their fingers.

But me? I was more or less a beginner who still needed training wheels to cast magic. I finally settled on a wind summoning that I thought I could cast with only a word and a gesture. Even though a microburst of wind wouldn't push me out of the stasis field, it could send the hood flying into me. I focused intently so I could cast the spell with the bare minimum of audible and physical cues.

Once I was certain that I'd worked out the spell sequence in my head, it was merely a matter of exerting my will. I began to shape my fingers into the proper form, forcing air out of my lungs to say the command word for the spell.

Damn it if it didn't take forever, but a minute or so later, the spell released. A huge gust of wind lifted the truck hood, sending it hurtling down toward me at the speed of gravity.

This is going to hurt.

As I suspected, the fact that most of the hood's mass remained outside the stasis field meant that it exerted its inertia on objects inside the field—namely, me—at normal speed. The edge of the hood struck me in the very same shoulder that Elmo had injured, and the force of that collision pushed me toward the ground. As soon as I felt my body escape the stasis field, I rolled away to avoid being completely crushed by the hood.

Strangely, that never happened. I landed on my side, rubbing my shoulder as I looked at the hood, which was now suspended in midair. *I guess enough of its mass got caught in the stasis field to keep it there. Interesting.*

I pulled my sleeve up to look at the spot where the hood had hit me. Nothing was broken, but between the bruise I'd soon have and the leftover aches from my previous injury, I was going to be on the gimp list for a while yet.

I sat up, leaning against an ugly brown Pinto that rested close to the ground on flat tires. "Fucking fae," I muttered, to no one in particular.

SIX

After a liberal application of one of Finnegas' healing poultices, I took some time to rest and heal, and then I called my girlfriend, Belladonna. Bells was one of the best hunters the Cold Iron Circle had on their payroll. I valued her opinion, and I figured getting a sharp set of eyes on the evidence might help me move the case forward.

As much as I loved and respected Bells, I didn't think much of her employers. The Circle was a centuries-old organization, created by humans to protect the human race from supernatural threats. Or, at least, that's what they claimed to do. In reality, they allowed a lot of supernatural harm to come to average everyday humans, and typically only took an interest in high-profile cases... when they felt like it.

I suspected there were powerful people at the highest levels of the Circle who had a vested interest in the cases they chose to work. But all that shit was above my pay grade; my business actually *was* with the little people. I left the Circle to their intrigues, minding my own business so long as the Circle jerks left me alone as well.

I met Bells in the back room at Luther's coffeehouse. The place was close to Circle headquarters, which made it convenient. Plus, Luther headed up the local vampire coven, and he never missed a beat. If anyone decided to eavesdrop on us, he'd know about it and give us the heads up.

I could've met Belladonna at my place or at hers, but she'd been avoiding close contact lately. I suspected it had something to do with her recent trip to visit her family in Spain, but I was trying to respect her desire for "space" while I avoided looking desperate and clingy—so I didn't ask. She'd spent considerable time on that trip with my favorite frenemy, Crowley, who happened to be her ex. I could've kicked myself for sending Crowley to look for her, but I'd been caught between a rock and a hard place at the time.

See, my buddy Hemi had died during our trip to Underhill. I'd blamed myself for his death, and had promised him I'd return his body to his mom in New Zealand. So, as soon as I'd recovered from nearly starving to death, that's the first place I went. I might not have necessarily trusted Crowley *with Bells*, but I did trust him, so I'd sent him to track her down in my place.

Stupid, I know. But then again, I'd never claimed to be wise in the ways of love. The one good thing that came out of it was finding out that Hemi's mother was a Maori deity, and she was able to bring his spirit back from the land of the dead. He was still recovering, but at least he wasn't gone for good.

Anyway, I was an idiot and deserved whatever fallout came from sending Bells' ex to track her down, instead of going myself. So there.

All that nonsense bounced around my skull as I waited for her to show, but it all faded into the background when she walked in the room. Bells was an absolute stunner. It was a mystery to me why she'd worked me so long and hard after my ex-girlfriend Jesse passed on—but she had, and eventually I'd fallen for her.

Looking at her now, I couldn't understand for the life of me how I'd resisted her for so long. She was maybe five-six on a good day, but she always wore boots with heels so high they could double as stilts. Bells once told me that all her cousins were built like models, so I figured that was why she wore the heels. Of course, you wouldn't catch me complaining.

As for her cousins' looks, Belladonna was nothing like them—she was all lean, hungry, graceful power, muscled like a Crossfitter with the balance and reflexes of a cat. With her long dark hair, full pouty lips, smoky eyes, and smile that always seemed to promise more, she was every guy's dream. And considering how she could fight and shoot, she was also every monster's nightmare.

I stood and wiped my hands on my jeans as she sashayed over to my table, a dork move that elicited a giggle from her. I leaned in, and she stood on tiptoe to kiss me lightly on the cheek.

"Sit down, silly. You're acting like one of those 'thropes or vamps who grew up a century or two ago, all manners and chivalry. Except you're not smooth enough to pull it off, so it just makes you seem awkward."

"Ouch," I replied with a frown.

She smacked my arm lightly. "Oh, don't be so sensitive. It's perfectly endearing, actually."

"Um... thanks, I guess," I said, frowning. I'd known Bells

for a few years, and we'd been dating for a couple months now, but she was still a mystery to me. I was pretty sure that it was in her nature to keep men on their toes, but sometimes I wished her intentions and feelings were more transparent.

Like I said, I'd never claimed to be an expert on matters of the heart.

I waited for Bells to sit down before I took my seat, even though she rolled her eyes slightly and shook her head for my doing so. Luther came by and dropped off a frap for her—he enjoyed anticipating his customer's requests—and after a few pleasantries, we had the space to ourselves.

"It's, uh, good to see you, Bells."

She screwed her mouth to one side as she regarded me through slitted eyes. "Alright, let's just get this right in the open."

"Okay..."

"First off, nothing happened between Crowley and I —*nothing*. Second, I am still head over heels for you, lover boy, and frankly it's nice to see you with your undies all in a wad, thinking you might have lost your mojo. And third, even though we haven't made out since I got back from Spain, I do in fact have a strong desire to jump your bones."

My eyebrows nearly touched my hairline, and I blinked several times in surprise before gathering my thoughts. "Honestly, that's a relief. But about the bones-jumping thing—"

She cut me off, and her response was curt and to the point. "Girl stuff."

THAT SHUT ME DOWN. I cleared my throat as I

awkwardly changed the subject. "Um, alright then. So—about the reason I asked you here."

A smile played across her lips as Belladonna crossed her legs. She interlaced her fingers, resting them on her knee as she leaned forward slightly. The position she'd taken put her cleavage on full display. I looked, and she noticed.

"Consider me to be at your disposal, handsome," she said, batting her eyes coquettishly.

I had to laugh despite myself. Bells was pushing all the right buttons, and she knew it. I figured there had to be some sort of payoff for putting up with her games, and decided to allow myself to be played.

"Okay, first up…" I reached into my Craneskin Bag, pulling out the arrow I'd plucked from Elmo's calf. "The arrowhead has been poisoned, so watch your fingers."

Bells picked the arrow up, turning it over in her hands and examining each end, looking down the shaft. She set it down on the table, shaking her head. "That's not a normal arrow. Look at it carefully—where's the nock?"

She was referring to the part of the arrow that had a notch to hold it in place on the bowstring. "I don't know… I figured it was broken off in the battle."

"Nope. Look carefully at the butt end. That arrow never had a nock mounted on it. It was left hollow for a reason, and that's because it was designed to be shot from an airbow."

"An air-what?" I asked, truly perplexed.

She sat back and crossed her arms. "An airbow. It's relatively old tech, applied in a new and unusual way. Think of a high-compression airgun, designed to shoot arrows instead of lead pellets. It'll shoot a 375-grain arrow at 450 feet per second, or about twice the speed of your typical recurve bow.

You can put down a bison with one of those things, which is probably why they chose it."

"And I take it that it's completely silent," I stated.

Bells nodded. "Oh yeah, definitely. All you'd hear is a whoosh of air, right before you got skewered by 26 inches of broadhead and aluminum. I'm sure it did quite a number on your friend. Heck, I'm surprised it didn't go right through his leg."

"Nah, it got lodged in the bone. Had a hell of a time taking it out."

Bells must've read something on my face, because I soon felt her hand on mine. "Hey, I know this is upsetting you. Sorry for speaking about it in such a clinical manner."

I coughed in my other hand. "It's alright. I really didn't know Elmo that well, but he was such an innocent soul, you know? Anyway, the sooner you help me sort out the evidence, the sooner I can catch the creep who killed him."

Belladonna looked at me, her eyes showing just the slightest bit of sympathy—enough to let me know she cared without being unprofessional. She was deadly serious about her work, and I respected that. I packed away whatever I might be feeling about Elmo's death, compartmentalizing my emotions so we could get to work.

Bells ran her tongue across her lips—a gesture that I used to think was pure flirtation, but she actually did it whenever she was working out a problem in her head.

"You say the arrow was poisoned?"

I nodded. "Yeah, with something I can't identify."

"Hmm... you mind if I take it, to have it analyzed?"

"Be my guest." I gestured at the arrow, lip curling with disgust at the knowledge that the weapon had been chosen specifically to take Elmo down. "Do you have any idea who might use one of those airbow things? Sounds like something that might stand out, if you saw that sort of thing in someone's kit."

"If you're asking what I think you're asking—no, the Circle doesn't use or issue them. But there are several independent hunter teams who work the central Texas area. I can ask around, to see if anyone at HQ knows of an indie outfit that might use that sort of weapon." She looked at her phone. "Speaking of which, I need to get going."

"Thanks, Bells." As she gathered her things, I stirred my coffee while pointedly avoiding eye contact. "So, when am I going to see you again?"

She stopped what she was doing to flash me a wicked grin. "You mean to say, when are you going to get some nookie?"

Luther laughed loud enough for us to hear him, even though he was manning the front counter. *Nope, that vampire doesn't miss a thing.* My face flushed, even though no one else was listening to our conversation.

Belladonna leaned in and pinched my cheek. "You are so cute when you're embarrassed. And to answer your question —soon, very soon. I promise, your patience will be rewarded."

I nodded in acquiescence as I stood. "Hey, I can be patient. But just so you know..."

Bells cocked her head at me. "Yes?"

"Well, it's not like we have to have sex to get together. I mean, I like being around you just because. So, if you have the time—"

My girlfriend planted her hands on her hips. "Why,

Colin McCool, are you asking me on a good old-fashioned date?"

I drew myself up to my full height. "Why yes, Miss Becerra, I believe I am."

She stepped into kissing distance, grabbing my lapel as she tickled my bare chest with her finger. "I'm free tomorrow night."

"Then I'll pick you up at seven, sharp."

"Mmm, I like it when you take charge." She stood on tiptoe, planting a kiss on my mouth. I happily returned the gesture. "See ya tomorrow, druid boy."

"I look forward to it," I replied as I watched her go.

When I turned to sit back down and finish my coffee, Luther was leaning in the doorway, arms crossed with a bar towel draped over his shoulder and a sly grin on his face. The vampire was a bit of a queen, and like most queens, he enjoyed a touch of juicy romantic intrigue every now and again—even if it was by proxy.

"You have it bad for her, don't you?" he asked in his deep, yet slightly effeminate, voice.

"Yeah, I think I do," I replied.

He laughed. "Oh, boyfriend, you have your hands full with her. But, that's not necessarily a bad thing."

"Indeed it's not, Luther. Definitely not a bad thing at all."

I WAS on my way home doing fifty on South Lamar when my brakes failed.

What the actual hell? I thought as depressed the brake pedal to the floor.

I swerved my way through a stoplight, horns blaring as I narrowly missed a couple of cars crossing the intersection ahead of me. They didn't see me until I was right on top of them because of the look away spell. If I hadn't cut the wheel in time, it would have been a bad wreck for all involved.

To make matters worse, when I took my foot off the gas pedal, nothing happened. My accelerator was stuck with my engine pegged at around 4,000 rpm, and I was sailing down one of the busiest roads in Austin with no way to stop.

I tried pumping the brakes again, but got nothing. The brake pedal went all the way to the floor, which meant that either the master cylinder had gone out, or I had a busted brake line.

Or someone had cut my brakes. Considering that my accelerator was stuck, I suspected foul play. I could determine who'd done it later—right now, I needed to figure out a way to stop my car without killing myself or an innocent bystander in the process.

I kept the car in gear and turned off the ignition, hoping that I didn't throw a rod by engine braking at speed. The last thing I needed was to have to rebuild the motor or transmission in the Gremlin. Then I stomped on the emergency brake lever, but of course it went to the floor with zero resistance. Obviously, someone *really* wanted to put me in a body bag.

By this time, I was approaching the next intersection—and another red light, no less—at about forty-five miles an hour. Cutting the engine was slowing the car down, but not fast enough to keep me from colliding with another vehicle.

It was down to magic or nothing.

I thought up a quick spell on the fly—or, rather, the application of a spell. The way a car's brakes worked was by friction. The hydraulics in the brake cylinders put pressure on the brake pads or shoes, which in turn squeezed or pressed against the brake rotor or drums, which were firmly attached to the axle. That, in turn, slowed the rotation of the wheels around the axle, which caused the car to stop.

So, all I needed to do was to intensify the friction that was already there.

I quickly rattled off a spell to increase the density of air in a given space, aiming it at the area around my front wheels where the brake pads met the rotors. As I released the spell, the car immediately began slowing down.

Unfortunately, there were several cars crossing the intersection ahead, and it was clear I wasn't going to stop in time. Not only that, but a woman was pushing a tandem jogging stroller into the crosswalk. Due to the look away spell on my car, she was completely oblivious to the two-ton metal missile of death heading straight toward her and her children.

Shit!

I did some quick calculations in my head, redirecting the energy of the spell to a spot that was roughly twenty feet in front of my car. Instantly, dirt and debris from the road ahead swirled into a small dust devil. The litter and dust coalesced in midair, freezing into a vertical column a foot across and slightly taller than the Gremlin's hood.

Lord, have mercy, I thought, just before my front bumper made contact with the dense, highly compressed pillar of air and debris that my spell had created ahead of me. I may as well have hit a light pole, because that's exactly the effect it had on my vehicle.

The car came crashing to a halt as the front bumper and hood wrapped around the mostly invisible barrier I'd created.

Of course, when the car stopped I didn't. I was thrown forward in the most violent manner imaginable, only to be stopped by my shoulder harness and seatbelt... sort of.

My head hit the steering wheel, and then everything went black.

SEVEN

I awoke to bright lights, puke-yellow curtain dividers, a disinfectant-over-urine smell, and the distinct beeping noise of a three-lead EKG monitor. A nurse was injecting something into an I.V. tube, which happened to be attached to my arm, while Finnegas and Maureen hovered behind her. Someone was coughing nearby, a Dr. Simes was being paged over the intercom, and my face felt like I'd gotten kicked by an angry centaur.

I pulled the I.V. line out of my arm, then dropped the siderail on the bed so I could sit up. This elicited a chuckle from Maureen and a gasp from the nurse, who immediately began trying to push me back into bed.

"Young man, you are in no condition to get up. You've been in a motor vehicle accident and you have a concussion."

I gently pushed her hands away. "Lady, I've had concussions before and I heal fast. Tell her, Grandpa," I said, looking to Finnegas for confirmation.

"I resent that," he said under his breath, low enough so

only Maureen and I would hear. He cleared his throat and addressed the nurse in a louder voice. "My grandson has indeed suffered a great many concussions—and based on his behavior, I can assure you that he's no more brain-addled than normal. I believe his main concern is the fact that he doesn't have insurance, which is probably why he's so eager to leave his hospital bed."

"Yup, that's right. I can't afford a hospital stay, so if you'll just bring me a release form to sign, I'll be on my way."

The nurse spent the next five minutes trying to convince me that I needed to be admitted. By the time she'd finished, I'd gathered my wallet and a few other personal articles from the clothing the paramedics had cut off me, and was headed out the door with my ass cheeks flapping in the wind. Hospital gowns were terribly breezy, as it turned out.

The nurse stepped in front of me. "At least let me get you some scrubs from surgery," she pleaded.

"Fine, I can wait." She headed out the door in a flustered rush. "And bring me that release form to sign!" I hollered after her.

"My, but someone has their panties in a wad," Maureen commented drily.

I sat on the gurney and shrugged. "Being the object of an attempted assassination will do that to you. How's my face?"

Finnegas grabbed me by the chin, turning my head this way and that as he examined me. "Well, the stitches aren't too bad, and thankfully your facial structure is intact. It's nothing that your fast metabolism and some druid healing magic can't fix."

"Did you grab my Bag?" He nodded. I rubbed my head,

wincing from the tender condition of my flesh. "How's the car?"

Finnegas pursed his lips. "Do you want the good news, or the bad news?"

"Both."

"Front end is totaled. It'll need a new bumper, new fenders, a new hood—and the engine will need to be looked at before it's drivable again." He crossed his arms and tsked. "Brake lines were cut—expertly, in fact. Plus, I found some kind of fancy mechanism under the air cleaner that was designed to freeze your throttle once you hit a certain speed. Whoever did this knew their work."

"You think it was the fae?" I asked, raising an eyebrow and instantly regretting it as my face protested.

"Naw, 'tis not their style," Maureen stated. She'd taken a seat on a doctor's stool nearby, and was flipping through a page-worn issue of *People* magazine. "If the fae had wanted you taken out, they'd have sent a hit squad to do you proper, with swords and the like." She glanced up over the top edge of the magazine. "If you're asking me, or even if you aren't, I'd say this has 'humans' written all over it."

I nodded, sucking air through my teeth. "Finnegas, you think our technomancer assassin is responsible?"

He pulled out his tobacco pouch. Maureen leaned forward and smacked him with the magazine, pointing at the "No Smoking" sign on the wall. The old man scowled as he put the tobacco away.

"Meh, it could be. Maybe he couldn't get to you via magical means, so he opted for more modern methods."

I thought about it for a second as I pulled my hospital gown together in back. It was starting to get really drafty, and the more I pulled out of my brain-concussed stupor, the more self-conscious I became.

"I don't know, Finn. If Elmo's killer really was the rich guy I met at the junkyard, he didn't really strike me as the type to get his hands dirty. In fact, he even said as much to me. No, I think if he was behind it, he'd have hired someone else to do it."

"Maybe the same crew who killed the ogre," Maureen said, just as the nurse walked in with a clipboard and a mint green set of scrubs. The nurse cleared her throat as she looked at each of us nervously.

"We're screenwriters, ma'am. We were just discussing a script we're working on."

She nodded, eager to accept my explanation as a matter of fact. Humans were always ready to accept any explanation for things that didn't fit their worldview. Confirmation bias was convenient that way, when you dealt with the world beneath.

"Well, Mr. McCool, I brought those scrubs as promised. Our attending would like to take a look at you before you leave, but he's busy at the moment treating another patient who has more serious injuries." As soon as she handed me the clothes, I began slipping them on. "If you could wait a few more minutes—"

"Sorry, miss, but I have places to be and people to kill." The nurse looked at me, eyes wide, as I realized my faux pas. "On paper, I mean. The, um, producer is breathing down our necks."

Maureen snickered from behind her magazine. "Oh for sure, and we don't want to keep her waiting—that's a fact."

The nurse looked at us both as she smoothed out her

nurse's smock. She glanced around, grabbing the clipboard off a bedside table and shoving it toward me.

"Well then, if you'll just sign here and here..."

I took the pen and did as she asked, waiting for her to bustle out of the room before speaking. "Alright, take me home so I can change. I really do have people to kill, and right now I'm damned eager to get started."

"Now, there's a plan I can get behind," Maureen quipped as she tucked the magazine into her handbag. Finnegas and I both stared at her. "Oh, you talk about killing folks, and that's just fine... but let Maureen snatch a magazine, and everyone has a cow! Fine! I'll put it back, ya pussies."

I WAS PRETTY BANGED UP, but later that afternoon I borrowed the yard truck from Ed and headed out to work the streets for information. My first stop was Rocko's bar, a little dive set well back from the curb in an industrial area in South Austin, near a bunch of other bars and strip joints. The place was popular with the seedy underbelly of Austin's supernatural community, so it was a good place to dig for intel.

It was mid-afternoon when I walked in, and besides a couple of regulars, the place was mostly empty. The odor of stale beer, cheap cigar smoke, and freshly-brewed coffee mingled in the air, while Sinatra played a little too loudly on the vintage jukebox in the corner. The walls were plastered with mob movie posters—some signed, some not—and black and white images of infamous gangsters and famous crooners from the 50s and 60s. The occasional cracked picture frame or skull-sized hole in the drywall indicated this was no trendy hipster bar; it was a place where you watched your wallet and your back at all times.

Rocko was sitting at the bar drinking black coffee and reading the paper. He was dressed in smart gray dress slacks, white patent-leather shoes, and a black silk *guayabera*. A cheap cigar smoldered in the ashtray next to him, filling the air with a noxious odor that was somewhat akin to old-school tear gas and burning leaves.

Sal's on-again, off-again human girlfriend, Cinnamon, stood behind the bar, drying beer mugs with a dish towel of dubious provenance. As always, she was dressed in a skirt that was almost criminally short, and a skin-tight top that showed as much of her cleavage as possible without being pornographic. Although I couldn't see behind the bar, I would have bet the Gremlin's pink slip that a pair of stripper shoes finished her ensemble.

Rocko looked up as I sat at the bar next to him. "You look like shit, druid. Come to ask for the job back, now that they're after you too?"

"Oh, I'm on the job, Rocko—but it's personal now. So no, I'm not here looking for a paycheck. I just need some info."

He set his newspaper down and tapped on his mug. "Warm this up for me, would you, Cinnamon?" She shrugged and walked to the end of the bar to fetch the coffee pot. After she'd filled his mug, Rocko shooed her away. "Sweetheart, go find something in the back to keep you busy."

"Aw, c'mon, Rocko. The T.V.'s busted, and there ain't no wifi here!"

"Just do it, and tomorrow I'll make sure to bring you some of those trashy rags you like to read."

"Whatever," Cinnamon replied as she adjusted her bra in

a very unladylike manner, before marching off to Rocko's office.

"Nice girl, but not much going on upstairs. Reads *The Enquirer* and believes it. Thinks aliens are real. Aliens! Never occurred to her that it might be the Fair Folk cutting up cattle and abducting farmers."

"Is it?" I asked.

"How the hell should I know what those country fucking fae do with their spare time? Wouldn't put it past 'em, though." He folded his paper and took a sip of his coffee, setting the mug down with a grimace. "Tastes like she made it with yesterday's grounds. Alright, druid, what can I help you with?"

"You know they killed Elmo at the junkyard two nights ago, right? And that they tried to off me this morning?"

He nodded. "Word gets around, especially when some college kid crashes his car into a big chunk of nothing in front of a dozen witnesses."

The Gremlin's crumpled front end had damaged the runes I'd written the see-me-not spells into, revealing the wreckage to passersby. Thankfully, none had gotten video footage of the wreck.

I crossed my arms. "It's a big weird world out there. Just ask *The Enquirer*."

The red cap paused to snag his cigar. "Word is they cut your brakes and jammed your throttle. Izzat true?"

"You're surprisingly well-informed as usual, Rocko."

He shrugged. "I got a few cops on the take. Now, what's this got to do with me?"

"Nothing. I got a lead on a hunter outfit that might be

involved in the killings. Humans, who use guns that shoot arrows."

"What, like crossbows or something? Must be half a dozen crews in the area who use 'em."

I shook my head. "No, I'm talking about a gun that shoots arrows using compressed air—kind of like a pellet gun, but a lot more powerful."

Rocko rubbed his chin. "Honestly, druid, I've never even heard of such a thing. But I'll put some feelers out, see if it rings any bells."

"You know how to reach me," I said as I pushed away from the bar and stood. I didn't thank Rocko, because that was always a dumb thing to do when dealing with the fae. His voice stopped me when I was halfway to the door.

"Oh, druid—one last thing. Let's say, theoretically speaking of course, that I had the need to hire people with certain... skills. Of course, this is just a rumor, mind you. But I hear there's this chat room on the dark web where you can *theoretically* find people who do jobs of a *less-than-legal* nature." He wrote a web address on a napkin that ended with "dot onion."

I pocketed the napkin. "Always a pleasure, Rocko."

"Likewise, druid. Try not to get yourself killed before you catch that piece of shit, alright? The boys got a pool going, and I got two-fifty that says you catch him by the end of the week."

"Huh. What kind of odds are they giving me?"

"Odds are on you getting offed, twenty-to-one. So, I stand to make a pretty penny if you manage to collar this freak."

"Well, it's nice to know I'm well-loved around here," I said, turning toward the exit. I yelled over my shoulder as I headed out the door. "Trust me, Rocko—you're going to clean up on that bet."

I WAS EXITING the bar when I heard movement on either side of me. A glance left and right revealed two tall, thin fae were approaching me, one to each side. They were dressed head to toe in hooded black leathers, and strapped with blades of various sizes six ways from Sunday. Their boots were covered in gravel dust, so I assumed they'd been waiting for me since I'd entered the bar.

Even though they each had a good twenty feet to cover, they were nearly in fighting range by the time I drew my sword from my Craneskin Bag. My feet crunched against gravel as I backed up into the parking lot to keep them from flanking me. I held my blade at eye level as I moved it back and forth between us. They didn't seem too impressed by me, at least not until one of them got a little too close. That's when the blade decided to burst into flames, which certainly got her attention.

"That's far enough," I stated.

The female fae in the lead stopped, as did her companion. She tossed her hood back and stared down her nose at me imperiously. Like all higher fae, she was supernaturally beautiful, with pale skin, high cheekbones, platinum blonde hair pulled back in a tight ponytail, and gray eyes so bright they were almost silver. Both she and her male counterpart were tall—a few inches taller than my six-one—and built like ballet dancers, all lean muscle and fluid grace.

They were a fae hit squad, likely trained from birth in

every deadly discipline imaginable. Hand-to-hand, blade craft, poisons, projectile weapons, explosives, and magic. They'd almost certainly been training, fighting, and killing together for centuries, so my chances of walking away alive were nil unless I hulked out on them... an option that didn't especially appeal to me.

Their presence was somewhat of a shock, since I couldn't recall a time when Maeve had felt the need to bring out her first string. If I hadn't known better, I'd have been tempted to think that this pair had been the ones who'd tried to kill me earlier. Except Maureen was right—slicing brake lines just wasn't their style.

But jumping someone outside a bar and slicing them up like confetti? Yeah, that was *definitely* their style.

"We were sent to relay a message from the Queen," the female assassin said in a voice both razor-thin and hauntingly beautiful. She was the type of fae that truly scared me, the old-school kind who didn't even bother masking their appearance. When fae didn't hide their identity from humans, you could bet that any human who saw them was a dead man walking.

"But we weren't instructed as to how we might deliver it, were we, Lucindras?" the male said.

The female smiled, but her eyes were tight. "Quite so. Therefore, Eliandres and I thought we'd deliver it in the universal language."

"Love?" I asked, just to be a smartass.

"Pain," the male fae hissed as he blurred into motion, tossing three knives at my face, one right after the other.

I dodged one, blocked the second, and took a shallow cut across my cheekbone from the third. I hoped it wasn't poisoned as I took a leap toward Rocko's restored seventies-era Olds 88, half-sliding and half-rolling across the trunk. Hell if I was going to fight both of these fuckers at once, so anything I could do to make them come at me one at a time was worth a little extra effort.

The good news was that my move forced the female to come around the front of the car to get at me. The bad news was that her buddy was circling around the other side. I switched my sword to my left hand and pulled my Glock from the small of my back with my right, snapping off three rounds that I aimed at the female's stomach, chest, and head, in that order.

The chick already had a wicked-looking pair of curved short swords out, and she was spinning them in dizzying patterns when I shot at her. Defying all expectations and the laws of probability, she blocked the first two rounds with her swords, and dodged the third. I only knew she blocked the first two bullets because I heard them ping off her blades as they ricocheted off into the distance.

And as for dodging my shot at her head? Well, she twitched like she was popping her neck, and then she didn't sprout a hole there. That pretty much indicated she'd dodged my shot, likely by anticipating my aim and timing my trigger pull. I was less than ten feet from her, and at that distance I simply didn't miss a head shot. I had to accept that she'd pulled a Neo on me.

"You know what, Lucy? I think I might be in love if I didn't think you were trying to kill me," I said as I back-kicked her partner in the chest.

He didn't think I was paying attention, so he caught it clean in the solar plexus. I don't care who you are—taking a combat boot to the xiphoid process will fuck you up. Eli fell back on his ass a few feet away, sucking air through his pie-hole like a fish out of water.

Pain indeed, I gloated to myself, just before I nearly got my head taken off by Lucindras' blade. I barely parried the cut with my off hand, firing another four shots with my right that caused the deadly assassin to spin away and take cover behind the 88's front grill.

Given a moment's reprieve I took it, leaping up to catch the driver's side door handle on Rocko's car under my boot. I pushed off, springing to the roof of the adjacent car parkour-style, then I leapt to the next car's roof to pull me out of reach of Lucy's blades.

Knowing I was outmatched by these two, I spun and put a bullet in the still-gasping Eli's gut, and another in his leg near his femoral artery. For the most part, fae anatomy was similar to ours, and I knew the injuries would be fatal if not seen to immediately.

Lucindras' eyes narrowed and her mouth curled into a scowl as she stalked toward me. "You'll pay for that with your life!" she screamed.

I pointed the barrel of the Glock at her partner. "And he'll die if you don't treat his injuries," I stated. "So, why don't you go ahead and relay that message, and we can all be on our way?"

She looked back and forth between Eliandres and me, finally sheathing her swords with a frustrated growl. "The Queen wants you to know that, while she still intends to punish you for your betrayal, she supports you in your quest to find those who are killing the fae. So, she will not stand in your way until the killers are found."

I twirled the tip of my sword to take in the entire vignette around me. "And just how does this little scene fit into the Queen's plans?"

Lucindras scowled. "Many of the Queen's most loyal subjects feel her interests would be better served if you were dead." She glanced at her partner, who was bleeding out a few feet away. "My advice to you, druid, is that you do not assume all her majesty's subjects will heed her commands where you are concerned."

"Noted," I said. "And fuck you very much for that info."

"I'll see you dead, druid. I swear it," she replied as she moved to assist her partner.

"Not if I see you first, Lucy. Ciao!" I gave them both a half-hearted salute before I beat a hasty retreat to my vehicle.

EIGHT

I'd gotten lucky with Lucy and Eli, and I knew it. Even with their magical wings clipped, it wouldn't take long for Eli to get healed so they could come back after me. That knowledge made me even more antsy, because now I had a fae hit squad *and* a serial killer gunning for me.

Leave it to me to keep things nice and simple, I thought as I drove to my next destination. The War Wolves' clubhouse was on the other side of town, but I had some time to kill. Besides, after running into Lucy and Eli, I didn't mind the idea of having a few dozen 'thropes watching my back, if only for a few hours.

It was getting close to dark, so things would be hopping at the clubhouse soon. If there was one thing the Pack loved to do, it was to party—and rest-assured there'd be a crowd on hand at the Pack's private hangout tonight. I'd have plenty of backup if the Wonder Twins decided to come at me again.

I was officially a member of the Pack, based on my status as a shifter who'd passed the Pack's trials—and the fact that

I'd saved their alpha from being killed by a nasty bunch of fae who'd infiltrated their organization. Even so, it wasn't like I was completely accepted by the rest of the Pack—my other half was Fomorian and not an animal like most shifters, and "Fomorian" was just the same as "fae" to most 'thropes.

So, I'd kept my distance since all that shit had gone down with the attempted Pack coup, and that was how I liked it. This was in spite of the fact that I owed the Pack's alpha, Samson, a debt of gratitude I could never repay for helping me get my Hyde-side under control. As I pulled into the parking lot, I silently hoped there weren't any hard feelings because I hadn't been around much lately.

I parked the truck in the back of the building, mostly to keep any prying eyes from knowing I was here, but also because certain Pack members had once been fond of letting the air out of my tires. *Yeah, Patrick Swayze's got nothing on me*, I thought as I walked in the service entrance to the clubhouse. No sooner had I entered the kitchen did I hear a dusky female voice call out to me from across the room.

"Well now, look what the coyotes dragged in—as I live and breathe, Colin McCool himself." I turned to see Samson's daughter, Fallyn, leaning on the safety rail above the basement stairs, a huge grin on her face and a mischievous look in her eye. "And here I was starting to think you didn't love us anymore."

I walked over to greet her, picking up a couple of cases of beer on the way. I'd had to bar back for the clubhouse when I was a prospect, so I knew the drill. I also knew they must've been shorthanded for Fallyn to be helping Mitzy, their bartender, get ready for the night.

"Hiya, Fallyn. Where do you want these?"

She smirked. "Just like that, huh? You're going to act like you haven't been avoiding us, and just pick up where you left off?" I shrugged. "Fine, you know where they go. And there's a dozen more cases downstairs, if you don't mind."

"No sweat, I got it," I said as I headed to the bar.

"I knew you were good for something, besides killing fae," she said as I walked away. "Come see me in Samson's office when you're done."

There were a few Pack members already in attendance when I stepped into the main hall. I got a few nods and a couple of, "Druid, how's it hanging"-type greetings as I finished helping Mitzy prep the bar for the night. Mitzy was a pretty redhead with a ready smile who liked to tell bawdy jokes. I'd liked her from the start back when I was new to the Pack, and she'd given me advice a time or two that had saved me from embarrassing myself. So, when she stopped me with a hand on my arm, I paid attention.

"Hey, champ, just an FYI—believe it or not, Sonny still has a few fans left 'round here. None of 'em will cause any trouble, at least not while Samson's around. But, just between you and me, keep an eye on your drink and sit with your back to the wall tonight, alright?"

"Thanks for the heads up, Mitzy."

I dropped a fiver into her tip jar. She nodded and gave me a playful wink, the kind most female bartenders did reflexively as a matter of course. Far be it from me to blame a woman for wanting to get better tips, and if guys were stupid enough to see it as flirting, well... that was on them.

Me? I just trusted that Mitzy wouldn't let anyone Mickey my drinks if she could help it. Plus, I knew how hard she worked. For those reasons, I considered it a moral obligation to tip her, even when I wasn't drinking.

I didn't see anyone in the clubhouse I cared to chat with, so I headed straight to the office. Inside, not much had changed. The walls were still plastered with girly calendars and posters, and the place still smelled of sex, weed, and liquor. The Pack's makeshift indoor shooting range was obviously still seeing regular use as well, albeit with a new mannequin to serve for a target.

As always, Samson sat behind his desk, face hidden in shadow as he sipped his whiskey and did his whole "zen biker" thing. He was leaning back in his chair with his boots kicked up, whiskey tumbler in his lap as he considered the paint peeling from the ceiling.

Fallyn sat on the edge of his desk, sharpening a huge Bowie knife with a stag handle. She looked up as I entered, continuing to run the edge of the blade across the whetstone in her hand. One slip and she'd lay her wrist open, but she was a 'thrope so she didn't have much to worry about.

"See, Dad? Told you I wasn't lying. The little shit actually decided to grace us with his presence." She said it with the same friendly smirk as before, but based on the tension in the room, I knew something was up.

Samson twitched his Chuck Norris mustache as he took a sip of whiskey. "Kid, you got some nerve coming in here unannounced."

I FIGURED Samson might be a little cross, what with me making myself scarce after I'd helped him and Fallyn stop

Sonny's coup. But I didn't think he'd do more than chide me a little and call it even. From the look on his face, I knew I was in for a major ass-chewing... if not an ass-kicking, as well.

Samson was an old, old wolf, and I'd seen him in action. No way did I want to face him down in a fair fight. My Hyde-side could take him, sure—but I wouldn't like it. Nope. So, I'd just take my licks if it came to that.

"Look, Samson, I'm sorry I haven't been around—"

He laughed out loud, and it wasn't an amused laugh. "Shit, son, you think I'm mad because you haven't showed your face lately? Hell, it was the best thing you could've done, considering how jumpy everyone was after you killed Sonny the way you did. Only a few things scare 'thropes, and death by fire is one of 'em. Naw, that ain't it at all."

My brow furrowed as I tried to think of what I might have done. "Sorry, I'm drawing a blank here. Do you two care to fill me?"

Fallyn stopped sharpening her knife and stuck it tip-first in the desk, drawing a sigh from her dad.

"I told you to stop doing that, Fallyn. Furniture costs money, damn it, and this desk is an antique."

"Oh, get over it. Thing's a piece of shit anyway." She sheathed her knife and turned on me. "As for *you*, what were you thinking, kicking the fae in the nuts like that? Do you know how close we came to all-out war with those pointy-eared fuckers after that stunt you pulled with Maeve?"

I mentally backpedaled for a moment, speechless. "I, um..."

"You didn't think about it, right?" she said with a smug look on her face. "Because Colin McCool, mightiest fucking druid apprentice in the free world, never stops to think anything through. He just barrels his way through life, kicking hornet's nests over, never considering how his actions might impact the people around him. Well, like it or not, you represent the Pack now, and—"

"Fallyn, enough," her father said in a low voice.

She turned on him in a heartbeat. "What do you mean, 'enough'? All the trouble he's caused, and you're not even going to chew his ass for it? If it was any other Pack member, he'd be eating his teeth."

He raised a hand, slowly. "Yeah, but he's not any other Pack member. When things went sideways, who else stepped in to set things right? Who backed us up against Sonny and his stooges? Hell, who could've, and lived? That's right, no one. And who saved your life, Fallyn? Sure, I healed you— but if it wasn't for shit-for-brains here I'd still be mourning the loss of my daughter."

Fallyn began to protest, but her father cut her off. "No, I don't want to hear it. Colin's a special case, whether you like it or not. He could never fit in here, not if he wanted to, but he's sacrificed more for the Pack than any ten of us." Samson turned his cold eyes on me, and I shivered a little as they flashed red in the lamplight. "You get one pass, kid. One. But next time, you'd better consult me first before you do something that could start a war. Understood?"

I gulped and nodded. "Yeah, Samson, I understand."

He nodded in kind, signaling to me that it was settled. Fallyn sighed, shaking her head as she gave me a smile that was just barely friendly. "I'd have gotten my ass chewed, golden boy, so don't think you're off the hook with me."

I smiled and nodded. "I get it, I screwed up and caused you grief. I'll make it up, I promise."

She chuckled as she walked by me on her way out the office. "No, you won't—at least not as long as you're still sharing a bed with that little hunter chick." Fallyn patted me on the cheek. "But come see me when you get bored with her, and I'll show you how a she-wolf takes out her frustrations."

Fallyn left, and I stood there in stunned silence for a few seconds before speaking. "Samson, I—"

"Don't," he said, and the warning in his voice was clear. "My daughter does what she wants—always has, always will. But you and her can never be a thing, am I clear? She needs a wolf, not a wildcard. As much as I like you, I want better for my daughter."

"Again, understood."

Samson spun in his chair to grab another glass and a bottle of whiskey. He poured one for each of us, sliding a tumbler to me before kicking his feet up again.

"Good. That's settled—why don't you tell me why you're here?"

SAMSON SAT with his fingers steepled, giving me his full attention as I shared the events of the last several weeks. When I was done, he took a sip of whiskey then stared off into the distance while I waited for him to speak.

"You sure know how to step in it, don't you, kid?"

I gave a rueful smile and cocked my head to the side. "It's a talent, but not really what you'd call a gift."

He chuckled. "Yeah, well—that's what you get for being young and idealistic. You get a little older, and you start to realize that every fight ain't your fight. You gotta pick your battles, else you'll never live to see old age."

My first thought to Samson's advice was, *Who wants to see old age?* But I kept that opinion to myself. "Well, I have a soft spot for underdogs, I guess. That ogre never hurt anyone —besides me, of course—and he got caught up in a mess that ended in his death, all because he was trying to help a defenseless teenage girl."

"A fae girl," Samson observed. "So it's not like she was completely defenseless, or pure as the driven snow either."

I tongued a molar and tsked. "Be that as it may, I'm still determined to see the killer—or killers—caught. And something tells me there's more to this than meets the eye."

Samson sipped his whiskey and sniffed. "Could be a power play—someone making a move on the fae's power base. And after the number you did on them, they're not really in a position to prevent it right now."

"Didn't you just say that the fae aren't exactly defenseless?" I asked.

"I did, but you're missing the point. Think about what keeps the world's superpowers from destroying each other. It ain't good intentions, I'll tell you that. Nope, it's self-preservation, because an all-out nuclear war would mean mutually-assured destruction for all involved. Nobody wins that scenario, which is why we're not all living in a nuclear winter.

"Well, the supernatural factions here in Austin are a lot like the world's superpowers. Nobody wants to start a war, because if it happens everyone loses. Each faction, be it the Pack, the Coven, the Circle, or the Fae—all of us agreed long ago that it was better to keep the peace than risk an all-out war.

"But, kid, you upset the balance of power when you cut the fae off from their giant magic battery in Underhill." I began to protest, but he raised a hand to cut me off. "Now, hear me out. I know for a fact that Maeve's not completely vulnerable. That old fae queen is crafty as all hell, and she has more aces up her sleeve than a six-armed card sharp."

"But..."

He kicked his legs off his desk, leaning forward on his elbows as he fixed me with a cold stare. "But some other factions might have been preparing for this day. Maybe they've been planning ahead for decades, waiting for the right moment to strike. Or maybe they have some sort of magic hidden that they think gives them an edge." He sat back and waved a hand in the air as if shooing a fly. "Hell, I don't know. But what I do know is that, if I had designs on eliminating the fae, I'd strike now."

"So, this is all my fault."

"Yup." Samson sipped his whiskey, staring at me with hooded eyes. "Question is, what're you going to do about it? Cause I can tell you, kid, whoever is going after the fae has designs on all their artifacts and talismans. And once they have them, who do you think they'll go after next?"

"The other factions," I said, finally realizing the implications of my actions. I leaned back in my chair, downing my whiskey. "Shit."

Samson raised his glass to me. "You got that right, kid. And a whole mess of it." He poured himself another three fingers, offering me the same. I declined. "So, again, what are you going to do about it?"

I thought for a moment, knowing that Samson was steering me toward a conclusion that I hadn't yet reached.

"Samson, if you were in my shoes, who would you finger for these killings?"

A smiled played at the corner of the old alpha's mouth. "Well, first, I'd ask who stands to gain the most from taking over Maeve's shit. It ain't us, that's for sure. What the hell are a bunch of werewolves going to do with fae artifacts?"

I swirled the last remaining drops of whiskey in my empty glass. "And it's probably not Luther. He tends to discourage his coven members from practicing magic."

"That's right," the old alpha replied, "because he wants to keep the balance of power—maintain the status quo. If the fae or the Circle got wind that he was training up a bunch of vampire mages, well—that shit just would not stand."

"So what you're saying is, The Cold Iron Circle is probably behind this."

Samson frowned unconvincingly. "Now did I say that? I distinctly recall *not* saying anything about who might be behind this whole mess. I only said who likely *wasn't* behind it. The difference is subtle, but important... especially when you're trying to stay neutral and keep your Pack out of a shit storm like this one."

"Right, I understand." I set my glass down on his desk and stood. "I think it's time I went to speak with Luther."

"Hell, he'd have been the first person I'd gone to if I were in your shoes. Anyway, while you're there tell him I'm running low on coffee beans."

"Um, okay. But, uh—can't you just pick up the phone and tell him yourself?"

"For once in your life, Colin, just do as your told."

"Alright, anything else?"

"Nope. Except don't go starting a war with the Circle

without speaking with me or Luther first. Chances are good that there are just a few people involved here, and not the whole bunch."

"Roger that, Samson. And thanks for the whiskey."

"Anytime," he said, tilting his glass to me as he kicked back even further in his chair, until his face was hidden in shadow once more. He was staring at the ceiling again by the time I reached the exit. "Shut the door behind you as you go, kid."

NINE

It was late, so I called Luther's before heading over. Not that
Luther ever answered his phone; he was so old he was a
virtual Luddite when it came to modern technology like cell
phones and the like. But someone always checked his
messages, either a member of his coven or a human assistant,
so my most important voicemails and texts always got
through.

Now, you'd think that a vampire who owned a coffee shop
would keep it open 24/7, but not Luther. He was all about
keeping up appearances, and these days he closed at 9 pm sharp,
opening at 5:30 am every day of the week. He liked to be present
whenever the shop was open, but he also thought people would
start to get suspicious if he was behind the counter twenty-four
hours a day. So he took nights off, just to be safe.

Honestly, I didn't think that Luther slept all that much.
From what I understood, older vampires didn't need much
rest, and Luther was likely the oldest vamp in the Austin

area. I'd never seen him anywhere but at the coffee shop or his apartment on the second and third floors of the building, except in the days after I'd first met him. We'd teamed up to deal with an ancient Nosferatu back then, one that had been older than Luther by many degrees. Since then, I'd only ever met Luther at his shop or home, so I assumed that's where he'd be.

I was about five minutes out from the coffeehouse when I got a call from an unknown number. "Colin's Mortuary. You stab 'em, we slab 'em," I answered.

A woman with a very proper-sounding Boston Brahmin accent responded. "Ahem. Luther is not at home. However, he requests your presence at the following location, at your earliest convenience." She rattled off an address that I recognized as being in a stylish upper-crust neighborhood on the west side.

"I can be there in twenty minutes," I replied.

"And, Mr. McCool?" she said with her Tuesday Weld voice. "Do come armed."

The caller hung up without another word. I drove the rest of the way to the address she'd given me, humming Lesley Gore's "You Don't Own Me." It seemed appropriate, for more than one reason.

I pulled up to the address, a sprawling mid-century modern that had obviously been patterned after a Frank Lloyd Wright design. I recognized the design cues because I'd done a paper on Wright in high school. This home bore more than a passing similarity to the Marshall Erdman Prefab homes, some of my favorites among the smaller houses he'd designed.

"Oh, to be well-heeled and immortal," I mumbled as I turned off the ignition and scanned the scene.

From where I'd parked I could see that the backyard had been lit with paper lanterns, and my hyper-sensitive hearing told me there were people milling around on the other side of the backyard fence. Some coffeehouse pop artist's latest ditty played softly in the background, and the sounds of pleasant conversation and glasses clinking echoed across the finely manicured front lawn.

I looked down at what I was wearing and sighed. Not wanting to embarrass Luther, I pulled my combat boots off, then dug around in my Craneskin Bag for something to change into that looked less careworn.

I ducked behind the truck and stripped out of my t-shirt and grease-stained Levi's, exchanging them for a clean pair of jeans, a plain white V-neck t-shirt, a newish pair of Doc Martens, and a fitted leather jacket that I saved for special occasions. I clipped my Glock's holster and a spare magazine carrier behind my back, then strapped the flaming sword over my shoulder, just to be safe.

Of course, I grabbed my Craneskin Bag... no way I was leaving it behind, uh-uh. It had a habit of letting things out that were better kept locked away—sentient magical items and such. I could only imagine what it might toss out at a vampire's soirée.

I walked up to the door and rang the doorbell, hoping this was indeed a vampire's home and not some society debutante's dinner party. If it was, I was about to play hell explaining why I had a sword strapped across my back.

Thankfully, the person who answered the door was most

definitely a vampire. He was a bit shorter than me, maybe five-ten, and Latino, with a dancer's build and a model's good looks. He wore a Jacquard silk dinner jacket and a pleated white dress shirt like he'd invented the term "black-tie-optional." The man looked me up and down with more than a professional interest before greeting me.

"Well, Luther said he had a plus-one coming, but in your case, I'd say you're a plus two-point-oh." He spoke in a very manly voice, yet his mannerisms had just a touch of the laissez-gay flair I'd come to expect from Luther's male friends. The man flashed me a grin filled with perfect white teeth, including a set of canines that extended ever-so-slightly as he smiled. "This way, please."

I pointed over my shoulder at the sword hilt. "Is this okay?"

The vamp stepped back, crossing his arms elbow-to-hand as he cupped his chin with his left finger and thumb. He looked me up and down again.

"Hmm..." The vampire reached out, almost too quick for me to react, straightening my clothes here and tucking them there. "That's better. Definitely keep the sword. The guests will love it."

Suddenly remembering my manners, I extended my hand. "I'm Colin, by the way."

"Mateo. Now, come, before they all wonder where I ran off to." He began walking away, looking back over his shoulder to serve me a friendly warning. "And do keep that sword handy. I have a feeling you'll need it before the night is done."

I loosened my sword in its scabbard as I followed after

him, wondering just what in the hell Luther was getting me into.

THERE WERE several party guests scattered throughout the house. Most displayed the unsettling affectations of young vampires, a kind of lack of natural movement that put them just on the wrong side of the uncanny valley. Older vamps learned to make themselves look human, most going so far as to breathe like normal humans, even though vampires required very little oxygen to survive. But the young ones, well—let's just say they were more than a little creepy to look at.

As Mateo led me through the house, conversations stopped and heads turned as I passed. Once we were gone, those conversations recommenced in hushed tones. I strained to pick up snippets of what the party guests were discussing, and soon realized they were talking about me.

Mateo gave me a knowing smile as we entered the industrial-sized kitchen, which was devoid of guests. "Don't let that concern you. Vampires tend to enjoy a bit of gossip and intrigue, and this crowd is no exception."

"I still don't quite get why I'm here," I said.

Mateo narrowed his eyes and his smile faded as he reached for the door. "I'll let Luther explain that to you." His face immediately lit up again as we exited the house, but I could tell it was for show. "And there he is!"

I followed Mateo across a flagstone patio, around a built-in fire pit where Luther stood conversing with a few other guests. I tried to avoid rubber-necking as I approached, but I couldn't help it—the backyard was huge, and it looked like it had been recently remodeled by the crew from *Yard Crashers*.

The guests who'd been talking to Luther slipped away as we approached. Luther half-scowled and half-smiled as I greeted him. "Oh, don't look so impressed, Colin. Mateo's boyfriend runs a landscaping company—it's not as if he did all this himself."

"Please," Mateo remarked. "You're just jealous because you had your eye on Tom before I did. It's not my fault you were slow to make your move."

"Luther, slow to make a move? Somehow, I find that hard to believe," I said.

Mateo laughed. "Believe it. He talks a good game, but he's way too old-fashioned at heart. It's put a cramp in his dating life since the sixties, at least."

I chuckled at the thought, much to Luther's chagrin. His scowl became genuine as he spoke. "Watch it now, young man, or I'll start telling stories about you and that sweet young thing you've been seeing."

"Do tell," Mateo said, as he snagged a glass of champagne from an attractive human server passing nearby. He sipped it and looked over the rim at Luther expectantly.

I cleared my throat nervously. "Um, not to change the subject—"

"Although you are," Luther interjected.

"—but does anyone want to tell me why I'm strapped for a fight at a vampire party?"

Mateo smirked. "Gets right to the point, doesn't he?"

Luther gave a small eye roll. "Alas, there's no sense for the dramatic in this one. He's all punch and no panache, I'm afraid."

"Sorry," I replied. "It's been an interesting day, and it has my hackles up."

"Should we tell him?" Mateo asked.

"I believe we should," Luther said. He turned to me with a casual smile. "We need you to referee a small dispute. It's nothing major—just a little spat between old friends."

I pointed my finger back and forth between them. "You two?"

Mateo chuckled. "Oh, heavens no. Actually, there's a vampire coming in from out of town. He's old—not as old as Luther here, but old."

"You wound me, Mateo," Luther said.

"As if you looked your age," Mateo replied. "Anyway, this vampire is very unpleasant, and he has a grudge of sorts against Luther."

"Should I know the source of this grudge?" I asked.

Mateo looked to Luther. "Oh, vaunted coven leader, would you care to divulge the cause of this long-standing feud?" he asked with a wicked grin.

"I slept with his wife," Luther replied. "It was during one of my hetero phases. Sue me."

Mateo gave Luther a sideways glance, then continued. "So, this rather unseemly person is coming here tonight, to challenge Luther. He intends to take Luther's coven away from him—"

"That's not going to happen," Luther interjected.

"—and we need you to referee the duel, as a neutral party," Mateo finished.

I pursed my lips as I looked at them both and nodded.

"Okay. Right. So, I'm supposed to referee a death match between two master vampires, and what? If you guys get out of hand, I'm supposed to break it up?"

Luther examined his fingernails. "Actually, your job is to make certain no one cheats, and that's it. You're not to get involved physically at all, else it will void the results of the match."

"What if someone else jumps in?" I asked.

Mateo waved off my concern as he sipped his champagne. "Oh, that won't happen. Both Luther and Cornelius will have their seconds on hand, to ensure that it's a fair fight —but if a second jumps in they forfeit the match."

"Cornelius?" I said. "Really?"

Luther smiled slightly. "It was a different time. Now, will you referee this duel, or do we need to call someone else in?"

I thought about it for a split-second, then shrugged. "Aw, what the hell—yeah, I'll do it. But I'm going to need some caffeine first, because I'm dead on my feet."

"Now, that we can take care of," Mateo said, snapping his fingers to get a nearby server's attention. "Charmaine, darling, could you bring me a double-shot cappuccino and some warm towels for our sword-bearing friend here? Thank you, dear."

The pretty girl scuttled off and returned in record time. Soon, I was fully-caffeinated and enjoying a hot towel facial and shoulder rub from the lovely Charmaine herself.

"I could get used to this, you guys," I mumbled from beneath the towel.

"Don't get too comfortable, druid," Mateo replied. "Here comes Cornelius."

I PULLED the towel off and stood, handing it to Charmaine. "Thank you," I said with a smile.

"My pleasure," she replied with a wink. "If you require further attention later, you have only to ask Mateo." I stared after her as she left.

"Is he blushing?" Mateo asked.

"Oh yes, he does that often," Luther replied. "I haven't decided if it's charming or droll, but the ladies seem to think the former of him."

"Ah, the fleeting innocence of youth," Mateo observed.

I cleared my throat, waving my hand to catch their attention. "Um, guys? Please tell me she's not...?" I let the uncomfortable question hang in the air, unwilling to offend the two vampires standing beside me by stating it out loud.

Mateo scowled. "Oh, of course not. We're not savages here. Besides, Luther outlawed the practice of keeping human slaves shortly after he established his rule in central Texas. No, Charmaine is a paid employee, and she's simply taken a shine to you, is all. Now, tuck your prick in your pants and attend the task at hand."

He inclined his head to a spot across the yard, where three shadowy figures were floating down to the ground from the dark night sky beyond. Mateo's yard backed up to a green belt, but I still wondered whether the neighbors might have seen.

"Well, that's a damned impressive entrance," I remarked.

Luther rolled his eyes. "Oh, good heavens. He always was a show-off."

"And the neighbors?" I asked.

Mateo waved my question away. "I own both houses to either side of this one—my staff members occupy them, currently. Besides, we have an illusionist on hand to ensure no prying eyes or cell phones catch anything untoward."

I shifted into the magical spectrum for a moment, just to spot the magic user. She was a goth-looking girl, sitting off by herself sipping a beer while she scrolled through her phone. When I spotted her, she glanced up from her phone long enough to flip me off.

"Fae, I presume," I said, failing to hide the distaste in my voice.

"She's talented. She works cheap, and still has some magic," Luther said. "So don't go starting any fights with the hired help, alright? I personally don't care to go looking for another illusionist who doesn't mind working with vampires. Good help is so hard to find."

"Shhh," Mateo whispered, nearly inaudibly. "Here he comes."

A gruff voice full of pretension and Southern charm called from across the yard. "Luther, I'm surprised to see you here."

Luther ignored the jibe, barely registering the other vampire's presence. "It is my territory, after all, and Mateo is one of my oldest friends. Why would I not attend a party held in my honor?"

"Dying is hardly an honor, although at my hands, your death may qualify," Cornelius replied. Again, Luther ignored the barb.

Luther's challenger stepped into the light as he approached, allowing me to get a good look at him. He was short—Napoleon short, in fact—but he carried himself like a lion, despite being rather rotund as well. He had a long, flowing mane of golden hair, reminiscent of Custer in his final days, and wore a finely-tailored three-piece suit, bespoke leather shoes, and a pocket watch and gold chain to top off the ensemble.

The suit was cut in a style that was modern, yet reminiscent of a bygone era—like something you'd expect Rich Uncle Pennybags to wear, were he a real person. If he'd been carrying a cane, I wouldn't have been surprised at all. Instead, he held a small, black, winged serpent, no larger than a small dog, which he stroked and petted as he spoke.

Well, that's interesting.

The reptile had its body wrapped around Cornelius' forearm, and it seemed to enjoy his ministrations. The vampire whispered to the creature before handing it off to one of the vamps who'd arrived with him. His companions were twins, and they looked like taller, thinner versions of their master. *His sons, perhaps?* I noted that the serpent obediently slithered onto one of the twin's arms, as though obeying its master's commands.

Just for grins, I checked the serpent out in the magical spectrum. The damned thing was throwing off magic like crazy—and not the bright and airy fae kind, either. This magic was dark, and it smelled like rotten eggs and meat left out too long. I wasn't sure what the serpent really was, but I was damned certain it was evil. I made a note to keep an eye on it.

Cornelius returned my stare with a slight sneer. "Is this the referee you've chosen? What is he, some hedge wizard reject from the Circle?"

"He's perfectly capable of fulfilling the duties required of him," Luther responded. "As the challenger, you had the right to choose the time of this duel. And, as the incumbent coven leader, I got to choose the place as well as the referee."

Cornelius clucked his tongue. "Fine, I'll not dispute your choice. It'll only forestall the inevitable. Besides, the lad looks harmless enough."

Mateo coughed in his hand, while Luther maintained a straight face. "The rules are simple," Mateo said in a loud voice. "Both combatants will enter the designated dueling area, and at the referee's command the duel will commence. They may use any weapon on their person, and any form they command. However, they may not leave the boundaries of the dueling square. Any such action will be considered a willful concession of the duel. Questions?"

Luther and Cornelius stared at each other, their mutual hatred evident. I shook my head.

"Fine then. Let's begin, shall we?" Mateo gestured to me. "Since I am serving as Luther's second, I'll hand the proceedings over to the referee. Colin, the floor is yours."

Great. Just fucking great. Luther, you better not get yourself killed.

A square area had been marked off on the lawn, roughly forty feet to a side. The party guests all congregated around the perimeter on three sides, leaving one side open for the combatants to enter. I pointed to the dueling ring.

"Gentlemen, are you ready?" I asked, feeling like a dork.

"Just get on with it, blood bag," Cornelius spat.

Luther sighed. "Yes, I'm ready. Once we enter the ring, just say the word. And when the victor has been made clear, simply call the duel complete and declare the winner."

The two vampires entered the designated area, squaring

off on either side of the ring. I walked to the boundary, raising my hand in the air like a kid flagging the starting line in a street race. I felt utterly stupid standing there with my arm in the air, but it was too late to take that goofy move back now.

I brought my hand down in a chopping motion. "Begin!"

TEN

The two master vampires wasted no time getting down to business. I'd seen Luther move before, but it still surprised me when the two of them sprang into action. Or as Cornelius sprang, that is.

The pudgy little blonde vampire launched himself through the air at Luther, quite literally flying across the ring at him. He covered the distance in the blink of an eye, and to be truthful I found myself straining to see the details of the fight.

"How am I supposed to declare a victor if I can't even tell what's going on?" I mumbled.

Click's voice replied from somewhere nearby. "The one that's left standing—that's the one you pick." A quick glance revealed him to be standing at my right elbow. He took a large and rather loud bite from an apple, chewing and swallowing before continuing. "Bet you're wondering why I'm here. Seeing two master *fampir* duel to the death, well—that's hardly something I could pass up. Plus, I have wager with their illusionist that Luther bites it."

"You bet against Luther? Seriously?" Click opened his mouth to reply, but I cut him off. "You know what? I don't want to hear it." I turned my attention back to the ring. "Gah! I still can't see anything."

Click crunched on his apple, spitting flecks of pulp as he spoke. "Hang on." He snapped his fingers in front of my face, and suddenly the action slowed considerably—but only inside the ring. Everything else seemed to be moving at normal speed.

I watched the duel unfold. "Neat trick. You're a chrono-mage, aren't you? I thought that branch of magic was outlawed by the Circle centuries ago."

He took another bite of his apple, tossing the core away. It bounced off a vampire's head, and the vamp looked around in vain for the culprit. "Don't worry—they can't see me, except for the illusionist. Although people might be wondering why you're talking to yourself. That is, if anyone is watching anything right now but the duel."

"You didn't answer my question," I replied.

"Yes, well, trickster magic has always been off-limits to human mages. They can't understand it, and that's why they fear it." He tapped a finger on the side of my skull. "But you, young man, you're a bard who croons to another tune entirely. In fact, you might actually be able to grasp the basic principles of chronourgy. I could even see you achieving a small measure of skill in the art... sometime far in the future, that is."

I glanced sideways at him. "Oh yeah?"

"Sure." He winked at me. "Just don't ever get caught using it."

We turned my attention back to the duel. Thus far, the fight had followed the same pattern. Cornelius would fly at Luther at supersonic speeds, and Luther would turn himself into shadow and smoke, reappearing on the other side of the ring unharmed. I had a feeling that Luther was trying to wear Cornelius out, but based on Luther's expression, things weren't going to plan. Not only was Cornelius not becoming fatigued, but he actually seemed to be getting faster as the duel continued.

All vampires had limited stores of energy based on how recently they'd fed, their age, their pedigree, and their natural abilities. Luther had once mentioned that his maker had been a very powerful and ancient vampire, so he could probably keep using his powers longer than most. But eventually he would tire, and if Cornelius had somehow found a way to circumvent that issue then Luther was royally fucked.

"Click, what do you know about the rules for these vampire duels?"

He shrugged. "Rules are simple. Stay in the ring, use any weapon or power you have on you when you enter, and don't die or else you lose. Old rules, created for simpler times. Ah, but how I miss those days."

At that moment, Cornelius flew across the ring at Luther for the umpteenth time. However, this time Luther did his smoke and shadow teleport thing just a little too late. He caught a vicious blow to his ribcage just as he was dematerializing, which elicited a small squeal of delight from Click. When the coven leader appeared on the other side of the ring, his stance was a little off. It wasn't much of a tell, but it was there.

Luther couldn't keep this up much longer.

I switched my vision back to the magical spectrum, because I needed to understand what was going on if I meant to save Luther. I searched Cornelius for some magical talisman or device, one that might be fueling his increased stamina. As far as I could tell, he had nothing of the sort on him. *Shit.*

Then, I spotted something. Just the faintest wisp of aether tethering him to his pet, who was currently wrapped around the arm of Cornelius' second outside the ring. When I focused on the tether, I determined the serpent was feeding Cornelius through that wisp of aether, much like a mother sustaining her child through an umbilical cord.

Cornelius was cheating via magical means. *Fuck me.*

As soon as he realized what I was looking at, Click's face fell. "Finally saw that, did you? I was hoping you wouldn't, being as I have money on the cheating bastard."

"You're incorrigible," I muttered as I stormed toward the twin vamps who'd arrived with Cornelius. I pointed my sword at the one holding the serpent. "Turn it off. Now."

The little fucker tried to play coy with me, giving me a smug grin as he replied. "Turn what off, human? I have no idea what you're talking about. Do you, Gaius?"

His twin shook his head as a smile tugged at the corners of his mouth. "No, Lucius, I haven't the foggiest."

"Fine," I seethed. I looked directly at the serpent, who displayed more intelligence in its eyes than both twins combined. I pointed the sword directly at its head, willing it to burst into flames. "Whatever you're doing to help

Cornelius, stop it now, or I lop off your head and Lucius here loses a hand. Your call!"

BESIDES FLICKING its tongue at me with a hiss, the serpent failed to respond to my demands. A gasp from the crowd caught my attention, and I looked over my shoulder in time to see Luther fly across the ring, propelled by a wicked backhand strike from his opponent. He landed on his feet, but I could tell he was hurt.

From that moment forward, it was *on* between the two vamps. Click's time differential spell was still in full effect, so I was able to see everything that was happening inside that ring. Cornelius fought like an Irish traveler, boxing bareknuckle in a manner that was both brutal and efficient. He threw combination after combination at Luther, launching blow after blow without pause.

Luther, on the other hand, fought more like a classic French *savateur*. *Boxe française savate* was the kickboxing art of the French, more commonly known simply as *savate*. Originally created by French sailors who'd held onto the rails and ropes of their ships to kick at their opponents while balancing on one leg, savate had evolved into a complete striking art over time. Savate was both beautiful and deadly, and Luther displayed true mastery of the art as he fought off Cornelius' attacks.

For every few punches Cornelius threw at Luther, Luther avoided most of them. As for the ones he missed, he'd take those on his arms and shoulders, covering and shelling up to prevent taking a punch on the jaw or temple. In response, Luther would return a dazzling combination of kicks that came from all angles, striking at multiple targets.

Yet Luther was already injured and quite exhausted while his opponent was still fresh, so Cornelius easily slipped, dodged, and blocked Luther's kicks. And while Luther was obviously the more skilled and savvy fighter, currently Cornelius possessed an advantage that Luther simply could not contend with. From experience, I knew that all those punches Luther was taking on his arms and shoulders were having an effect. Eventually they'd weaken him and slow him down. Then, one of Cornelius' jackhammer punches would land and it would be over.

I spun back on the serpent, menacing it with my sword. "You heard what I said, snake. Stop whatever you're doing to help Cornelius, or things are going to get ugly between us and fast!"

As I raised the sword to strike, I heard a thickly-accented voice inside my head.

I, Kulkulkan, have made a pact with Camazotz's offspring, the one who calls himself Cornelius. Know you now that the gods do not break their bond at the whim of mortals. Begone, lest I reveal my true form so I might crush you where you stand.

I racked my brain, trying to remember where I'd heard that name before. I knew it was a deity of some sort, because they were the only ones who spoke with that much pretention. Then I remembered: Kulkulkan was a winged serpent deity to the Mayan people. It was also the name of a powerful Mayan priest who'd lived several centuries ago, a man who was more than likely a mortal avatar of the deity. Chances were good that the creature before me was that guy, and not the deity itself. Or so I hoped.

"I've killed a god before," I said, stretching the truth a bit. Actually, I'd killed a Norse deity's son, a demigod. I'd also just barely fought off Whiro, the Maori god of death, but I almost didn't survive that encounter. Still, this Kulkulkan entity didn't need to know that. "You should know, it's no skin off my nose to kill another."

Do your worst, little pale skin. No matter how you struggle, I promise that your bones will litter my nest tonight.

By this time, a few bystanders were starting to pay attention to what was going on between the twins and me. I also noticed that Click was speaking to the fae illusionist in hushed tones. The fae girl nodded, then the two shook hands —I could only guess as to whether Click had bet on me, or the Mayan serpent deity. A quick look at the duel told me Luther wouldn't hold out much longer, and if I kept arguing with the twins someone was bound to step in on their behalf, which could complicate matters considerably.

Well, I guess I'd better light this candle or call it a day.

"Your funeral, serpent," I said as I swung the flaming sword at the snake.

Although I moved at full speed, I had a sneaking suspicion that the snake would evade the cut, and I was right. The serpent disappeared in a puff of smoke, just as my blade was about to strike. Lucius, however, wasn't so skilled or lucky. The flaming sword sliced his hand off cleanly mid-forearm. As the severed appendage flopped to the lawn, the pretty blonde vampire screamed like Miss Muffet in a tarantula store.

"My arm, father, my arm! The human has cut off my arm!"

"Oh please, it's just your hand," Click shouted.

I swiveled my head frantically, more to search for Kulkulkan than to anticipate an attack by Cornelius or Gaius. I wasn't worried about the vamps; it was the snake deity that concerned me. Even so, Cornelius stopped fighting with Luther—who was losing, incidentally—to speed to the edge of the dueling ring.

Lucius clutched his arm, whimpering while his brother seethed at me. I shook my head at Gaius, serving him notice that I wasn't having it.

"I'll kill you!" Cornelius screamed behind me.

I turned on him, pointing the flaming sword in his direction. "Ah-ah-ah! You leave that ring and you forfeit the match."

Cornelius stayed put, while Luther caught his breath on the other side of the ring. I sensed movement from the twins so I spun around, just in time to catch Gaius preparing to pounce.

"Don't try it, pretty boy," I said, "or they're going to be calling you two Stumpy and Hook from here on out."

Gaius froze mid-step as he reconsidered his options, and I kept a close eye on him for a moment just to be safe. Suddenly, his eyes grew wide and he pointed over my shoulder, backpedaling away from me and dragging his brother along with him.

I laughed. "Oh, like I'm going to fall for that old trick—nice try." Then, I noticed Click waving his arms frantically and pointing behind me from across the lawn. I looked at

Gaius and Lucius, who were nearly falling all over themselves to create as much space between us as possible.

"There's a giant winged serpent behind me, isn't there?" I asked them. The twins responded with almost simultaneous nods. "Shit."

———

VAMPIRES AND HUMANS scattered in all directions—some screaming, others cursing, and still others calmly stepping back to observe what would happen next. I supposed that when you were semi-immortal, anything out of the ordinary was a welcome distraction, even if being an innocent bystander might get you killed. I dove and rolled out of the way, narrowly missing being snapped up in a giant serpent's jaws.

I came to my feet quickly, pivoting to face the threat. Whether he was the deity's avatar or the real McCoy, Kulkulkan was a sight to behold. Fully thirty feet long from nose to tail, he sported deep green iridescent scales on his back and a lighter greenish-tan coloring on the underside of his torso. A huge set of wings had sprouted just behind his head, with bright, multi-colored plumage reminiscent of a macaw's feathers. As he towered over me, he spread his jaws wide, displaying a set of foot-long fangs that dripped with venom.

"See my true form," Kulkulkan roared at me, "and tremble!"

"Oh, fuck this," I replied, tossing my sword into my Craneskin Bag and throwing the Bag across the lawn to Click. "I'm going to want that back!" I yelled.

Click bobbled the Bag in his hands, finally ending up holding it suspended away from him with the strap pinched between his finger and thumb. His expression soured with distaste as he yelled back at me. "Be quick in dispatching the serpent, druid—this thing has never liked me!"

"Noted!" I said as I shifted into my Formorian form, screaming in pain and relief as the transformation commenced.

As my Hyde-side emerged, my bones grew and shifted, my skin split and reformed, and I gained at least a few hundred pounds of mass and a good eighteen inches in height. My clothes, of course, were shredded instantly, and they hung off in tatters—all except my Jockeys, that is. I'd learned the hard way to wear lycra underwear, just in case I needed to shift. Nothing was worse than fighting in public in your shifted form with your dangly bits flopping all over the place.

I felt my bones and skin thicken, my forehead protrude, my knuckles enlarge, and my muscles swell. My right arm grew until it had much more girth than my left. I flexed my right hand, squeezing it into a fist that resembled a mace on the end of a tree trunk. My left hand curled into a claw-like appendage instead, more suited for ripping and tearing than it was for pummeling. Finally, my back hunched slightly and my left eye bulged nearly out of its socket, giving me a sinister, Quasimodo-like appearance.

And when the transformation was complete, I felt it— that tug inside me, urging me to commit mayhem and violence on an epic scale.

I roared my fury to the skies. "Now, serpent—let us see what kind of *god* you are!"

The thing about snakes is, they're very, very fast. As I leapt at the giant serpent he struck, latching his jaws on my right shoulder and sinking his fangs into my flesh. Then, he began wrapping himself around me, stacking coil after coil that squeezed the breath from my lungs and caused my joints to creak.

"Oof!" I groaned, forcefully exhaling to avoid being popped like a grape.

Kulkulkan hissed, releasing me from his jaws to gloat. "Never before have I seen your like, creature. But despite your size and strength, none can withstand the fury of Kulkulkan!"

In response, I smiled. And in this form, I knew that smile wasn't pretty.

Opening his jaws was Kulkulkan's first mistake. As he reared his head back to crow about his impending victory, I managed to squirm my right arm out of his coils. Soon, I was hammering at his anguiform body, and despite my lack of leverage I was still hitting the serpent hard enough to crush its ribs.

Kulkulkan roared like a jungle cat, then he struck at me again. This time I was ready for him. I snapped my hand out, snagging the serpent around the throat with my massive, deformed hand. Then, I squeezed.

"Do you see? Two can play this game, worm," I croaked.

While Kulkulkan was crushing the life from me, I was squeezing hard enough to cut off his air, and perhaps to even snap his spine if I was lucky. He squirmed and squeezed even tighter, but I held onto his neck for dear life. Then, I began pulling him in toward me.

Kulkulkan's eyes bulged, his vertical pupils going wide.

With one final yank, I drew his neck to my face and bit down, hard. Cool black blood gushed into my mouth, the taste stoking my thirst for gore and death.

The great serpent thrashed violently as he realized the tactical error he had made. Soon he released his hold on me to try and escape, whipping his tail left and right, up and down, slamming it against the ground and beating his wings in a frantic attempt to dislodge me from his neck.

But instead of letting go, I simply reached around the serpent with both arms, pulling him closer as I bit him again, and again, and again. Thick dark wetness gushed into my mouth, choking me as it clotted, but I didn't care. The Formorian, monstrous, bestial side of me was in full control, and it *hungered*. Before I knew it, the serpent had stopped struggling, and I was crunching on his spine. Seconds later, his head plopped to the ground, splashing thick black blood in all directions.

Having vanquished one foe, I looked around for others. As my gaze swept across the crowd, vampires fled in all directions.

"Fight me, cowards!" I roared. None took me up on the invitation.

I searched nearby for a worthy opponent, until I spotted a tall dark-skinned man across the lawn beating a pudgy blonde-haired man's head into the ground. His arms moved with superhuman speed, and his fists landed like jackhammers, pulverizing the other man's skull into bloody grey and white gibbets.

There lies a battle worth fighting, I thought as I dropped the serpent's lifeless body to the ground.

As I took a step toward the dark-skinned man, a booming voice exploded inside my skull.

-Colin, no.-

I recognized that voice. It was the Eye, a destructive force even greater than my own. Now I remembered. I had lusted after that power, craved it like that weak fool Balor. He'd been slain by Lugh for his ambitions, but I would not fall so easily. I would tame the Eye, conquer it by will alone, and together we would destroy and kill and burn the world to ash.

-No, I'm afraid that is not my purpose. My apologies for this.-

A searing heat exploded inside my head, like a nuclear bomb going off in my brain. And with it came a pain like a mountain crushing my skull, agony so intense that it brought me to my knees. I clutched my head and screamed loud enough to make the ground tremble.

Then a darkness fell over me, and I remembered nothing more.

ELEVEN

"Uhhh... ow, that hurts." I cracked an eye open, and was thankfully met with darkness and not light. Even my eyelids hurt, and I suspected sunlight would only make my pounding headache worse.

"Hey, look who's back in the land of the living!"

That was Click's voice, coming from somewhere nearby. I sat up, much too quickly in fact, my gut churning like the Drake Passage. I turned to the side and expelled the contents of my stomach all over the lawn. Based on what I hurled, it was entirely possible that I'd slammed a couple quarts of dirty motor oil before I'd blacked out.

Nope, not motor oil. My vomit smelled like musk and old, rotten fish guts. I took a whiff full in the face, triggering an extended dry-heaving session. A few minutes later, my body decided that I'd purged as much as humanly possible, and thankfully my roiling stomach calmed enough to allow me the power of speech again.

"Oh man," I said as I wiped my mouth on the bare skin of my arm. "I feel better."

Click squatted down next to me, carefully avoiding the puddle of blackish sludge I'd hurled out on the grass. "Well, you ought to feel better. You must've had at least a pint of god blood in you, and that's potent stuff. Probably why you're still alive though, after that thing inside your skull gave you an aneurism—not to mention the serpent's venom. I s'pose it's a good thing you kept all that gunk down as long as you did."

I looked down at my shredded clothes and bedraggled appearance. I was covered in more of the black, tarry stuff I'd vomited, and my skin was bruised and purple all around my torso. I glanced around to get my bearings but drew a blank. Then I noticed the giant headless serpent on the lawn nearby.

"Click, why is there a ginormous dead snake over there?"

"Don't remember a thing, do you? Well, some *haliwr*—that's wanker, to you—wanted to off your friend, the one that heads up the local *fampir* clan. Turns out the fellow was cheating, and had you not noticed I'd have made some serious coin. But you did, and then you took offense, and after that you killed an avatar of a Mayan deity that was helping the wanker cheat. That's it over there—what's left of it, anyway. I think that about covers it."

"Ah. And the headache?" I asked.

"Are you daft, or did you suffer permanent brain damage? I just told you not two minutes ago, that thing inside your skull burst a blood vessel in your head."

"Right." I paused as the nausea started coming back. I managed to belch a little, and thankfully it went away. "Um, just why did the Eye try to kill me?"

Click threw his hands up in the air. "Well, isn't it obvious? It's because you went all Fomorian to kill the serpent, and then you wanted to kill everything else in sight. T'was quite a glorious display of unbridled rage, it was, but a bit unnerving for the guests. You should really speak with a professional about your anger issues. They have drugs for that sort of thing, you know."

I rubbed my head, thankful that the headache was subsiding slightly. "I'm quite familiar with the modern field of psychopharmacology, believe me." I looked around, again drawing a blank on my surroundings. "Where are we, by the way?"

"Back garden of some vampire who goes by Mateo. Old one, not as old as your friend though. He won, by the way—Luther, that is."

I heaved a sigh of relief. "Finally, some good news."

"Cost me a wad of gold, but I made it up by betting against the Mayan snake. Although I was rather surprised at how eager you were to dispatch him, considering that you're a snake person and all." He paused, rubbing his chin and squinting at me. "Still haven't figured out where the vorarephilia comes from."

"What? Never mind, I don't want to know. Where's Luther?"

Click tilted his head in the direction of the house. "In there, but Mateo said you weren't to enter his house until you'd hosed off and changed."

"Ah. I think it's all coming back to me now."

"Then I guess you'll be needing this again." He tossed me my Craneskin Bag, looking at it like a pawn broker eyeing a fake Rolex. "Oh yeah? Well screw you too, ya flea-bitten crap basket."

I wasn't quite ready to ask Click why he was talking to my Bag, so I stood and pointed at the rear of the house, ignoring his outburst. "I'm, uh, going to go clean up."

Click crossed his arms as he turned his nose up at my Bag. "Then if you don't mind, take that moth-eaten haversack with you. Damned thing's been insulting me since you started your fight with the serpent."

"Right," I said, sagely deciding to save that discussion for another day. I shouldered the Bag and headed to the back of the house. It took me a good fifteen minutes to get all the dried serpent blood out of my hair. On the plus side, once I'd toweled off and brushed it out, my hair felt incredibly lush and silky. *Clairol, eat your heart out.*

When I walked back around the side of the house the serpent was still there, but Click was gone. *Just as well—trouble seems to follow him like a bad smell.* I knocked on the kitchen door, waiting patiently until a very pale-faced Charmaine answered.

"Uh, hi. Are Mateo and Luther inside?" She nodded, tight-lipped and avoiding eye contact. "Then, may I come in?"

Another nod.

"Right. If you'll excuse me?"

I smiled at her as I walked past, but she was having none of it. That happened a lot when people saw my *other* side. I'd thought I still had it under control, but as the evening's events had demonstrated, that was far from the case.

And just what am I going to do about that little problem? I wondered. But that was trouble for another time. Right now, I was more concerned with discovering how and why I'd been manipulated into taking out Luther's trash.

AS I ENTERED the living room, Mateo and Luther were laughing and drinking wine as if nothing out of the ordinary had happened. Luther looked none the worse for wear, freshly dressed and cleaned up. By the way they were joking, you'd have thought there wasn't a dead Mayan deity on the lawn out back.

Mateo announced me as I walked in. "Ah, our hero returns from the land of slumber!"

I was more than a little cross, what with being kept in the dark about the whole situation until the very last minute. I ignored Mateo's ebullient welcome, instead opting to plop down on the couch and brood.

"I told you he'd come through for us," Luther said to Mateo before turning to look at me. "Oh, stop pouting—it simply does not become you."

"Shit, Luther—wouldn't you be pissed if you were in my shoes? Your girl told me to show up, and that was all. And while she did say to come armed, she didn't mention that I'd be fighting a giant snake."

"Oh, but I *do* throw the best parties," Mateo interjected, a self-satisfied grin on his face. "The coven will be talking about this one for ages."

"I'm so glad I could be the evening's entertainment," I huffed.

Luther gave me a chiding look. "Colin, I asked for you because I don't trust any other human—at least none who are local to Austin, that is. We've been friends for a while now, have we not?" I nodded while attempting to look disagreeable as he continued. "Then correct me if I'm mistaken, but I believe the way friendship works is when a friend calls, you come. And vice versa."

"Well when you put it that way—"

"You feel like a heel for bitching and complaining?" Mateo asked.

I sighed. "A little. But you have to understand, I'm a bit touchy about having my chain yanked. I only just extracted myself from Maeve's machinations, you know."

Mateo snorted. "As if. When that old bitty gets her claws in someone, she hangs on for dear life. Sorry to inform you, but if you ask me she's far from through with you."

"Great," I muttered. "Anyway, you can see why I'm miffed about being used as a tool by you two."

Luther bristled. "First off, we had no idea it'd be that bad. I just figured you'd spot him cheating, call him out, and that would be that. I never expected things to escalate—and for that, I am sorry."

I certainly couldn't argue with that explanation. It wasn't like Luther could have known Cornelius had made a deal with Kulkulkan. I mulled it over for a few seconds and decided that the Luther I knew wouldn't intentionally place me in harm's way.

"Apology accepted, Luther. You know I have your back."

"I do." He looked me over quickly, like a physician examining a patient. "All things considered, you seem to be in one piece—a bit green around the gills, but otherwise intact. When you collapsed we were ready to call Finnegas, but a disembodied voice insisted that you'd be fine, so long as no one pumped your stomach."

My face flushed as I suddenly remembered Luther had seen me in all my Fomorian glory for the very first time. "Ah, yeah—about that..."

Luther waved my concerns away. "Pish-posh, I've seen weirder things in my time, disembodied voices notwithstanding. You know, it's rare that I can hear but not smell someone, even that fae illusionist who was here earlier. I take it Mr. Disembodied Voice is a friend of yours?"

"More like a business associate," I said.

Luther took a sip of wine, his eyes narrowing slightly. "Perhaps you can tell me about him some other time. For now, know that you have my eternal gratitude for executing your duties as referee in a most admirable fashion."

Mateo frowned slightly. "I'll admit I had my doubts, but my oh my... you certainly live up to your hype, druid."

I'd never been good at taking compliments, so by way of deflection I grabbed their wine, dispensing with the need for a glass by drinking straight out of the bottle.

Mateo sighed as he fixed me with a look of displeasure. "That's a '90 Chambertin Grand Cru. I do hope you enjoy it."

I held the bottle up, examining the label. "Not bad, for an expired bottle of vino. A little too fruity for my tastes, though."

"You don't say," Mateo deadpanned.

I took another swig. "So you two knew Cornelius was up to no good? Why didn't you tip me off that he'd be using magic to cheat?"

Luther gave the room a lazy sweep of his hand. "Lots of

sharp ears around earlier. If we'd said anything word would have gotten back to Cornelius, and he'd never have shown."

"Which would have been a shame," Mateo replied.

"I'll say. It was high time I scraped that piece of shit from my shoe," Luther said. He looked at me and raised his glass. "Thanks again, for that."

"Ah, don't mention it." All their gratitude was making me uncomfortable. I suddenly remembered why I'd tracked Luther down in the first place, and saw a means of extricating myself from the conversation. "By the way, there was something I wanted to discuss with you."

"Hmm, about the murders I take it?" he asked after a sip of wine. I nodded. "Check the security footage."

I scratched my forehead, confused. "What security footage?"

Luther smiled. "The security footage from the system your uncle had installed, after he kept having nightmares about being attacked by ninjas in his place of business. I have it on good authority that a local security company gave him an excellent deal on the installation."

"And that would be a security company you own, I presume?"

"Got it in one," Mateo said. "My, but he is sharp."

"Sharp would've been spotting the cameras," Luther stated drily.

"I killed an immortal avatar tonight, so I think that gets me a pass on missing the security cameras." Unwilling to banter with the two vamps any longer, I decided to beg off so I could hit the hay. "Shit, I'd better go. By the way, Samson says he's getting low on coffee beans."

Luther perked up a bit at that. "Ah, you don't say? I'll send him a delivery at once," the old vampire remarked.

"I didn't know you sold coffee beans."

"I don't—good heavens, boy, don't you recognize code when you hear it?"

I pressed my palm to my forehead. "I do—I figured— never mind, it's not worth the trouble."

"One last word of advice," Luther said. "Watch your back for a while, because Cornelius' boys will be out for blood, especially after you hacked Lucius' hand off."

Mateo clapped silently. "Well done, on that particular point. Little prick had it coming."

"And Cornelius?" I asked.

Luther considered the last few drops of wine in his glass. "Neutralized, but not deceased. It's a lot harder to kill a master vampire than you might think. Also, there are councils to lobby and committees to bribe before a coven leader can take out another prominent member of our kind. So, let's just say he's on ice and leave it at that."

I nodded. "And about the, uh—corpse, in the backyard?"

"Oh don't worry, we'll dispose of the serpent," Mateo said. "It isn't every day you get to fertilize your lawn with a god's corpse. Trust me, you did me a favor by leaving that thing there. My flowerbed is going to be simply amazing next year, I'm sure of it."

I ALLOWED myself a few short hours of sleep, but only until Ed got to the office. He showed up at the same hour every day, so I set an alarm to wake me up in time to greet him when he arrived.

I caught my uncle just as he was huffing and puffing his way up to the office door. "Morning, Ed."

Ed eyed me with suspicion. "You have that, 'I need something from Uncle Ed' look."

"Well, I do have a favor to ask."

"If it's an advance on your next check, no can do. I have a big shipment of cars coming from auction, and until we flip them I'll be running a little low on operating cash. But if it's time off, you know you don't have to ask me. Just make it up on Saturday."

"Naw, it's not that. I just need to take a look at the security footage from the other night."

That got his attention. He stopped fumbling with his keys and leaned in, whispering in hushed tones. "How'd you know I had a security system installed? I specifically had the security company install it when no one was around—and I had them hide the cameras, too. Didn't want any of the employees to think I was spying on them."

"I don't think anyone would blame you for getting a security system. Rufus and Roscoe are getting a bit long in the tooth."

Ed blew a short puff of breath from his lips. "Still, a pair of growling and barking mutts is a pretty good deterrent." He rubbed the scar around his wrist absentmindedly. "Naw, I'm not getting rid of the dogs. It's just that—well, I felt like it was time to increase the security around here."

I merely nodded in response, at a loss for words that might reassure him. According to Maureen, it would take time for Ed's latent memories to fade.

Maureen was the one who wiped Ed's mind, at the hospital after a fae assassin from Underhill had lopped off his hand. Ed had been rambling, and it had to be done right then. Unfortunately, Maureen didn't have Maeve's millennia of experience, so the job she did wasn't exactly thorough. And even though he never mentioned it, based on his recent jumpiness and the dark circles under his eyes, I was certain Ed had been having nightmares about the incident.

Ed was silently staring into the distance, so I touched him on the arm. "Uncle Ed? The security footage?"

"What? Oh yeah, right. Come on in and I'll pull it up." Ed unlocked the office and I followed after, listening to him wheeze as he set his coffee thermos down and switched on the computer. "What do you need this for, anyway?"

"I'm trying to catch those punks who keep tagging the front fence." Ed nodded once, satisfied with my explanation. "Is it on DVD or something?" I asked.

"No, nothing like that. The guy who installed it said they don't need DVD recorders or whatever to store video now." He made quotations marks in the air. "Everything's stored 'in the cloud' these days. Hell, I don't even know where the cloud is—you think it's safe?"

I didn't have the heart to tell my uncle that since 9/11, the NSA could get any information they wanted on anyone at any time, Snowden's revelations be damned. "Safe as houses."

Ed nodded and settled in behind his desk as the office workstation whirred to life. "Alright, let me see..." He pulled out a Post-It note with a series of instructions scrawled all over it, including a web address and login info. I watched patiently as he pecked the keys and hit enter several times, failing each time to enter the proper URL.

"Here, let me try," I said. Ed moved and I sat down, immediately logging into the site he had written down. I quickly located the video file for the evening Elmo was killed, and sent a copy to my email. "Thanks, Ed."

"What, you aren't going to look at it?" he asked.

"No, I sent it to my phone so I can look at it later. I don't want to be in your way while you're working."

"Damned technology—I swear we're living in Star Trek. Back in my day we had VCRs. Let me tell you, searching for a video clip on a VCR was a pain. My buddy and I wore out the fast-forward and rewind on his parents' VCR, watching Phoebe Cates step out of the pool over and over again." Ed paused and a mischievous grin played across his face. "Say, this doesn't have anything to do with your girlfriend, does it? Did you accidentally get caught on camera, chasing her around the yard in your birthday suit?"

"I'm going now," I said, a little too loudly. "And don't bother checking the footage—you're not going to see anyone in the buff on there, I promise."

Ed chuckled as I exited the office. "Whatever you say."

If you only knew, Ed. If you only knew.

TWELVE

I wasn't worried about Ed seeing something on camera, like Elmo's true form or the events that led to his murder. For one, fae magic had a way of screwing up modern cameras. It was nearly impossible to get a clear image of anything supernatural, unless you had tech that was charmed.

And besides that, any mage or hunter team worth their salt would have used magic to brick the cameras before they entered the yard. That was why I didn't expect to see the actual murder on the video footage, any more than I was worried about Ed seeing it. But what I did hope to find was something that might lead me to Elmo's killers.

I pulled the footage up on my laptop, hoping I might catch more details on the larger screen. As I suspected, the cameras inside the yard showed nothing but static at the time of Elmo's death. But one camera had remained working the entire time, and that was the camera Ed had pointed outside the front entrance.

Got you, you piece of shit.

Sure enough, the camera caught a van driving by—right about the time I'd been watching Elmo bleed out. The van was unmarked, but all I needed was a license plate number, and thankfully Luther's people had installed some killer cameras. The plate number was clear as day, so I wrote it down and texted it to Belladonna along with the dark web address Rocko had given me. Bells could put the geek squad down at Circle HQ on it, and if there was a connection to be made they'd find it for sure. Bells had them wrapped around her finger, and they'd do anything to get her attention.

Bells called me back a few hours later. "You're not going to like this," she said.

"Just give me the news," I replied. "Who's it registered to?"

"Group of hunters who operate out of Bastrop. Carver's crew."

"Carver... that fucking piece of shit!"

"Yeah, and it gets better. From the looks of it, Carver advertises his services on that dark web page you sent me. The nerd herd did some digging, and they say he's been doing hits for years. Low-level stuff, but he's definitely dirty."

It made sense that Carver was involved. He was one hunter I refused to work with because he'd take any job, no matter how immoral. He'd kill relatively harmless creatures, even the highly sentient ones, instead of trying to find alternative solutions for getting rid of them. Killing was simply a faster way to a paycheck, which was why he always opted for that route.

We'd brushed into each other a few times and it had been hate at first sight. Knowing that he'd been involved in Elmo's death, I was looking forward to having a nice long chat with Carver. A painful chat.

"Colin, he has a pretty big crew—maybe six or eight strong. I don't want you going after him without backup. Wait until I get off work and I'll head out there with you."

"No can do. These guys work at night, so the chances of me catching him at their compound after sundown are minimal. Naw, I need to head over there now. Besides, they might have someone monitoring their data in the system. If they get wind that someone searched their plate number, they'll know I'm coming."

"You are such a hardhead."

"That's why you love me," I said.

"'Love' might be a strong word when I'm this frustrated with you. You sure I can't talk you out of doing this alone?"

"Sorry, Bells. This is the first solid lead I've gotten on the case, and I want to follow it up right away."

"Fine. But don't do anything stupid, okay?"

"I promise I won't," I lied.

"Speaking of which—"

"Yes?"

"There's a rumor going around that an ogre killed a snake deity at a house party on the west side last night. You wouldn't happen to know anything about that, would you?"

"The only ogre I've ever known was Elmo, and he's dead. So no, I wouldn't know a thing about it."

She chuckled. "Listen, stud, you keep going around kicking immortals' asses, and eventually someone really important is going to take offense. You know how the major players are about mortals who make them look bad."

"Again, I have no idea what you're talking about." I decided to change the subject. "So, dinner at my place?"

"Your place is a dump. How about my place? Eight sound good?"

"Wouldn't miss it."

"Mm-hmm. By the way, you're not off the hook. I expect to hear the whole story at dinner tonight. ¿Entendido?"

"When you put it that way, sure. You know it drives me crazy when you speak Spanish to me."

"Don't change the subject. I want a full report, no excuses. I can't watch your back if I don't know who might be coming after you."

I sighed in exasperation. "No one's coming after me, Bells. Relax."

"Yeah, and that's why your car and house have been double and triple-warded for the last few months, and why you're always looking over your shoulder now, and why you jump out of bed at the slightest noise. I think if we just started marking off who isn't coming after you, it'd be a much shorter list."

"Some people collect cars, I collect enemies. What do you want me to say?"

She laughed humorlessly. "Say you'll be careful when you go after Carver's crew."

"Yes, I'll be careful. Trust me, there's absolutely nothing to worry about."

"Isn't that what Custer said, just before Sitting Bull handed him his ass on a platter?"

"Custer was cocky, and that's what got him killed. Me? I'm cautiously self-assured."

"Whatever. If you get in trouble, just text me a 911 with

your location." She paused. "And Colin?"

"Yes?"

"If I have to skip picking up dinner to come save your ass, you are *not* getting laid tonight."

———

IF I'D BEEN MERELY LOOKING for evidence, I'd have gone to Carver's compound while he and his crew were out on a job. That would have been the safe bet—to recon their place, find proof that they were behind the murders, and then take that info to the fae to let them handle it. But I wasn't just searching for proof. I was out for revenge.

Okay, so maybe revenge wasn't the right word. Out for justice? Naw, that just made me sound like a Steven Seagal wannabe, and that guy was a dick. Chuck Norris never had to make his movie titles that freaking obvious, except maybe *Forced Vengeance* or *An Eye for an Eye*. But *Good Guys Wear Black, Code of Silence, The Octagon*... now those were classic action film titles that lacked the pretentiousness of Seagal's craptastic films.

Martial arts movie classics aside, justice *was* what I was seeking. This wasn't really a personal vendetta, not by a long shot. I hadn't known Elmo for more than a few days, and I'd only known Jeretta in passing. Even so, I couldn't stomach the idea that someone would kill a gentle creature like Elmo just to cover their tracks. Someone had to stop them, and since they'd decided to kill Elmo on my turf, that someone was me.

Bastrop was a good long drive from Austin, so I took the opportunity to run through my options. I could try talking with Carver, but I doubted he'd admit to any wrongdoing. I could take him and his crew head on, but that'd get messy and possibly trigger another Hyde-side appearance. I didn't want to think about what might happen if I let *him* loose again, so that approach was a no-go.

So, it looked like I was going to take the sneaky approach instead. The address Bells had given me for Carver's place was way out in the sticks, near Bastrop State Park. Most of the area had been burned to cinders several years back, turning what was once endless miles of loblolly pines to ash. The area around Carver's place appeared to have been spared, so I'd have plenty of cover to work with as I reconned their hideout.

I parked about a mile from the location and headed through a densely forested area toward Carver's compound. According to Belladonna, he owned thirteen acres that was bordered by the state park on one side and a Christmas tree farm on the other. That meant it was plenty private, which was exactly what any hunter crew would want in a hideout. I hoped I could use that privacy to my advantage.

As I got closer, I checked my Glock to make sure I had a round in the chamber and a few spare magazines ready to go. Chances were good that if I got into a firefight with these chumps, it'd get ugly fast, so I wanted enough firepower on hand to make a quick escape. I had no illusions about winning that sort of confrontation, though. I'd be outnumbered and they'd have shotguns and rifles. No, I'd avoid a direct confrontation if possible. At least, that was the plan.

I reached into my Bag and pulled out a toy I'd picked up a while back. It was a police-style taser with a thirty-foot range and enough juice to take down a bear. My plan was to sneak up to the compound, taser one of Carver's crew, and then take the unlucky soul somewhere private to interrogate them. Once I had an idea of what I was dealing with, I'd set a trap for Carver, maybe try to catch him when he was alone and vulnerable. Then I'd get Elmo the justice he deserved.

I crept to within twenty-five yards of the compound, my senses on high alert. The place wasn't exactly Fort Knox, but it was well-guarded. The main building was a metal barn that had been converted into a two-story dwelling of some sort, and there were two other similar structures that had been set up in a wide-mouthed U shape on either side of the house. One of those structures was an open front pole barn, and the other looked to be a multi-bay garage.

There were tall sections of chain-link fence topped in barbed wire connecting the buildings in the back. I also spotted at least three security cameras trained on key approach points. And to top it all off, a large manmade pond sat in front of the building, acting as a sort of moat to protect that side of their compound. The only way in and out of the place was by a narrow one-lane drive that wound through the woods from the main road. It was protected by more chain link fence and a tall gate capped in more barbed wire.

This is going to be harder than I thought.

I didn't see much activity around the place, which wasn't surprising considering that most hunters worked at night. I waited patiently, knowing that eventually someone would show their face. Sure enough, my patience was rewarded when a large, slightly overweight man walked out of the house. He looked around for a moment, then stretched and lit up a cigarette, just before he unzipped his trousers and took a piss off the front porch of the house.

There's my target of opportunity. Now, to snatch this guy and get out of here.

I waited until he headed into the garage before making my move. Slipping toward the house as silently as possible, I relied on the thick layer of pine needles underfoot to mask the sounds of my passing. Once I hit the pond, there were only two ways to go. I chose left and stuck to the trees as I skirted the water.

I was nearly to the garage when I stepped on something that felt *off*. Rather than the spongy feel of the forest floor, my foot hit something hard that yielded under pressure.

Shit.

I shifted my weight to jump clear, but it was too late. Pine needles exploded from the ground around me as the trap triggered and lifted me fifteen feet in the air, catching me fast in a steel mesh net. Before I could find a way to free myself, I heard a switch trip. The net became electrified, sending me into convulsions while the smell of burned hair and clothing filled my nose.

I MUST HAVE BLACKED OUT, because the next thing I knew I was trussed up hand to foot and spitting pine needles out of my mouth.

"And just what the hell do we have here?" a man's voice said nearby. It was a deep voice, gruff, with a strong central Texas accent. "Well now, it looks like we caught ourselves a druid."

I spat out more pine needles as I cracked an eye open. "Carver, what a pleasant surprise." Or, at least, that's what I meant to say. What came out was more like, "Carrrgghh, whuffa prez an shurpish."

This elicited a round of laughter from my captors, who were gathered in a semi-circle around me. They'd bound me up good, first tying my hands and ankles together, and then wrapping a noose around my neck that was cinched behind me to my limbs. They'd even bound my hands into fists, the crafty bastards, which prevented me from casting spells. I was completely immobilized, not that I could move if I wanted to—the residual effects of being zapped by their net made sure of that.

Carver walked into view, kneeling in front of me. He was six feet and 240, all of it muscle, and he wore khaki tactical pants, desert tan combat boots, and a dark-green button-down over a black t-shirt. The hunter's arms were thickly muscled and decorated with military-style tattoos, including a globe and anchor, an eagle gripping a flag in its talons, and a battle-field cross. His flaming red hair was cut Marine Corps-style high and tight, but he sported a thick man beard and mustache that he obviously spent a great deal of time grooming and oiling.

His icy blue eyes stared into mine as he replied with amusement in his voice. "Now now, don't exert yourself on our account. You got hit with enough amps to down a large horse, so you're going to be a bit woozy for a time. We set those traps up in case anything supernatural came looking for us, and Bubba here made sure that if something landed in one they'd never escape."

"I hooked it up to 220," said a fat man wearing hunter's coveralls and a Houston Texans ball cap. "Shoulda stopped your heart. Must be one tough sum' bitch. Or spelled." The man spat tobacco juice off to one side as he regarded me with equal measures of respect and distrust.

Considering the results of my previous attempt at witty banter, I figured I may as well size up the situation. There were seven hunters standing around me, plus Carver. Two were female and the rest were male, six were Anglo, one of the men was Asian, and none of them looked happy to see me. The crew was dressed in a patchwork wardrobe made up of random pieces of tactical gear, camouflage hunting clothes, military BDUs, and casual wear. They looked like extras from an episode of *The Walking Dead*, but with better hygiene.

A painfully thin female wearing desert camo fatigues and a Garth Brooks concert t-shirt spoke up. She had an AR-15 casually pointed in my direction, and she looked like she knew how to use it. "Carver, now that we got him, what the hell are we going to do with him? I mean, ganking monsters and shit is one thing, but killing humans is another."

Carver continued to stare into my eyes, as if he was trying to plumb the depths of my soul. "Oh, McCool here isn't human—not by a stretch, Sissy. No, he's a shifter. Not any kind y'all have seen, but a shifter just the same. Don't you feel bad at all about treating him just like we would any other crypto or supe." He stood and his eyes swept his team. "That goes for all of you."

His team responded with a series of grunts and nods. Bubba cleared his throat, hocking a loogie and spitting it off into the trees nearby. "Still haven't told us what you intend to do with him, Carver."

Carver crossed his muscular arms, scanning his team with a slight scowl before looking at the fat man. "And just what do you think we should do with him, Bubba? I have some ideas, but I'm willing to hear what you think about it."

Bubba wiped the side of his nose with a grubby thumb. "Kill him and bury him out in the woods, deep. No sense in stretching it out. He ain't got nothing we want, and we already know who he works for. So, let's just put a couple of holes in him and be done with it."

Carver considered his subordinate's words, tapping his chin. "I agree with you about how to dispose of him. But you're wrong about McCool not having anything we want. That Bag of his is supposed to be full of all kinds of magical artifacts. I'm sure you all remember how we made out when we killed that striga last year."

A slight man with stringy blonde hair and a wispy beard nodded. "Damned straight. I ate good for six months after we sold all her shit—paid off my truck and the double-wide both. Hell, I say we kill him and crack that thing open to see what the fuck he's got." The man belched loudly when he finished —whether for emphasis or on general principle, I wasn't certain.

Carver stroked his beard. "Eloquently said as always, Dicky. Thing is, we can't kill him until he tells us how to get inside that Bag. Ain't that right, McCool?"

He pulled his leg back and soccer kicked me in the gut. My body involuntarily doubled over, choking me when the spasms in my gut stretched the rope taut around my neck. After I stopped convulsing and strangling myself, I stared up at him with all the hatred I could muster.

I am so going to fuck this guy up, I thought. *Just as soon as I figure out how to free myself and overpower eight trained hunters. No pressure, McCool. No fucking pressure.*

THIRTEEN

A few hours later, I was hanging from a rafter in Carver's garage, wrists bound tight and tossed over a hook and hoist chain overhead. I was shirtless, bleeding from a dozen cuts, and missing several fingernails. I'd been burned multiple times, had battery acid poured in my wounds, and I'd had red hot needles stuck deep into my muscles. Without a doubt, Carver sure knew his business when it came to torture.

On the bright side, he hadn't started in on my teeth yet, so that was something.

He pulled a round metal tub across the floor, lifting my feet to place them inside. I tried dropkicking him in the chest, but I was too exhausted from holding myself up to even lift my legs. Most people don't know that when you hang someone by their arms, hanging there is just as much torture as the torture itself. Your own weight pulls your shoulders up, making it difficult to breathe once your muscles fatigue, and pretty soon it's all you can do to take a breath. I was way past that point, which was why I was finding it so hard to fight back.

Carver brought a hose in from outside, leaving one end in the tub. He walked back outside, and soon the tub filled with water. A few minutes later, the water shut off and Carver returned.

"I can't understand why you're fighting me so hard on this, McCool. You're going to die, one way or another. Why not just make it easy on yourself, and tell me how to get in that fucking Bag?"

I laughed softly, which turned into a coughing fit, causing my head to bounce off my chest. "What makes you think you *can* get in it? Hell, what makes you think you *want* to? I swear, Carver, you're mean as a sunburned rattlesnake, but you're not near as smart as you think."

My Craneskin Bag sat on a chair nearby, where Carver had flung it after turning it inside out and searching it for hidden pockets and who knew what else. Of course, to him it just appeared to be an old, worn, empty leather satchel. The Bag only worked for the descendants of Fionn MacCumhaill, so no matter how much Carver searched it, there was no way it would reveal its secrets to him.

"I know there has to be some trick to making the Bag work," he said as he attached a set of jumper cables to a car battery. He clacked the ends together, making them crackle as sparks jumped from the metal. "All you have to do is tell me, and I'll make it all stop."

I considered my options and determined I didn't have any. I hadn't tried to shift in order to escape, mostly because I couldn't trust my other self at the moment. Sure, I might change and kill Carver and his whole crew, but what if I couldn't control it again? Everyone in a ten-mile radius of this place would be in danger. I'd rather die than risk it.

But eventually Carver was going to make me hulk out, and then I'd kill him and who knew how many others. Chances were I might not come back to myself if I transformed involuntarily—not with the way my Hyde-side had been taking over lately.

Or, Carver might actually kill me. As messed up as that was, I thought it possible. The Eye had done something to me after I'd killed Kulkulcan's avatar, so it stood to reason that I might not be able to shift at all. Despite all the torture I'd endured, I hadn't noticed a single sign to indicate my Hyde-side was trying to come out. I speculated that what the Eye had done might have cut me off from my ability to shift. And if that was the case, if Carver decided to cap me it'd be permanent.

So, I figured I may as well try to get something out of him before that happened. Either way, I wasn't going to get another shot at him. It was now or never.

"Tell you what, Carver. I'll make you a deal."

He placed both jumper cable clamps in one hand, crossing his arms while carefully avoiding shocking himself. "Alright, I'm listening."

"I just want to know why you did it. If I'm going to die, then I at least want to know what the hell I died for. So, you answer my questions, and I'll tell you how to activate the Bag. Deal?"

He considered for several seconds, but I knew I had him. "Deal. Ask away."

"Why kill all those fae? Were they hits, or did you just do it for fun? Clue me in here, because it just doesn't add up."

Carver responded with a genuine laugh. "Oh, shit—you think we killed all those fae? Seriously?"

I coughed and spat out a wad of bloody phlegm. "Just a working theory, but yes, that's what I thought."

He chuckled. "I admit I would've enjoyed it, and that's a fact. But no, we weren't the ones who took all those fae out, and we didn't cut your brake lines either. We had nothing to do with any of that shit, except the ogre—that was our work."

I kept an eye on him, doing my damnedest to detect any falsehood in what he was saying. As far as I could tell, he was telling the truth. *Damn.*

"Alright, then if you didn't do it, who did?"

Carver shook his head. "Hell if I know, and even if I did I wouldn't tell you. Someone contacted us through the usual channels, and they hired us to kill the ogre. They paid us in gold by dead drop after the work was done. We never saw their faces or spoke to anyone—everything was arranged via chat through a secure connection."

I hung my head. "Damn it. All this and I'm no closer to finding who's behind everything."

Carver scratched his balls. "Sorry to disappoint you, McCool, but that's the truth. Now, are you going to tell me how to get in that Bag?"

I glanced over at the chair, which was now conspicuously absent my Craneskin Bag. This was no shock to me, since I'd watched it disappear just a few moments before. The Bag had a mind of its own. Either it had decided to make itself scarce out of some vague sense of self-preservation, or Click was nearby and he'd snagged it. I thought the former more likely than the latter, but one could hope.

I gave Carver a smart-assed grin. "Yeah, about that..."

———

CARVER beat me mercilessly after I told him the Bag was gone, convinced that I'd somehow double-crossed him. Now, I was being dragged by Bubba and Dicky through the woods behind their compound as daylight faded into dusk. Each man held a shovel in one hand as they pulled me by my ankles with the other. At least I knew I'd have a brief respite while they dug the hole.

When they'd dragged me away, Carver had been questioning the remainder of his crew, trying to figure out whether one of them had snagged the Bag. I'd told him I hadn't seen what had happened to it, that it was there one moment and gone the next. Which was sort of true, although I'd actually seen it vanish. I hadn't needed to lie much to plant a seed of doubt in Carver's mind, which showed how little these low-lives trusted one another.

Bubba and Dicky discussed the situation back at the compound while they hauled me to my intended eternal resting place. "Bubba, did you take that bag? Be honest now, I won't snitch. I just want my share. Heck, we can even start our own crew and get the hell out from under Carver's thumb."

Bubba scowled. "Dicky, I didn't steal no damn bag—and even if I did I wouldn't tell you. You think I'm stupid? First thing you'd do is go run back to Carver and rat me out."

Dicky stood a little straighter as he replied. "I sure in the hell wouldn't. Uh-uh, no sir. Dicky Schumacher ain't no snitch."

"How many times I gotta tell you not to speak of yourself in the third person? It makes you sound like an asshole."

Dicky visibly shrank at Bubba's criticism. "That's harsh, man. Why you gotta be such a dick all the time?"

Bubba ignored his protests. "And what the hell kinda name is Schumacher, anyway? Sounds Jewish or sumthin'."

"It's German, asshole. And I ain't no Jew. My grandpa was with the *Luftwaffe* in World War II."

"What the fuck is a lift-waffle? I think you're just talking out your ass."

Dicky looked like he was about to blow a gasket, but apparently he thought better of picking a fight with the much larger man. "Never you mind. Anyway, we're here. So, how you wanna do this? Do we kill him now, or later?"

Bubba scratched his ass through his pants. "Supposed to bury him alive. Carver was pissed about that bag going missing, so I guess he wants this asshole to suffer. Sounds cruel to me—if he's a shifter it'll take him days to die. But I ain't the one in charge."

"I could give a shit one way or the other." Dicky looked around the proposed grave site. "Let's talk division of labor—do we take turns digging, or what?"

"Division of what? What kind of commie bullshit talk is that?" Bubba farted, waving his hand behind his ass. "Oh man, that Mexican food is coming back to haunt me. Naw, if we take turns we'll be out here all night. You dig one end and I'll dig the other. Carver said he wanted him buried deep, but I think three feet oughta do it."

"Sounds good to me—oh holy shit, Bubba. That is fucking foul."

Bubba had a good laugh, then the two of them got to work digging my grave.

Well, Colin, you fucked up this time, I thought. *Now, how in the hell are you going to get out of this mess?*

Out of desperation I'd tried a partial shift, just enough to break my bonds. It wasn't working, which added credence to my theory that the Eye had blocked my ability to shift somehow. And my Hyde-side sure in the hell wasn't coming out on its own, else it would have done so while Carver was working me over. I couldn't work magic, not with my hands bound closed and my mouth taped shut. I was more or less completely screwed.

Or am I? I thought back to the lessons Finnegas had been teaching me lately, about tuning into nature with druidry. I wondered, if I could amplify the raw forces of nature to work magic, shouldn't I be able to tap into it in other ways?

I had no idea what I was going to do, but right now it appeared that was my only option. I closed my eyes and slowed my breathing, settling into a trance just as Finnegas had shown me.

It took a while to get in the right state, simply because I had to block out the pain from the hundred or so injuries Carver had inflicted on me. Yet minutes later, I began to sense the energy of the earth and air around me.

Now, what is here that I can use to free myself?

The challenge I faced was that I needed the use of my hands to work druidry. So, creating a fireball out of a pinecone or sending a gust of wind to knock a tree over on Dicky and Bubba was completely out of the question. That meant I needed to use what I'd learned in an entirely new way.

All I have to do is improvise a little magic to save myself from a horrible and premature death. No pressure.

Out of options, I did the only thing I could do, which was to sink deeper into the trance than I'd ever gone. Time slipped away, and moments or minutes later I began to sense more than the elements around me. It was like I became a part of the area's ecosystem. I felt the pine trees swaying in the wind, the smaller yaupon and farkleberry trees reaching for the last few rays of sun, and even the moss growing on a rocky outcrop nearby.

Then, another presence became known to me—countless presences, in fact. Like little fireflies lighting up the vast empty reaches of my consciousness, I suddenly became aware of dozens upon dozens of forest creatures, including birds, rabbits, squirrels, moles, raccoons, and even a fox and a pair of skunks. It was amazing and somewhat overwhelming, because I'd never felt that in touch with nature.

The question was, could I use it to my advantage?

I CONSIDERED how druid magic worked, by amplifying the forces that were already present in nature. I wondered, what if I amplified the natural instincts and urges of the animals around me? Could I even touch the mind of an animal, or was that something that was beyond the skills of an apprentice druid?

No time like the present to find out, I thought. I searched my mind to locate the closest animal, then I tuned into its presence.

It was a grey squirrel, a species quite common to the area, and it was jumping around from tree to tree looking for food to eat and store away. At first all I got was static, but as I focused in on the creature I began to sense its thoughts.

Jump. Look. Noise. Freeze. Wait. Run. Food. Eat. The squirrel thought in simple directives, like a little ADHD nut-finding machine. Finally, I'd discovered something I could use to my advantage.

I concentrated on sending a specific message to the squirrel—specifically, where it could find the biggest, juiciest acorn it had ever seen. This incredibly large acorn was located inside a human's hands, where he lay at the foot of the squirrel's tree. Sure, there were other humans around, but this one was asleep and quite harmless. If the squirrel was careful, he could get the acorn and be gone before anyone noticed him.

Once I'd planted the idea in the little squirrel's mind, I gently withdrew and waited to see what would happen. At first, the squirrel just sat there on his branch, and I worried that I'd failed. Then, he began to crawl down the other side of the trunk, out of sight.

Come on, little guy. You can do this.

The squirrel reached the ground and poked his head around the tree trunk. Bubba and Dicky were still arguing about how deep the grave needed to be, but they had their backs turned. The squirrel thought he was safe. He scrambled across the forest floor, right up to my tightly bound hands.

For a moment, I worried that the squirrel would chew

through my fingers to get to its expected prize, but my concerns were unfounded. The little tree rodent was incredibly efficient, gnawing through the thin rope my captors had used to bind my hands in record time. Soon, the little guy had freed my hands. Although my fingers had fallen numb from being tightly bound, at least I was closer to freedom.

I wriggled out of the remaining ropes that secured my hands and wrists, sending the squirrel scurrying as I slipped free. I opened and closed my hands to get the circulation back, waiting several painful minutes as a small measure of sensation returned to my fingers. Then I reached into my waistband, pulling loose a tiny razor blade that I kept as back up for just such an occasion.

I fumbled it once or twice, nearly letting it slip through my numb fingers, but eventually I managed to cut my ankles free and loosen the tape over my mouth as well. The tricky part was making sure I kept my movements hidden from Bubba and Dicky—but the two hunters were deep in a discussion about the relative merits and drawbacks of truck stop Viagra. For the moment I was safe, but I still had to decide how I was going to make my escape.

On any other day, I could have easily taken those two bozos out barehanded without breaking a sweat. But right now, I was in no shape to take on two hunters empty-handed. Carver had worked me over good, and between the blood loss, concussion, and trauma, I put my chances at sixty-forty against me walking away from a fistfight with Dicky and Bubba. Besides, they were armed with knives and pistols, so unless I took them out quickly I'd be toast.

I racked my brain for a plan, then heard a soft *plunk* nearby. I turned my head, and the most welcome sight ever greeted me. My Craneskin Bag was sitting on the ground next to me, flap open like it had been waiting for me there all along. I reached inside for the one weapon I knew to be within easy reach—the flaming sword I'd found in its depths when I'd been trapped underground in Maeve's portal chamber.

I pulled the Bag under and behind me, keeping my arm hidden inside with my hand firmly wrapped around the sword's hilt. Then, I waited for Bubba and Dicky to finish the grim work of digging my grave. It had grown dark and the two men had been working by flashlight, so I hoped they wouldn't notice I'd cut my bonds until it was too late.

Finally, the two hunters climbed out of the hole they'd dug. Dicky wiped his hands on his pants before picking up the flashlight. "Well, Bubba, let's get this over with so we can go have a beer."

Bubba sat on a log facing away from me. He stuffed a huge wad of snuff between his cheek and gum, chewing for a moment before spitting a stream of juice out the side of his mouth. "Aw hell, Dicky, you toss him in. I'm too damned tired to do it."

"Alright, but you owe me." Dicky walked over to me, not even looking to see if I was still securely bound. He grabbed an ankle to drag me over to the hole, and as he did the ropes I'd cut fell away in his hand. "What the fuck—?"

Dicky never had time to finish his question. I stabbed upward, piercing his throat from the front and bisecting his spinal cord as the sword's tip exited the back of his neck.

"What'd you say?" Bubba asked from where he sat on the log. "Dicky, quit fucking around and toss him in the hole so we can finish this shit and get back to the house."

I kicked Dicky's body off the tip of my blade, causing him to land across the log next to Bubba. "Dicky's taking a break," I said as I pulled the sword back over my shoulder. "Maybe you should join him."

I swung and cut Bubba's head clean off his shoulders, then watched as it rolled and tumbled into the grave in front of him. *Well, that was convenient. Now, to take care of the rest of these fuckers.*

FOURTEEN

I knew more of Carver's crew would come looking for Dicky and Bubba eventually, so I laid in wait with a silenced pistol I'd pulled from the Bag. Soon, two more members of Carver's crew lay dead on the forest floor. But silencer or not, chances were good the sound had traveled back to the compound. I had to assume the rest would be waiting for me, which was why I'd waited for Bells to show up before I went after Carver.

I'd called her with Dicky's phone, just as soon as I'd taken care of him and Bubba. As luck would have it, she'd been texting me all afternoon, and when I hadn't responded she'd left work early to come look for me. She was already close by when I called her, and had shown up armed to the teeth.

"Remember, we need Carver alive," I whispered as we took cover behind a tree.

"Yes, I'm well aware," she replied. "But once you're done with him, I get to kill that son of a bitch."

"Deal. But I get to watch."

"For a pale-ass ginger-headed white boy, you sure are kinky."

I chuckled, thankful for the painkillers Bells had brought. One of the perks of working for the Circle was access to their field trauma kits. Man, they had the best drugs. She'd given me an opiate mixed with a modafinil derivative, magically-enhanced to prevent dangerous drug interactions. Right now, I felt much better than I looked—but when it wore off I was going to be hating life.

Of course, Belladonna had gotten angry as all hell when she'd seen what Carver had done to me. I'd told her not to worry, since it would all heal the next time I shifted. What I didn't tell her was that I couldn't shift right now. I'd just have to rely on Finn's healing magic when I got home—but she didn't need to know that.

"Alright, Bells, just clear a path for me and I'll take care of the rest."

"Trust me, I got this."

Belladonna flipped out the bipod on her Remington Defense concealable sniper rifle. Developed for the U.S. military, it could be broken down and carried in a briefcase or backpack, and reassembled in seconds without the need for zeroing in the scope all over again. That rifle cost more than I made in a year working at the junkyard, so it was a sure bet she'd borrowed it from the Circle's armory.

As Bells settled into a prone position, I tapped her on the shoulder. "Are you sure you're okay with taking out humans —fellow hunters?"

"They don't qualify as human, not any more than those fae sex traffickers you hunted down. So yeah, I'm good. Now, quit flapping your jaws and go get that fucker, because all this talk of violence is making me horny."

"Yes, ma'am," I said with a wink as I slipped off into the darkness.

I cast a quick cantrip to enhance my eyes with night vision, and another to silence my footsteps. Carver and his hunters would likely be using night vision goggles and FLIR cameras to spot me, so I cast one more cantrip to chill the air around me, which I hoped would make me invisible to their infrared optics. They'd still be able to pick me up on night vision, but at least I wouldn't stand out like a sore thumb on their FLIR screens.

What I was really counting on was for Bells to take them out as I approached the compound. I hadn't gone far when I heard the report of a suppressed .300 Blackout round, followed by a grunt and a crash up ahead. *One down, three to go. Thank you, Belladonna*, I thought as I continued toward the barn.

I saw a flash of movement around the corner of the building ahead, so I dropped to the forest floor. A round whizzed past, but the shooter's muzzle flash gave away their position. I knew that Bells didn't have a clear shot, so I snapped off three rounds from the silenced pistol. I heard someone drop, followed by Sissy's voice calling out in the dark.

"I'm hit! Oh, son of a fucking bitch—Carver, I'm hit!"

"Is it bad?" a man's voice called back. Not Carver, but another member of the team.

I rolled to cover behind a large pine tree. "Does it matter? Your team is already down by five, and Sissy will make six if you don't get her some medical assistance. I suggest that you two leave now, and I'll let you live. The only one I want is Carver."

Carver's voice called from somewhere within the small compound. "You run and I'll kill you myself!"

"Fuck you, Carver!" Sissy yelled. "I didn't sign up for this shit. Druid, you should know that Carver's the one who went in and killed that ogre. The rest of us didn't want no part of it, not after what we heard about you."

"Shut up, Sissy!" Carver yelled.

"I'm fucking bleeding out, you coward! What, are you going to shoot me ag—?" A shot rang out in the dark, cutting off Sissy's retort.

"Screw this shit, I'm out of here," the nameless and last member of Carver's team shouted.

A car engine turned over inside the compound, then a large four-wheel drive truck crashed through one of the metal garage doors. Gun fire and muzzle flashes came from one of the windows in the house, but a few rounds from Belladonna's rifle stopped that as soon as it started.

The truck ran the gate over and sped down the drive. It made it just past the pond, then the dirt road underneath it exploded, lifting the truck several feet in the air as it continued moving forward at speed. As it landed, the truck careened over on its side, sliding into a pine tree with a loud crunch of metal. Seconds later, the gas tank caught fire, and soon the night was lit up as the vehicle exploded in a massive fireball.

"CARVER, you are one coldhearted son of a bitch," I yelled as I ducked into the shadows behind me.

"He had it coming, the yellow bastard!" Carver yelled back.

That gave me pause. "Wait a minute... do you mean that as a racial slur, or are you using 'yellow' to indicate general cowardice?"

Carver voice dripped with indignation. "Huh? Cowardice, of course. I'm an asshole McCool, not a bigot. Give me a little credit at least."

"Fair enough—but I'm still going to kill you if you don't give up!"

I slunk from tree to tree through the forest, edging my way closer to the back of the house. Every so often, I'd hear the telltale crack of Belladonna's rifle, followed by the sound of a round hitting the metal exterior of the house. Bells would keep Carver pinned down—now I just needed to get to him without getting shot.

I peeked around a tree trunk at waist level, crouching to keep a low profile. The house was just a few yards away, and from what I could tell the coast was clear. There were only a couple of small windows on this side of the house, and both were closed. Foregoing all pretense of style and grace, I sprinted out from behind the tree toward the back wall of the house. I was halfway across the open area between the house and the woods when I spotted movement in an upper window.

Shit, I'm a sitting duck here, I thought, just as Belladonna's rifle sounded in the distance behind me. Glass shattered and I heard Carver cussing as I silently thanked Bells for changing position to cover my approach.

"I only winged him," she called from the woods. "He should still be able to talk."

I chuckled as I crept around the corner of the house, still wary of gunfire. Getting "winged" by a subsonic .300 Blackout round was akin to getting "nicked" by a chainsaw. No matter how casual the contact, it would still ruin your day.

I opened the front door of the house, staying hidden behind the exterior wall. I wasn't greeted by gunfire, but I did hear Carver calling out to me from the second floor of the house.

"Alright, McCool, I give up. Come upstairs and we'll talk. I have some shit you're going to want to hear."

I peeked inside the house. It was an open floor plan, with a living area dead ahead and a loft over the kitchen and bathroom toward the back of the house. A staircase led to the second floor along the wall to the left, ending at a landing at the farthest corner of the house. I'd be blind heading up the stairs, an easy target if Carver decided to play dirty.

"I'm warning you, Carver—you pull any tricks and my partner out there is going to come in here and finish the job. And you should know, she's not as nice as I am."

"Yeah, yeah," he replied. I heard a lighter flicking open and took cover behind the wall again, half-expecting a stick of dynamite or Molotov cocktail to come flying down the stairs. Moments later, the smell of cigarette smoke wafted down to me. "You coming, or what? I ain't got all day here. Your girlfriend shot me through the biceps and I'm bleeding like a stuck pig. Either get up here and talk or kill me already."

I rubbed my forehead as I considered the wisdom of

trusting a guy who had just tortured me and ordered me buried alive. "Fuck it," I muttered. "Alright, I'm coming up."

I side-stepped up the stairs, pistol at the ready, as the second floor slowly came into view through a metal railing that bordered the stairway. As I peered over the floor's edge at the top of the stairs, I saw Carver sitting against the far wall, smoking a cigarette in a pool of shattered glass and his own blood. He'd taken his belt off and used it as a tourniquet, but he hadn't pulled it tight enough to stop the bleeding completely.

A tricked out HK416 rifle was propped up against the wall beside him. I crossed the floor over to him, kicking the rifle just out of his reach as I neared him. Carver seemed content to sit there bleeding and smoking his cigarette. He took a drag, breathing the smoke deep into his lungs before pointing at me with the cigarette and his index finger.

"I hunted supes for two decades before you came along, you know that? I was killing fae and vamps and 'thropes when you were still in diapers." He shook his head. "You know what I learned in all that time? They're killers, every last one of them. Shit, look what they did to you. Why you want to save them is beyond me."

"I don't want to save them all, Carver. Damned few are worth the trouble. But that ogre, he didn't deserve to die. And you killed him in my junkyard to boot. Did you think I'd let that stand?"

"He said you'd take offense if we did it there, warned me against it. I couldn't even get my crew to come with me that night. But I didn't put much stock in your inflated reputation, so I did the job anyway. Figured I'd just put you down when you came, just like I did the ogre. Thought I'd have a nice payday to boot after I got inside that Bag." He paused to take another drag on his cancer stick. "Guess I was wrong."

I stood facing him, pistol held loosely at my side. "Just tell me who hired you. I won't let you live, but I'll make it quick."

CARVER LAUGHED. "You think I'm scared of you? Yeah, well, maybe I am. But there ain't no way I'm more scared of you than I am of those fuckers. You'll just kill me, but they'll stretch it out for decades. You don't know these people, McCool. They ain't like you and me."

"I'm not like you at all," I spat.

He sneered. "You're just like me. You kill them for money —the fae, vamps, and 'thropes. Maybe you think you're all noble for picking and choosing your jobs, but you're not. Hell, you've been doing their dirty work since you landed in Austin. Naw, you and me are two peas in a pod."

I stared at him silently. What he was saying wasn't exactly a lie. What *did* make me different from Carver, when all was said and done? Was it because I protected humans? If that was the case, then what made one sentient life more valuable than another?

Certainly, most of the fae I'd met were outright sociopaths, except for the half-breeds. But did that give me the right to kill them? When all was said and done, they were only following their inner nature. How was hunting fae different from hunting animals like lions and bears for sport?

Because lions and bears don't kill to be cruel or for amuse-ment. Animals killed for survival, unless there was something wrong with them. But the fae? They raped and killed and tortured humans for pleasure, and had for as long as they'd shared this world with humans. And for that reason alone, I really didn't think killing the fae made me evil.

And as for all the rest?

Among the other supernatural races, vampires were the closest to the fae, because they lived lives that were long enough to allow the loss of their humanity. But many of them chose to remember, vamps like Luther and Mateo. And as for the 'thropes, it was rare to find one who killed for pleasure—in fact, most 'thropes were indistinguishable from humans, morally speaking.

The bottom line was, I'd only ever killed creatures who preyed on humans. But hunters like Carver didn't care about those distinctions. And in that regard, hunters like him were just like the fae.

Carver snickered. "Got nothing to say, McCool? Guess I must've hit a nerve."

"Nope. I was just reflecting on all the reasons why I want to kill you. But as it turns out, I promised to let Belladonna here do the honors. As I said, she's not as nice as I am."

I'd heard Bells enter the house moments before, and as she topped the steps she took a small bow. "I can take it from here," she stated simply.

"Be my guest."

Belladonna walked up to Carver, who eyed her warily. "You're with the Circle. What the fuck are you doing here?"

Bells tilted her head to one side. "I happen to like Mr. Tall, Pale, and Ginger over there." She squatted next to Carver, her high heels snapping broken glass as she lowered herself to his level. "Which is why you and I are going to have words."

Carver blew cigarette smoke in her face. "Uh-uh. I'll talk to pretty boy there, but not you."

Belladonna moved with a speed I'd never seen her exhibit before. I saw a flash of silver as she hit Carver in the shoulder, then she pulled her hand back quick enough so I couldn't tell what she'd done.

"Bitch!" Carver yelled. "What the hell was that?"

Belladonna shrugged. "I don't know, exactly. The lab geeks over at HQ said it was like formula SP-17, the stuff the KGB used to interrogate captives during the Cold War. Except this stuff is supposed to work way better."

"Peachy," I said.

Carver tried to get up, but whatever Bells had injected him with seemed to be a very fast-acting drug. He made a few half-hearted attempts to stand, then he plopped down again and hung his head.

"Fucking bitch," he mumbled.

I walked over and stooped to tighten his makeshift tourniquet properly, which earned me a sour look from Bells. "Hey, if he dies before we get the info we need—"

She held up a hand. "Say no more." Bells slapped Carver on the cheek a few times, then snapped her fingers in front of his face. "Hey, shithead, wake up."

"Not... talk... you," Carver muttered. His head lolled from side to side, and he was starting to drool.

"Damn, Bells, what's in that stuff, elephant tranquilizer? Carver doesn't look like he's going to tell us anything any time soon."

She tapped her lip with her thumb. "Hmm, must be the blood loss." She slapped him again, much harder this time. "Hey, you! Who hired you to kill the ogre?"

Carver began to laugh as spittle ran down his chin. "That's funny—like you don't know." He cracked an eye to look at Belladonna. "Then again, mebbe you don't know. Mebbe you're not part of it."

Bells lifted his chin. "Part of what, Carver? What are you talking about?"

Carver tried to place his index finger on Belladonna's mouth, but she batted it away. "Sshh, it's a secret."

I tsked. "Come on, Bells, he's just babbling. I say we leave him—he's not worth the trouble."

The hunter cackled. "Oh, they'll come for me, and that's a fact. Now that you've tracked me down they'll think I talked, but they won't know for sure. Which means they'll make me suffer until they're sure I didn't expose them."

Carver started to drift off, so Belladonna slapped him again to wake him up. "Who's coming for you Carver? Who would want you dead?"

"Same people who wanted the ogre dead." He pointed at me. "They'd have done it themselves, but they're afraid of him. Guess I should've been too, huh?" Carver mumbled a few more unintelligible words, then drifted off into heavy snoring.

I stuck my pistol in my waistband, for lack of a better place to put it. "I think he's done, Bells. Let's just leave him for his employers to sort out."

"Meh, I wasn't going to kill him." She wiped her hands off on Carver's shirt and stood. "Shit. I thought we'd get more out of him, though. That's why I asked you to let me kill him, so you'd leave him alive for me to question him."

"Smart. I'd have killed him by now." I gestured outside. "Should we bury the bodies?"

"Leave them. I can have a clean-up crew take care of it in the morning, after Carver's long gone. I have a feeling he's going to go on the run, just as soon as he wakes up."

"Thanks for coming to rescue me." I put an arm around her, kissing the top of her head as I pointed us toward the stairs. As we hit the top step, a thought occurred to me. "Um, won't the clean-up crew ask questions?"

Bells leaned into me, nuzzling my chest. "Not if I tell them Carver's team was killed in the course of a Circle investigation."

A gunshot rang out, causing us both to pivot and draw our weapons. Carver was slumped on the floor, his rifle barrel in his mouth and his brains splattered all over the wall.

"Damn," I hissed. "I guess he really was afraid of whoever hired him."

"Ugh, talk about spoiling the mood." Belladonna knuckled her forehead. "I have a really bad feeling about this case of yours, and it's giving me a headache. Rain check on our date?"

I gestured at my bruised, cut, burned body. "What, you don't want some of this?"

"You might be feeling frisky now, but when those painkillers wear off all you're going to want to do is curl up and die. Go home, heal up, and call me in the morning."

"You got it, boss."

"That's 'mistress' to you, loverboy."

I laughed and kissed her again as we headed for the stairs. Did it bother me that I'd just seen Carver kill himself? Not really—the fact that it *didn't* bother me was what really worried me.

FIFTEEN

I called Finnegas on my way back to the junkyard, explaining what had happened. "And you say you couldn't shift?"

"Nope. I think the Eye did something to my brain, to prevent me from hulking out and going on a killing spree."

"That's not necessarily a bad thing, considering how your change has been affecting you lately. Colin, did you remember what you did at Mateo's party?"

I paused to consider the question. "Not at first, but later it all came back to me."

"Hmm. Okay, head back to the junkyard and wait for me. I'll bring what I need to patch you up."

The painkillers Bells had given me were already wearing off when Finnegas arrived. "Oh, holy lizard shit, this hurts."

"It's going to hurt worse before it gets better. Strip down and let me get a look at you." I did as requested, and Finn whistled. "Well, this hunter was nothing if not thorough. You should be glad that everything is still all in one piece."

"I was more worried about losing teeth, but now that you

mention it…" I covered my junk with my hands out of reflex rather than modesty. "I suppose it's a good thing Carver wasn't a *complete* psycho."

Finnegas examined my wounds, shaking his head. "None of these wounds are life-threatening, but there are so many of them that I can't treat them individually." He dug around in a knapsack he'd brought with him, pulling out a stoppered glass bottle. "Here, drink this."

Again, I complied. "Tastes like ass, Finnegas."

"You'd know," he mumbled as he rooted around inside his bag. "It'll dull the pain, and help you go deep into a trance so the magic can fully facilitate your healing."

Finnegas pulled out a stone mortar and pestle, and soon he was grinding various herbs, leaves, and other ingredients into a thick paste.

"That smells like how the potion you gave me tasted."

"All magic has its costs. In this case, you'll smell like you've been mating with a she-troll for a few days."

"Great. Alright, let's get this over with." I raised my arms out to the side with a groan, and Finnegas started rubbing the paste into my injuries. "Ah, damn it, that burns!"

Finnegas snorted. "Stop being a baby. If you're going to rush into impossible situations, then you can't complain about suffering the consequences of your poor judgement." He rubbed more of the goop into my cuts and burns, taking his time in getting the concoction deep into every wound. Minutes later, he set the mortar down and took a seat. "There, all done. Now, tell me about what happened at Luther's duel. Leave no detail out."

I recounted the story as best as I could, and in as much detail as possible. When I finished, Finnegas sat stroking his beard. "And once your memory came back to you, you say you recalled the entire evening, with no blackouts whatsoever?"

"No, none. I remember the whole thing. Why?"

"Isn't it obvious? That means you were in control the entire time."

"But, how? I mean, that wasn't me who wanted to kill Luther—was it?"

Finnegas pulled his tobacco pouch out and began rolling a cigarette. "Remember, I was there to witness Cú Chulainn's trials and travails, and I saw how the *ríastrad* affected him. When the battle frenzy seized him, it was still Cú Chulainn at the helm—a darker and much more bloodthirsty side of him, but it was him nonetheless. He remembered every murderous act he committed while under the effects of the *ríastrad*, and it haunted him all his days."

I took a deep breath, considering the implications. "I guess I wanted to keep believing the beast was separate from me somehow, a different entity inside me—kind of like the Eye, you know?"

Finnegas blew smoke out his nostrils and shook his head. "I used to think so as well, but as your training with the Pack revealed, you have a split in your personality—one that occurred when you accidentally killed Jesse." Even now, recollections of that horrible night stabbed me right through the heart, and Finn must've read it on my face. "Now, now, I know you still blame yourself for that, but you mustn't. Even in the knowledge that it was you who killed her, and not something inside you."

"Finnegas, does it really matter if I was in control or not?

It was still me who did it, and I'll never forgive myself for Jesse's death. Never."

Finnegas stood up, patting me on the shoulder as he passed by to retrieve his things. "Never is a long time, Colin. Believe me, I should know. It's no platitude to say that time heals all wounds. Chances are that you're going to walk this earth a good long time, so trust me—this pain will fade, eventually."

"And you, Finnegas? Have you forgiven yourself for Jesse's death?" I said it not as an accusation, but an honest question.

Finnegas sighed heavily, avoiding my eyes as he packed his bag. "No, my boy. It's much too soon for that." The old man stood, more slowly than I would have expected. "Now, sit down, cross your legs, and breathe. You'll be spending the night in a druid trance—it'll help the medicine do its work, and when you're injured it's a much better way for you to regain your strength than sleep."

I sat cross-legged on the floor, closing my eyes and then opening them again. "Speaking of which, something happened when I was trying to keep Carver's crew from killing me. I went under, just like you taught me, but I went a hell of a lot deeper this time."

Finnegas took a puff of his cigarette, burning the cherry down to his fingers. His hands were so weathered and calloused he didn't even notice. "How so?" he asked with interest.

"Well, I sensed things—not just the elements around me, but plants and animals as well."

Finn's eyes widened slightly. "Now, that *is* interesting," he said as he stomped his cigarette out on the floor.

"Damn it, Finn, can't you use an ashtray?" I growled. "An empty beer can? Your pocket? You know, something other than my floor?"

"It's a concrete floor, so it's not like I burned an expensive Persian rug. Now, as for your trance—I want you to try to repeat that experience tonight. And remember that you're supposed to be in meditation, not counting sheep. Report your experiences to me in the morning."

"Yes, drill sergeant," I said.

He smirked as he licked and sealed another cigarette, lighting it as he walked out the door. "You should be so lucky. If what you told me is true, well—now the *real* work begins."

I DID AS FINNEGAS ASKED, taking myself deep into a druid trance. That is, after I grabbed a towel to sit on, because that floor was damned cold. I stayed in the trance all night, but this time it was much, much different than when I was in the forest waiting to be buried alive by Carver's goons.

Despite being under duress, back in the forest it was a lot easier to connect with the plant life and animals around me. Here, inside the concrete and metal of the junkyard warehouse, I found it difficult to find something to connect with. Eventually, however, I detected a plethora of life around me, much more than I had ever realized might exist within the confines of the yard.

There were ant colonies underneath the building, mice in the walls, rabbits and birds nesting deep within the stacks, rats everywhere—which kind of grossed me out—and of course, Roscoe and Rufus, guarding the yard as always.

Carver had trapped them in another part of the yard when he'd attacked Elmo, which was too bad because they'd have made him regret his trespass.

Just for grins, I made an attempt to touch Roscoe's mind, but all I did was frighten the poor dog. That in turn caused him to start barking, pacing back and forth like a tiger in a cage. I decided to experiment and see if I could send the dog a message to calm him down.

Roscoe! It's me, Colin. Settle down, already.

I heard a whine and a short "woof," but rather than sensing distinct thoughts all I got from Roscoe were impressions of his emotions. Maybe dogs were different than rodents—hell, I didn't know. But what I did know was that Roscoe soon quieted down while sending me feelings of vigilant calm. What was really weird was that, once he figured out that I was communicating empathically, he was completely okay with it. It made me wonder if dogs normally communicated in that manner, just as the Pack did.

I spent the remainder of the night letting my focus and awareness drift around the junkyard. I'd locate an animal, "feel" what it was thinking or doing, observe it for a while, and then move on. After a while I got bored, so I brought my awareness back to my own body and just kind of sat there feeling the mellow.

That's when I noticed something really weird; it felt as though there was another intelligence inside my room. The presence was just below the level of my conscious awareness, and was too subtle for me to notice normally. But when I was this deep in the druid trance, I was hyper-aware of my surroundings and every life-form present. Still, this wasn't so much a life-form as an intelligence.

Eye, is that you?

The Eye's response was different from what I was accustomed to "hearing" inside my head. It was muted, and sounded like it was coming from a great distance.

-No, although I am pleased that you've discovered a means for us to communicate when you're not in your Fomorian form.-

To tell the truth, this is a pleasant surprise for me as well. Okay, so if it's not you, then what is it?

-My inclination is to state how this should be obvious to you, but I also realize what is obvious to me is not always clear to mortals. The presence you are detecting is your Craneskin Bag. I would advise that you not attempt communication with it, as it is an intelligence that is wholly and completely foreign to the human mind.-

I would've said the same about you, Eye. Before I got to know you, that is.

The Eye paused before responding. *-I shall take that as a compliment. It is... peculiar for me to experience the companionship of others. However, after all these centuries alone I am coming to enjoy it.-*

I'll take that as a compliment as well. Now, getting back to my Bag—what exactly is it? The intelligence I'm sensing, I mean.

-It is an intelligence only in the vaguest sense of the word. Think of it as a simple AI made completely of magic. It was created for a specific purpose and with very clearly defined directives, in order to serve the MacCumhaill heirs for the length of its existence.-

Okay... so that thing is watching me all the time?

-Yes, and attempting to decipher your intentions as well as

anticipate your needs. In the past, when it released magical items of its own accord, it was likely making crude attempts to assist you. But make no mistake—it is a fae artifact, and therefore entirely unpredictable and completely capricious in nature.-

Capricious? Really? But I've always found it to be absolutely reliable.

-That's because the Bag likes you. However, I doubt it has performed so well for each and every one of your forebears, and I'm certain at least a few of those who carried it before you tried to rid themselves of it. Imagine if the Bag decided it didn't like you, and consider the havoc it could wreak if it was so inclined.-

I considered the Eye's commentary carefully before responding. Eye, what do you think it would take to make the Bag turn on me?

-Primarily, trying to harm its creator. Or doing something that misaligns with its creator's wishes.-

Any idea who or what made it?

-Lugh did, of course. Who else could've crafted such an item?-

So, don't piss Lugh off then.

-I would certainly not advise it.-

I CONVERSED with the Eye until it informed me that morning had arrived. Realizing it would be difficult to explain the dried green crap I had all over me, I brought myself out of the trance so I could shower before Ed and the morning shift arrived.

Interestingly, I wasn't nearly as sore and stiff as I would have expected, considering the state I'd been in the night before. I knew from experience that Finn's healing draughts and poultices didn't work that quickly, at least not unless he gave them a boost of his own magic. So, I could only assume it had been the trance that had accelerated my healing.

Oh, I was still beat up alright, but not nearly as bad as I had been. Moreover, I felt completely rested. Better than rested, actually. I felt alive.

Finnegas was waiting for me when I walked out of the warehouse to my outdoor shower. "Trouble. I found this pinned to the front gate with a fae arrow when I arrived this morning."

He handed me a rolled piece of parchment, made of a thin translucent material that almost felt like leather. I unrolled it, revealing a few lines of unfamiliar script written by hand in intricate calligraphy and scrollwork.

"I can't read this crap. What does it say?"

Finnegas spat. "It's a missive from the queen, requesting your presence. *Immediately*."

"Maeve?"

"Is there another queen I should be aware of?"

I tsked as I looked the document over. "Only the ones who hang out with Luther," I stated absently. "She sent for me once already, actually."

"Well, I can't say I blame you for not making an appearance."

"Considering that her messengers tried to kill me, I wasn't exactly inclined to pay her a visit." I waved the parchment at him. "You think she's going to try something?"

Finnegas' eyes narrowed. "No, I don't think so. A royal

invitation like this one comes with an inherent promise of safe passage. The high fae may be treacherous, but they do have manners."

"I'll go armed, just in case," I said as I handed the parchment back to him.

Finnegas took it, looking it over one more time. "Hmm..."

"What's up? See something you missed earlier?"

"Yes, this is human skin. See the tattoo? Fae don't mark their skin in that manner." He held up the parchment to give me a better look at the markings.

"Shit, I recognize that tattoo—Carver had one just like it. Damn it, they've been tracking my movements... or someone's been tipping them off."

Finnegas chuckled. "Surprised?"

I rubbed my face, exhaling heavily. "I guess I shouldn't be. Maeve's assassin squad sure knew how to find me quickly when they jumped me outside of Rocko's club."

"She sent assassins to deliver a message to you?" Finnegas sat down on a nearby bumper, reaching for his tobacco pouch. "Between that and the material she chose for this invitation, I'd say she's sending you a very clear message."

"Which is?"

Finnegas finished rolling his cigarette, lighting up and taking a long pull before answering. "You're not going to see her alone."

"Fine, I'll take Belladonna."

He spat a fleck of tobacco and shook his head. "No, she's out of her depth with Maeve. Besides, I'd say there's more than a little jealousy brewing between those two, considering how possessive they both are of you."

I snorted. "Oh, come on, Finn. Seriously?"

He pointed a finger at me as he blew smoke from his nostrils. "That's why the stunt you pulled with the Treasures wounded her so deeply. I think she actually cares about you, and frankly that scares the shit out of me. You think hell hath no wrath like a woman scorned? Tell that to someone who spurned the attentions of a faery queen."

"Finn, you're kind of grossing me out. I mean, she's like my grandmother or something. Not that she's not hotter than a two-dollar pistol, but damn—that's pretty much incest. No thanks."

The old man flicked me on the forehead with his fingers, making a loud thunk. "Think, Colin! She's not romantically interested in you—at least I don't think she is, although fae see acts of incest much differently than humans. No, I believe she has taken an interest in you because you remind her of Oisín."

"Oh, damn."

Finnegas stabbed his cigarette at me. "Exactly. When that idiot decided to go to Underhill with Niamh I told him not to do it, because I knew he'd miss his home eventually. And that would mean spurning her—or, at least, that's how she would've interpreted it."

I raised my hand. "Wait a minute—you knew Maeve was Niamh?"

"Of course I did. Now, stop interrupting me. Where was I? Ah yes, Niamh and Oisín." He took a drag on his coffin nail and blew it out the side of his mouth. "Let me ask you a question—do you think the steed she gave Oisín was a gift, or merely a device to ensure he returned to Underhill?"

"I don't know. I just figured it was to prevent him from staying here on Earth."

Finnegas tsked. "The opposite, actually. That horse was a trap. Even though Oisín fully intended to visit his family and then go back to her, Niamh couldn't stand the thought that he loved his family as much or more than her. That's why she sliced the horse's girth before gifting it to Oisín."

"Damn, that's cold."

"Colin, I've told you time and again, the fae don't think like us. Everything with them is about power and lording it over others. Maeve might care about you, but that's only because she wants to *possess* you. No, you absolutely cannot visit her alone."

I scratched at one of my wounds. The poultice Finnegas had applied was starting to itch. "Alright, fine. I won't go alone. But who should I take?"

"Me, that's who. It's time I reminded that faery queen why the fae have reason to fear druidkind."

SIXTEEN

When we pulled up to Maeve's mansion in the work truck, Finnegas placed a hand on my arm. "Listen, I know The Dagda gave you something in Underhill."

"You mean the—"

Finnegas clapped his hand over my mouth. "Ssh! I only bring it up to tell you that you should never speak of it or reveal it to anyone. I'll not say more on the matter, except that you should never gift or barter it away, nor reveal where you keep it hidden."

He removed his hand, and I eyed him warily. "Keep it secret and safe. Whatever you say, Gandalf."

"I told you years ago not to call me that. Now, things are bound to get heated in there. No matter what happens, I want you to act like you know what's going on. In other words, pretend like you have a clue. It shouldn't be hard for you, seeing how you go through life faking competence as a matter of course."

"Um, thanks. Alright, I'll be cool as a cucumber. No worries."

"We'll see," Finnegas said as he slipped out of the truck.

I took the lead as we headed up the walk to Maeve's place. Quite unlike my previous visits, this time the lawn was brown, anemic, and generally ill-maintained. The front walk had weeds growing up through the cracks, and the trellised gate was overgrown with ivy. Paint peeled off its every exposed surface.

I glanced at Finnegas, and he leaned in to whisper in my ear.

"Don't say a word about the house and grounds, no matter what."

I raised an eyebrow, then I opened the front gate. It creaked as it swung wide to allow us entrance. Just as I was about to set foot in the yard, one of Maeve's pet gargoyles leapt out in front of me, landing with a resounding crash. The beast roared at me, daring me to set foot in its designated territory.

I raised my hands in a gesture of peace. "Look, Adelard—"

The beast roared again, and despite the fact that I didn't think gargoyles needed to breathe, the force of it blew my hair back against my head. "Fine, Lothair then. Maeve asked me to show up, so I'm here. I don't like it any more than you do, but that's just how it is."

The gargoyle glowered at me, blowing puffs of dust from its nostrils every now and again and generally being intimidating as all hell.

I groaned. "Oh, for heaven's sake, are you going to let me in or not?"

Lothair growled, his expression conveying pure menace. That is, more menace than normal. All gargoyles had permanent bitchy resting face.

Finnegas tapped me on the shoulder. "Let me try."

"Fine, be my guest." I stepped out of the way to let Finn pass.

The old man walked up to the gate boundary and spoke three clipped words in a language I didn't recognize. If I were to describe it, I'd have to say it sounded a lot like Finnegas was coughing up a hairball. After the old man had spoken, the gargoyle cocked his head like a confused dog. Then, he backed off to one side, laid down, and went completely still.

Finnegas looked over his shoulder at me. "Let's go. I don't want to be here all day."

"Um, what did you say to him?" I asked as I followed Finnegas up the walk.

"I spoke the first three syllables of his true name. That was enough to get him to behave."

"How'd you learn a thing like that?"

Finnegas tapped his temple. "Foresight, my boy. Part of being a Seer is determining what knowledge might be useful in future days."

"And the other part?"

"Acquiring such knowledge without letting your enemies know you have it."

As we approached the front door, I noticed that the rest of Maeve's house was just as dilapidated as the front entrance. Paint was peeling everywhere, mold grew under the eaves and in every shaded place, and parts of the front porch were rotting away. In a matter of months, Maeve's home had gone from something you might see on HGTV to a shithole that had "senile cat lady hoarder lives here" written all over it.

Finnegas allowed me to take the lead again as we mounted the steps. Unsurprisingly, the floorboards creaked and groaned underfoot as we crossed the porch. I knocked loudly three times, then we waited for someone to answer. Perhaps a minute or two later, the door swung open, revealing Lucindras and Eliandres. They did not look happy to see me.

"Enter, druid, but tread carefully while you are in the Queen's home," Lucindras said. "One slip and you *will* suffer the consequences. Nothing would please us more than the opportunity to teach you some manners."

I yawned. "You guys are awful uppity for being the hired help. But hey, if you ever want a rematch, I'm easy to find."

Eliandres smiled in a most unfriendly manner. "I assure you, druidling, we fully intend to even the score after our Queen is through with you."

Finnegas laid a hand on my shoulder. "If this is how the queen treats her guests, we'll be taking our leave." By the time I turned around, he was already halfway to the truck. Lacking a better plan, I followed suit.

"Wait!" Lucindras exclaimed. "You may pass unmolested, as our Queen wills it."

Finnegas stopped. I looked at him, and he at me. "Well, I suppose we have a few minutes to spare," he said.

Lucindras allowed me to pass, but she barred the doorway with her arm before Finnegas could enter. "You were not invited, Seer."

The old man's eyes were two slits as he replied in a still, quiet voice that made the hairs on the back of my neck stand up. "Colin has a right to bring an advisor when summoned to the Queen's court, as do all envoys, consuls, dignitaries... and visiting royalty."

Lucindras laughed. "He is none of those."

Finnegas frowned slightly. "I beg to differ. He is a direct descendant of Fionn MacCumhaill, leader of the fianna, who were and are a power and tribe unto themselves. That makes him a *rígfénnid* of the fianna, which is tantamount to king-hood. He is also a plenipotentiary acting and speaking on behalf of all druidkind, and therefore carries the rights and privileges thereof, to advise, admonish, advocate, and adjure all races, mortal and immortal, as The Dagda decreed when he established our order."

Lucindras attempted to rebut Finn's argument. "That's not... I mean he can't... he has no standing—"

The old man spoke over her stuttering response like a bulldozer mowing down a flowerbed. "Finally, he is a descendent of your Queen, through the line of Oisín, making him at the very least a lord in the Fair-Haired Lady's court."

Lucindras was now at a complete loss for words. "I..."

Finn leaned in and whispered his last words with a subtle menace I did not think him capable of. "You have no right to bar me entry. Let. Me. Pass."

Eliandres stepped forward, gently pushing his now apoplectic partner out of the way. "This way, please," he said with all formality. "The Queen awaits."

I WHISPERED to Finnegas as we followed Eliandres and Lucindras at a distance. "What was all that bullshit about?"

Finn whispered back. "It's not bullshit. Every last bit of it is the truth."

"Wait a minute... I'm a lord?"

"Don't let it go to your head. As far as I'm concerned, you're still my bumbling apprentice."

"You say that now, but when I'm handing out titles and lands you'll change your tune."

Finnegas scowled, but remained silent as we walked further into Maeve's home. The place still seemed much larger on the inside than it did without, but the halls and passages no longer constantly shifted position in relation to each other. Despite the house's lack of its former *Alice in Wonderland* qualities, it was creepier now than it had ever been.

Just as it appeared on the outside, the formerly opulent interior of Maeve's mansion had decayed considerably. Wall paper curled away from the walls, paint and plaster had fallen in specks and chunks to the floor, the rugs were worn and threadbare, and the paintings and tapestries that had decorated the place were now moth-eaten and tattered. The place appeared to be the classic example of a haunted house, so much so that I half-expected an apparition to pass through the walls ahead of us.

Eliandres and Lucindras led us to a tall wooden door, intricately carved and iron bound, with a crystal knob and an ancient iron bolt keeping it shut. Unsurprisingly, Eliandres opened it with a gloved hand, as the fae were notoriously averse to iron and steel.

After opening the door, the two assassins took up stations on either side of the doorway. I looked through the entry to a large throne room beyond, complete with high ceilings, stone columns, and a long red rug that stretched across the flag-stone floor and up to a raised dais. Fae warriors lined both sides of the carpet, each dressed in tarnished but serviceable plate armor. The warriors were armed with matching spears and shields, and each had a short sword strapped to their waist.

At the end of the hall, Queen Maeve sat atop the dais. Her throne was carved from basalt and inlaid with precious metals and gemstones. She rested on a cushion, regally poised with her legs crossed and hands resting to either side. Maeve's appearance bore none of her past pretense; she'd shed her mortal disguise to reveal herself as the fae queen and Tuatha royalty she was.

The Queen wore a gauzy white gown, white slippers, and a blue sash about her waist. Besides the simple golden circlet on her head she was otherwise devoid of adornment, the otherworldly radiance of her pale skin and golden hair making trinkets and jewels superfluous. Despite the distance between us, her eyes drew me in as they swirled from the deepest sea foam green to the blue of a summer sky, to the indigo woad of glacial ice, then back to green again.

Finnegas nudged me with his elbow, and I immediately snapped back to reality. "Rather crass of you, Maeve, to attempt to charm my apprentice," he said as he approached Maeve's throne without command or invite. "I'd advise that you not try that again."

Maeve regarded my teacher as he crossed the room. "Your presence was not requested, Seer," she replied, her magically-amplified voice filling the hall. "My business is with Colin, and he alone."

Finn didn't miss a beat in responding, showing that

Maeve hadn't cowed him in the slightest. "As I reminded those footpads out there, Colin is allowed to bring an advisor when summoned to the royal court."

I tried to avoid looking dazed as I scurried after Finnegas, but I was still reeling from the spell Maeve had attempted to cast. That alone was enough to infuriate me, and the resulting release of adrenaline helped me shake off the residual stupor. I caught up with Finn without looking like I was in too much of a rush, and took up a position slightly behind him and to his right. While I was tempted to say something witty and inappropriate, I chose to remain silent, if only to see how this power play turned out.

Maeve waved off Finnegas' retort. "As you wish, but you will remain silent as I command Colin on how he is to proceed in his investigation. He owes the fae a great debt for his betrayal, which he will pay in servitude—"

Finn's stomped his foot and the ground shook as a huge crack opened in the flagstone floor. The crack opened wider as it zigzagged toward Maeve's dais, and Finn's voice roared like thunder, shaking the columns and bringing dust from the ceiling with his reply.

"You will command him on nothing! Nothing!"

FIFTY FOOT SOLDIERS surrounded Finn and me in a clatter of armor and weapons, as they moved to protect their Queen from Finn's wrath. Their spears formed a bristling wall around us, although we still had an escape route to our rear flank. The door to the throne room slammed shut, and a quick glance told me that Eliandres, Lucindras, and four more assassins guarded the exit.

Great. Now what?

Despite being trapped and outnumbered, Finnegas was unperturbed. He and Maeve locked eyes, and they engaged in a staring contest so intense, I swore I saw daggers flying between them. Finally, Maeve flicked a single finger. In response, her guard raised their spears and dropped their shields, coming to parade rest while maintaining their position in front of her throne.

Maeve gave us a serpent's smile. "So, the Seer hasn't become as decrepit and infirm as he led us to believe." She steepled her fingers in front of her. "Tell me, Seer—why should I not have you cut down where you stand?"

"Besides the fact that my apprentice could bring this place down singlehandedly? Or that I might command the earth to swallow your entire guard whole?"

"You'd still be dead, old man," she replied.

"Would you attack the last remaining druids, here while we stand as guests of your court, and break the pact The Dagda made when he created our order? Are you willing to carry that curse? Would you have it known that Niamh, daughter of Manannán mac Lir, is an oathbreaker who acts in defiance of the former leader of her people?"

"You go too far, Seer," Maeve hissed.

"On the contrary, I haven't gone far enough. You pounced on my apprentice, just as soon as you believed me weak and unable to intervene. While he was still reeling from the loss of his love, you used his mother as leverage to force him into your service. That, in direct violation of the promise we received from An Dagda—that no druid would ever be drafted into the service of his people."

"That promise was made long ago, by one who no longer leads the Tuatha," Maeve said. "As the sole living member of the Tuath Dé on earth, I now lead in his stead, and my decree stands as the will of the fae."

Finnegas raised a finger in the air. "Ah, but the fae are not the Tuath Dé, but only their offspring. And from what I understand, The Dagda leads *your* people quite handily from his farm in Underhill."

Maeve bristled at Finn's response, but she opted to abandon that argument to attack from another direction. "Nothing you say changes the fact that Colin betrayed his word to me, and in doing so he diminished the power of my people significantly. For that, he owes me a great debt, and by rights I get to choose the manner of repayment."

Finnegas calmly rolled a cigarette, oblivious to the fifty armed guards in front of us and half a dozen deadly assassins at our backs. He lit up and took several long puffs, arms crossed as he considered Maeve's words. Then he took another drag, blowing smoke as he responded.

"Actually, Colin didn't break his word in the slightest. In fact, he performed the tasks you set to him exactly as he agreed. And I quote: 'So, I have to travel to Underhill, avoid being killed by various powerful factions while I'm there, kill the Rye Mother, rescue the children, somehow acquire all four of the treasures of Ireland, and then make it back to the gate in one piece.' To which you replied, 'I'd say that sums it up nicely.'"

Maeve's eyes narrowed as Finnegas continued. "And with that, the pact was sealed. Colin stated the terms, and you agreed to them. Although you originally requested that he bring the Treasures to *you*, he only agreed to *acquire them and make it back to the gate*. A task which he performed admirably, I might add.

"To conclude, it is quite apparent that he owes you no debt at all." Finn stated. The old man puffed on his cigarette as Maeve fumed silently. "Any questions?"

Maeve mouth drew into a tight line as Finnegas finished, and tiny crow's feet appeared as her eyes narrowed. "Leave my presence this instant, Seer, and take your apprentice with you. Else I *will* break the Dagda's oath, even if it means bringing my kingdom down around me."

Finnegas took a few last drags from his lung dart before dropping it and stubbing it out on Maeve's carpet with his toe. "A pleasure as always, Maeve."

The old man turned and headed toward the exit. At first, I followed, then I paused. I could see Finn's shoulders hitch slightly when my footsteps stopped. I looked back over my shoulder at Maeve, locking eyes for just a moment.

"I will find whoever is killing the fae, Maeve. Not out of any debt to you, but because they killed an innocent. And frankly, I simply cannot let that stand."

Perhaps Maeve's expression softened slightly at that, or maybe it was just my imagination. Nothing more was said as I followed Finnegas to the door. Upon exiting the throne room, we were deposited directly outside the house on Maeve's decrepit front porch.

"I'd say that went well," I said.

"Not until we're in the truck," Finnegas hissed. "Come, we have much to discuss."

SEVENTEEN

I opened my mouth to speak once we were in the truck, but my dour-faced teacher raised a hand to silence me. Trusting that he knew what was best when dealing with the fae, I started the truck, put it in gear, and headed off down the road. A few miles later, I sensed the old man relax. When he cracked a window and pulled out his tobacco pouch, I knew things were alright.

"You're going to give me cancer with all that secondhand smoke," I jibed.

"I've been smoking leaf for over two-thousand years. Do you see me hurting for it?"

I chuckled. "Yeah, but I'm not semi-immortal."

Finn paused as he was lighting up. "The way you're headed, you will be if you're not careful."

"What's that supposed to mean?" I asked, truly confounded by what he'd said.

My mentor groaned softly as he readjusted in his seat. Working magic took a lot out of him these days. "Ask me about that some other time. For now, let's stick with the issues at hand."

"Okay, fine. What the hell happened to Maeve's house?"

Finnegas flicked ash out the window. Why he was so careful with the yard truck and not my bedroom floor, I had no idea. "That one's obvious, so you tell me."

I thought for a second before answering. "Either it all deteriorated after I cut the earthbound fae off from Underhill, or everything I saw before was an illusion."

The old druid wobbled his hand back and forth. "Eh, a little of both, actually. The high fae like to place spells on their possessions, especially things that can't easily be regrown or replaced. The magic distorts time, slows it down so the enchanted items decay and degrade much more slowly."

"Chronomancy—that seems to be popping up a lot lately," I muttered.

"That idiot Click's been showing off to you, has he? I'm telling you, stay away from that one. He's been known to start wars just to see what would happen."

"I'll keep that in mind. Getting back to the fae and how Maeve's place went all *House on Haunted Hill...*?"

"Right. Besides being skin-flints they're uppity bastards, so they lay glamours on top of everything to make it all look sparkly and new. But without access to Underhill?" He made two fists and opened his hands wide, mimicking an explosion. "Poof! All that magic went up in smoke. Serves them right."

"Well, that clears up one mystery. Now, about what you told Maeve—"

"The part about you being rígfénnid of the fianna, or the

part about you being a plenipotentiary of druidkind, or the part about you being a lord in Maeve's court?"

"All of it, actually," I said in a soft voice.

Finnegas scratched his cheek. "All true. Of course, there's only one fiann right now, and it consists of just one member."

"Me, I take it."

"Correct. However, you have the right to take on other members, to recruit and build your fiann's strength as you see fit."

I blinked a couple of times, unsure why I might want to build a small army. "Um, good to know, I think. What about the other stuff?"

"You're one of only two members of our order. Well, three, but the Dark Druid doesn't count. Anyway, that makes you second in command, and that affords you privileges that an apprentice wouldn't normally have."

"Such as...?"

Finnegas coughed in his hand, then he looked at his cigarette and tossed it out the window. "Such as being a representative of our kind—an ambassador, if you will. But it's more than that. When The Dagda founded our order, his intent was to even the scales between the supernatural races and mankind."

"Humankind," I interjected.

Finnegas frowned. "That's what I said, didn't I? Stop interrupting."

As adaptable as the old man was, I doubted I'd ever get him to be politically correct. I'd learned to pick my battles where he was concerned, so I let him continue.

"Now, the Dagda was a crafty old codger, and he knew that humans wouldn't like it if a bunch of magic-wielding forest rangers suddenly started messing around in their business. So, he taught us to present ourselves as advisors to the Celtic peoples. And where they went, we went, sometimes giving counsel, sometimes acting as protectors, and at other times, meting out justice when and where necessary. Some of us became advisers to kings, a dangerous business, while others were content to lurk behind the scenes, only making our presence known when it was absolutely necessary."

"Finn, what happened to the druids? If you were so powerful, how did your numbers dwindle over the centuries?"

"Rome had a lot to do with it, and as faith in the old gods faded, so did we. But it mostly had to do with the fae. When the majority of them retreated to Underhill, we thought we were no longer needed. How wrong we were."

"Why did you choose to stick around—until now, I mean?"

Finn clucked his tongue. "Because I'm an idiot, that's why." I raised an eyebrow, eliciting a chuckle from the old man. "Oh, don't be so sensitive. You know very well it's because I'd committed to preserving the MacCumhaill line. Being a Seer isn't all it's cracked up to be. Visions, prophecies, omens—pfah!"

"I don't suppose you care to expand on that topic?" I waited for him to elaborate, but he remained tight-lipped. "Okay, next question. Am I really a lord in Maeve's court?"

Finnegas wiped his hands on his jeans. "Sort of. She'd have to confer the title, rights, and privileges to make it official, but you do qualify. Trust me, though, that's the last thing you want, to be caught up in the high fae's court intrigues and whatnot. Which brings me to the point of this discussion..."

"Which is? I still don't fully understand what just happened."

"What just happened is, I freed you from Maeve's meddling. Although when you opened your trap, I was almost sure you were going to obligate yourself to her again. But the good news is you didn't. The better news is that, whether by accident or instinct, you outsmarted her with this last gig she had you do."

I shrugged. "News to me. I don't suppose it occurred to you to mention this before we went to see Maeve?"

"I'd been waiting for the right moment to throw it in her face, but the time was never right. Since you'd been avoiding her, I didn't feel the need to bring it up. And if I had told you beforehand, you'd have just gotten cocky and opened your mouth at the wrong moment. Maeve would've manipulated you into another deal, and you'd be right back where you were before."

"I wouldn't—"

Finnegas laughed. "Really? And have you forgotten every other time you've put your foot in your mouth?"

"Point taken," I replied, tapping the steering wheel nervously. All this excitement and intrigue was starting to make me anxious. "One last question... how did you know the exact words I used when I made that deal with Maeve?"

Finn's face split in a Cheshire grin. "I'm the Seer, remember? Seeing is what I do." He poked a finger in my chest. "And if there's one thing you should take away from this entire sordid affair, it's that magic isn't what made the druids feared by all the other races and factions."

"It isn't?"

"Not at all. What made them fear us was our *knowledge*,

and that we were cleverer than everyone else at using it to our advantage. Kind of like your modern attorneys, except we weren't such sodding pricks."

"Noted." My fingers beat a rhythm on the steering wheel as I considered all he'd said. "Hey, Finnegas?"

"Yes?"

"You think Ed would let me get a work shirt with 'Lord McCool' stitched on the name tag?"

"I knew I shouldn't have said that in front of you," Finnegas replied, cranking the stereo up. As Hüsker Dü's "Zen Arcade" blared from the truck's tinny speakers, I wondered if things would really ever be over between Maeve and me. Somehow, I doubted it.

THE NEXT DAY, I got up early to finish everything Ed needed me to do around the yard. After nuking a couple of burritos and washing them down with an energy drink, I washed up and changed into a clean set of jeans and one of my Kevlar motorcycle jackets. Then I gathered my gear, and with a forlorn look at the Gremlin, borrowed the keys for the yard truck from Ed and headed out to Bastrop.

There were a couple of things that bothered me about what we'd learned at Carver's compound. One was that we hadn't learned a damned thing, and the second was that Carver was no technomancer. The way Elmo had been killed reeked of technomancy, which meant that Carver had only been there to slow the ogre down.

Which also meant that Elmo's killer was still out there.

Just to be safe, I parked in the same spot I had the last

time when I got the Carver's place and hoofed it through the woods toward the compound. Staying low, I mounted a rise that brought the compound into view. I crouched behind a tree, hidden by undergrowth as I watched and waited patiently for any sign of movement.

Fifteen minutes later, all I saw were squirrels and some bubbles in the pond. *Probably turtles*, I thought. Chicken turtles and red-eared sliders were found everywhere near slow-moving creeks, ponds, and bogs in Central Texas. Nevertheless, I drew my Glock before creeping down to the compound.

On my approach to the front of the residence, I noted that everything looked as it had when I'd first seen the place. Bullet holes had been patched up, broken windows had been replaced, the garage door had been repaired, and even the wrecked and burned vehicle was now missing. In fact, I couldn't even tell where it had crashed. Circle clean-up teams were incredibly thorough, their job being to erase all evidence of a mage-hunter team's presence.

I rounded the pond on the west side, which was farthest away from the driveway. Taking my time and sticking close to the trees, I scurried toward the fence line on that side, sweeping the area ahead with the muzzle of my weapon. As I cleared the pond and came in full view of the buildings and central courtyard, I paused near the fence one last time.

Not a single sign of life. Outstanding.

I holstered my pistol and reached into the Bag, grabbing a heavy-duty pair of ratcheting wire cutters. They were loud, but they'd cut through the chainlink fence like a hot knife through butter. I snagged a piece of the fence in the cutter's jaws and went to work, wincing at the noise. Since I wanted to be in and out of here quickly, I was willing to sacrifice stealth for speed.

And that was my first mistake.

I heard a muffled sucking noise behind me, followed by a disturbance in the surface of the pond. Just a few ripples, nothing to be alarmed by, but I stopped what I was doing just the same. A few bubbles surfaced again, nothing more, so I chalked it up to a fish surfacing, or maybe a big alligator turtle that had taken up residence in the murky waters.

I went back to work on the fence, and that's when it surged out of the water and grabbed me.

The whole thing happened so fast, I really didn't understand what was going on when it pulled me under. One minute I was up on the bank of the pond cutting through the fence, and the next I was being pulled deep into the muddy waters. Something large and reptilian had latched on to my left shoulder and arm, and although its teeth hadn't cut through my Kevlar jacket, I was certain that was only a matter of time.

I'd managed to hold my breath when I was grabbed, but I knew that fighting amphibious creatures under water was always a losing proposition. Getting oxygen was my first priority, and getting back on dry land was next on my agenda. To do that, I had to make this thing release me.

I pulled my pistol and craned my neck to get a good look at it. The thing looked something like a cross between a salamander and a chameleon—or at least its head did. But unlike those two species, it had huge, curving horns coming out of its forehead. One large eye with a vertical pupil regarded me, then the creature proceeded to shake me underwater like a dog with a bone.

I nearly lost my grip on the pistol, but managed to hang on to it by holding it close to my body. My lungs were burning and my shoulder was being crushed, but as long as the thing thought I still had some fight left in me, I knew it'd keep trying to drown me. Instead of fighting I went limp and closed my eyes, hoping it would be enough to make the creature think I was unconscious.

Seconds later, the beast stopped thrashing me back and forth, and when it did I wasted no time in taking action. I opened my eyes and slammed the barrel of the Glock into its eye, pulling the trigger once, twice, three times. The gun had to be fired at point-blank range, else the rounds would be slowed by the water, losing all penetrating force before making contact.

By the third trigger pull, the thing roared and expelled me from its jaws. As soon as I was free I headed straight for sunlight above, gasping for breath. Then I swam like Phelps for the shore, which was only fifteen feet or so away. I was halfway there when I felt something snag my leg. This time, it broke the skin through my jeans.

I barely had time to scream before it started pulling me under again. Reflexively, I shoved the gun toward my leg until the muzzle hit something solid, then I fired it again twice. The beast held on, so I changed position and proceeded to empty the magazine. Six rounds later, I was free. I swam until I hit the shallows, then I half ran, half-dragged myself up onto the shore.

MY LEG WAS BLEEDING in several places, but how badly

I wouldn't know until I exposed the wounds. My left shoulder and arm were still functional, but it felt like something had torn inside my shoulder joint. Ignoring my injuries, I got to my feet and scrambled up the bank and away from the fence, far enough from the shore so that thing couldn't lunge up and pull me back under.

I holstered the pistol, not even bothering to change out the magazine. A nine-millimeter pistol wasn't going to stop something this large. In fact, I doubted that it would have even had an effect if I hadn't hit the monster from point-blank range. I reached into my Bag to grab my sword as I slowly backed away from the pond.

"Come on, you overgrown gecko—stop fucking around so we can get this over with." I saw a trail of bubbles hit the surface of the still churning water, and tracked them as they got closer to shore. "That's it, come to daddy."

If you've ever seen a crocodile hunting prey on television, that's exactly how this thing moved when it lunged out of the water at me. One second it was submerged, and the next it was on shore coming after me. And man, was it ugly.

The thing was at least fifteen feet from nose to tip, bluish-green, scaled, heavily muscled, and it had six legs instead of four. Now that it was out of the water, it looked more like a tegu lizard than anything else, in form if not in color. Those long horns on its head appeared to be more for protection than for fighting, since they were angled too far back to be used for much else. Two rows of ridges lined its back, trailing down to a long skinny tail I suspected might be used to grasp tree limbs.

Or its prey.

I made this entire assessment in a split-second as I scrambled back into the woods. The weird salamander beast roared as it slithered and crawled up the bank after me. I had wounded it, however, and the loss of its eye had slowed it considerably—or at least made it a bit warier of me. Rather than closing the gap completely it slowed about ten feet from me, then began to circle to my left flank.

"Oh, hell no. You are not getting me back in the water." Realizing what it was attempting to do, I waited until its back was to the fence.

Then, I charged it.

I don't think the beast had ever faced anything so aggressive before, because rather than attacking or retreating, it froze as I attacked. Rather than fight it face on, I cut to the right at the last minute so I could take advantage of its blinded left eye.

I was rearing back for a swing when I felt something snag my left ankle. Before I had time to react I was yanked off my feet, landing hard on the on the forest floor beneath me. Wasting no time, the thing began to pull me toward the pond again, scuttling with its six stubby legs as it dragged me behind with its skinny prehensile tail. The beast roared to announce its impending triumph, assured of victory once it had me underwater once more.

"Hell *no*," I spat as righteous anger flowed through me. As my emotions flared, the sword answered in kind, and I rolled up to raise the burning blade high. I brought the flaming tip down on the creature's tail just past my foot, slicing it cleanly. The giant lizard cried in pain and anger, and it turned on me with murder in its one remaining eye.

I rolled to my feet, kicking the tip of its tail from my leg as

I stood. The creature circled me again slowly, hissing and flicking its tongue as we danced around each other.

"Yeah, you *really* want to eat me now, don't you? Fine, here I am, big boy. Come get your supper."

The giant lizard's throat rumbled with a growl that shook the trees nearby, and it sprinted right at me as fast as those six stubby legs could carry it. I stood my ground, knowing that I needed to end this before my adrenaline wore off and the shock of my injuries kicked in.

Five yards away.

Four yards.

Three yards.

Now.

The creature leapt straight at me, mouth gaping wide. I knew it intended to snatch me in its jaws, bowl me over, and strangle me with what remained of its tail, killing me in one fell swoop.

Not today, Geico.

Once it was airborne and committed to its attack, I side-stepped and pivoted, bringing the flaming sword down on its neck as it passed. As the blade landed, the lizard's head tumbled away from its body. Although it squirmed and thrashed its tail after landing, I was certain it was dead.

Just to be sure, I walked up to the corpse and plunged the burning blade up to the hilt, where I thought its heart would be. I twisted it around, listening to the lizard's flesh sizzle as the sword did its work. Then, I walked over to the head to do the same.

As I kicked the head upright, I noticed something shiny, buried between the thing's horns. "What the fuck?" I mumbled, leaning in to get a closer look.

Implanted in a spot where one of the creature's scales had been removed was a small, shiny device, machined from metal and obviously a new construct. It was roughly diamond-shaped, about one-half inch thick and no more than three inches across. Its foremost corner had a tiny camera lens with a small, flashing red light beside it.

EIGHTEEN

They were watching me the whole time—probably controlling this thing as well. Now, I was pissed. It was obvious that the killer or killers had left their pet behind, just in case I decided to come back here and look for more clues. I grabbed the severed head by the horns, turning it so I could look directly in the camera.

"Listen, asshole—I'm going to find you, and when I do I intend to bring your entire world crashing down around you. That's a fucking promise."

The light blinked for a few more seconds, then it stopped. I raised my sword to smash the thing to bits with the pommel, then I thought better of it. Instead, I put the sword away and pulled out my hunting knife, which I used to cut and pry the device from the creature's head. Once done I wiped my knife clean, then wrapped the device in a rag and tossed it inside my Craneskin Bag.

"Hah! Try getting a signal from an alternate dimension, bitch."

I slung my bag over my shoulder, replaced the magazine in my pistol, and headed toward the house. As expected, everything inside the home was undamaged and undisturbed, as if nothing untoward had ever happened on the premises. There were no blood stains, no bullet holes, and zero evidence any act of violence had ever been committed here.

The good thing about having a Circle team clean the place up was that they were instructed to leave everything intact. Sure, they'd sweep the place for magical artifacts, because no self-respecting secret cabal would overlook an opportunity to increase its power. But otherwise, they'd touch only what was necessary to remove evidence of the Circle's presence, and that was all.

That meant there was a high likelihood of finding a clue to lead me to Carver's employer. I knew from experience that criminals always left evidence of their crimes in their homes—people who looked for an easy payday were generally lazy, stupid, and often egotistical enough to take trophies and souvenirs. But as I searched Carver's place up one side and down the other, damned if I could find a single scrap or token to reveal who'd hired the hunter to kill Elmo.

Next, I searched through his computer, but that was a dead end too. As far as I could tell, he only used it for surfing porn sites and doing his taxes. I suddenly wished I'd had the foresight to snag his phone before Bells and I had split, but I'd been under the influence of powerful painkillers and not in my right mind.

Having failed by normal methods, I scanned the place in the magical spectrum. Other than the usual wards and runes to keep unwanted guests out, there was nothing to indicate a hidden cache or safe, or any other such place where Carver might have kept information useful to my investigation.

Frustrated that I hadn't turned up anything, I decided to take a different tack. I sat down on the floor and closed my eyes, slowing my breathing as I dropped into a druid's trance.

Hope no one else shows up while I'm out, I thought as I slipped under. I must've been getting better at entering the trance, because this time it only took me a few minutes. Soon, I was in communion with the plant life and animals nearby.

My intended strategy had been to see if there was any place *absent* of life, which might indicate a magically-protected safe or other storage area. But the house and outbuildings appeared to be normal and mostly magic-free in every way.

I'll just push out farther, I thought. *Can't hurt to try.*

I stretched my senses out to the woods beyond the house, searching for anything out of the ordinary. Scanning the area carefully, I found nothing but the usual animal and plant life, and one large, dead tree.

Wait a minute. I went back to that tree, checking it for anything unusual. *Bingo.* It had been spelled with a powerful "look away, turn away" charm. I'd probably walked right by it on my previous visit and never even noticed it being there.

Marking its location in my mind, I exited the house and headed toward it, seeing in the magical spectrum instead of with my normal vision. Where the tree should have been there was a dead spot, showing that it had not only been glamoured, but masked as well.

Whatever's in there, Carver sure didn't want anyone to find it, I thought. I extended my perception, testing and tugging at the magic that had been cast on the tree until I snagged a loose end in the binding. Then, I pulled on it, working my way through the casting until I gently unraveled the spell.

I opened my eyes, and there in front of me was a large, dead oak tree, one that had been struck by lightning ages before. I grabbed a limb and climbed up to where it had been hit, where I found a large hole that led to a hollow in the trunk. Checking for traps and finding none, I reached my arm in and felt around until my hand landed on something cold and metallic.

I grabbed it and pulled it out, discovering a mid-sized fire-proof safe—roughly the size of a small briefcase. Whatever was inside, it was heavy. It was obviously also something flammable or perishable.

How curious.

Locks were no obstacle for someone of my skill set, and within minutes I had snapped the latch release on the case and flipped open the lid.

"Ho-lee shit."

Inside the safe were stacks of gold coins laid on their sides, nestled in foam compartments to keep them from clinking and rolling around. A pocket under the safe's lid held some legal documents, including the title to the land, a will, and a few other miscellaneous papers.

I pulled a coin from a stack, holding it high to examine it in the fading light. It had been stamped or molded with a curious design—eight cups or chalices in a circle around the center, along with markings indicating the purity of the gold and its weight in grams.

I did some quick calculations in my head. Each coin was an ounce of gold, and there were a couple hundred coins inside the safe. There had to be over half a million dollars sitting in my lap.

"Carver, what the fuck did you get yourself into?" I wondered aloud as I placed the coin in my pocket.

I closed the case and stuffed it in my Craneskin Bag. Later, I'd search the documents to see if I could locate Carver's heirs, to make sure the safe's contents got to them. I might be a lot of things, but I was no thief. For now, though, I'd keep it hidden until I figured out where the coins had come from—and who'd hired Carver to do their dirty work.

I WAS PRETTY BANGED UP, which had become a habit since I'd taken this case. I texted Finnegas and got a snappy reply, something about, "Time you learned how to do this yourself" and "I have a life too you know." So, I headed back to the junkyard, grabbed the first aid kit, and took care of my injuries the old-fashioned way.

Thankfully, the puncture wounds in my leg weren't too deep. The lizard thing's teeth weren't very long or sharp, as its mouth had been more frog-like than serpentine. Still, I was sure I'd gotten plenty of pond water and lizard saliva in those wounds. With visions of flesh-eating bacteria dancing in my head, after a quick shower I scrubbed the cuts with a povidone-iodine brush and applied a liberal layer of antibiotic cream before wrapping them in gauze.

My shoulder was another matter. It was injured, and that was a fact. The way it was popping and crackling, I figured I'd torn my rotator cuff. Wishing I could just shift and heal up, instead I iced it down for twenty minutes, then rubbed some *dit da jow* liniment on it and called it a day.

After that, I grabbed that funky coin and plopped back on my bed. I flipped the weird token over the backs of my fingers in one hand as I used my phone with the other to research gold coins. Nothing came up online about a coin with eight cups on it, so instead I searched for custom coin mints. I found a company in Dallas who minted personalized gold coins for gifts and such, but they didn't look like they dealt in volume. Another dead end.

I was still flipping the coin when I heard a knock on my door. Before answering it, I slipped the coin back in my pocket and grabbed my pistol.

Before I'd crossed the room, I heard Belladonna's muffled voice from the other side of the door. "Put the gun away—it's just me, silly."

I opened the door, and she was standing there with a couple of plastic takeout bags in one hand, a bottle of whiskey in the other, and a look that said I was about to get laid.

"How'd you know I grabbed the gun?" I asked, shoving it in my waistband.

"You'll shoot your balls off one day doing that," she said as she entered. "After I heard the bed creak, there was a pause before I heard footsteps. Plus, I can recognize the sound of metal on Kydex from a mile away." She handed me the takeout bags. "Grab this while I go wash out a couple of glasses."

"I'm not that much of a slob," I said. In truth, I kept my quarters pretty clean.

"Yeah, but you're lazy as shit about washing out your coffee mugs."

"Hey, the residue adds to the flavor," I replied.

"Don't I know it. The last time you made me a cup of coffee here, it had a rather... *piquant* quality to it."

"At Colin's Bed and Breakfast, we aim to please," I said with grin as I waggled my eyebrows, Groucho Marx style.

Belladonna grabbed a couple of mugs and headed out the door, but not without one final jab. "Do that thing with your eyebrows again, and no one will be pleased with how this night goes."

When Belladonna returned, she handed me the mugs and I poured us a couple of whiskey and Cokes. Bells usually bought the cheap stuff, bless her heart, so I went straight to the mix when she was buying. She took a long swig of her drink, then sat on the bed and patted a spot beside her. Mama didn't raise no fool, so I sat where indicated.

"So, tell me about your day," she said as she gave me a *look* over her glass.

"Look at me like that again, and you won't hear about it until morning."

"Promises, promises. That was actually the plan, but the way you're favoring your left shoulder and right leg, I figure there's a story I haven't heard yet."

I shrugged. "I went back to Carver's. I got attacked by a giant lizard. I killed it. End of story."

"That's it?" she asked.

"That's it." I considered mentioning the coins, but I was thinking with my other head by that point, so I decided to give her the details later. I slugged my drink and leaned in close.

"The food will get cold," she said with a twinkle in her eye.

"I have a microwave," I said, taking her drink and set it on said appliance.

"I thought I was going to be the driver tonight," she replied as she laid back on the bed.

I walked myself up her body, gently kissing her chest and neck. Nuzzling her ear, I took a moment to nip at her earlobes. "Second go-round. I promise to call you mistress."

"And scream my name?" she whispered, a smile playing across her full, red lips.

"First *and* last," I mumbled with a mouth full of earlobe. Belladonna immediately started laughing. "Too much?" I asked as I sat up.

"No, silly—it just tickled. Come back down here." She grabbed me by the shirt, pulling me on top of her. As I leaned in to kiss her, she pulled on my arm and bucked her hips, rolling me over so she was on top.

"You can be the driver next time," she purred.

"You're the boss... mistress."

AN HOUR LATER, I was heating the food while Belladonna went to the bathroom to freshen up. She walked in just as I was serving the food on paper plates.

"Ugh, you really need to get an apartment—something with its own shower, toilet, and sink. That place is disgusting."

"I clean it nearly every day, but it's a public—"

"*Ay, carajo,* don't remind me." She looked around the room, probably for some discarded piece of clothing, but her eyes stopped where my jeans had landed in the corner. "What's that?"

"What?" I turned to look, and realized the gold coin had fallen out of my pants pocket. "Oh, I was going to tell you about that... after, that is."

"You mean sharing the details of your day with me is less important to you than getting your rocks off?"

"Um... was it good for you too?" She slapped me playfully on the shoulder, hard enough for it to sting. "Hey, that was my injured side!"

"Yes, it was," she said as she knelt to pick up the coin. Bells turned to me, a serious look on her face. "Where did you get this?"

"At Carver's place. I found a whole stash of them in a hollow tree behind his house. He had some serious spell work in place so no one would find it."

Belladonna examined the coin, her eyes hard. "Colin, this is a Circle coin. We use them to pay outside contractors, because they're practically untraceable."

"Wait a minute—you're saying that Carver was working for the Circle?"

"If he had a bunch of these in his possession—then yes, he was." She snapped her hand closed around the coin. "Damn it!"

"What?"

"The high council are the only ones who have access to that much capital. There's no way they authorized all those killings, which means someone on the council is running ops off the books."

I took a deep breath, letting it out slowly as I considered the implications. "It was a lot of gold, Bells. A hell of a lot more than they'd pay for just one job. Maybe Carver was in on it all along, helping this council member track down and kill all those fae."

Bells shook her head. "Council members are very powerful, Colin. They have access to potent magic artifacts, and they wield powers we can only dream about. No, a council member wouldn't need a lowly hunter's help to take out a few fae. Whoever hired Carver, it was probably someone lower on the totem pole—a person who'd need backup to kill those fae and then cover their tracks."

"You think it was more than one person? That maybe there's a faction within the Circle who could be responsible for the killings?"

Bells looked at the coin again. "I don't know. If there really is a rogue council member pulling the strings, that person would want to have complete deniability. This is the sort of thing that could start a war between the fae and the Circle. I'd think they'd want to be several degrees removed from whoever they sent to do their dirty work."

"Shit. I can't imagine how this makes you feel." Bells was loyal to the Circle, through and through. She believed in what they did and loved her job, even if some of her coworkers were total dicks. I wished now that she hadn't seen the coin.

Belladonna flipped the coin to me. "That thing you killed at Carver's today—describe it to me."

"Let's see... bluish-green, six legs, looked like a giant tegu lizard with horns. Ring any bells?"

"Sounds like a bukavac."

"A buka-what? Sorry, I'm unfamiliar with the species."

Belladonna sat down on my bed, rubbing her knuckles as

she spoke. "It's a creature from Slavic folklore, a kind of supernatural assassin. They hide in rivers, ponds, swamps, and lakes, waiting for an unsuspecting person to happen by. Then, they leap out and drown or strangle them to death."

I let out a low whistle. "Wow, look at who knows her cryptids."

She ignored the tease, still massaging her knuckles. By the tightness around her eyes and the stiffness in her shoulders, I knew she wasn't just experiencing a sudden bout of arthritis.

"You forget, I was raised in Europe and taught how to fight the fae from the time I was young. Mother made us learn about supernatural creatures from all over the continent, because the fae we dealt with were fond of conjuration."

I rubbed the coin with my fingers, as if it might reveal its secrets via osmosis. "We don't have a large Slavic contingent here in central Texas. There are plenty of Czechs and Germans, but damned few people of Slavic descent."

Belladonna pursed her lips, eyes narrowing as she considered what I was implying. "So the question is, how does a creature from Slavic folklore get from Serbia to Texas?"

"And?" I asked, already knowing the answer but wanting to hear it from her lips.

She stood quickly. "Someone imported it, or they conjured it. Either way, it takes a great deal of resources to retrieve something that big from that far away." Bells started gathering her things, slipping on her boots as she spoke. "Everything here points to the Circle's involvement, Colin. Someone in the Circle wants you dead, and they're not going to stop until they get their way."

I leaned against the doorframe, arms crossed. "I take it you're going to start digging around, to find out if someone at the Circle is connected?"

"Yes I am, and don't look so cross. You know damned well that I'd do anything for you, even if it means losing my job."

I stepped forward, grabbing her hands in mine. "It's not your job I'm concerned with—it's you I'm worried about."

She stood on tip-toe to kiss me, planting her lips firmly on mine. "Don't you worry about me, Colin McCool. I'm a big girl and I'm perfectly capable of looking after myself."

"Of that I'm fully aware... but if you find something huge, call me right away and let me handle it."

She scowled. "By yourself? As if." She kissed me again lightly on the cheek before heading out. "Keep your phone close by. It won't take the nerd herd long to run a trace on Carver's communications. I'll call you as soon as they find something."

"Be careful," I admonished as she shut the door.

Belladonna's voice trailed off as she headed for the parking lot. "Right back at you, druid boy."

NINETEEN

At a loss for something constructive to do while I was waiting for Bells to call, I decided to ask around about Carver's coin. My first stop was to see Rocko at The Bloody Fedora, because something wasn't sitting right with me about him. Someone had told Eliandres and Lucindras I was at the Fedora, which meant that either Cinnamon had acted on her own, or Rocko had signaled her to do it. Cinnamon just wasn't ambitious enough to get caught up in fae matters, so I was pretty sure her boss was playing both sides, and I wanted to know why.

It was close to midnight when I pulled up, and the parking lot was packed. I parked the truck behind the building and entered through the back entrance. The light was on in the office, so I pushed the door open and went inside. Rocko was behind his desk smoking a stogie, a cheap bottle of Irish whiskey near at hand with three fingers poured in a glass. His expression turned from dour to neutral on seeing me, but one thing was for certain—he'd been expecting me.

Rocko pulled a glass from a drawer and served me a generous pour. "Freely given, no obligations attached and all that," he said as he pushed the glass toward me. "No magic, poison, spells, or tricks, on my word."

"I'll pass, if it's all the same."

"Your loss. I put the good stuff in empty well bottles—keeps the help out of my stash." He leaned back in his chair, sipping his whiskey as he squeezed an eye shut. "Damn, but that's good. Alright, druid, talk. To what do I owe the honor?"

I slapped the coin down on the desk next to the whiskey bottle. "Know anything about this coin?"

"It's not familiar. Looks expensive, though. Did you roll a leprechaun on the way in here?"

"I'm not in the mood for jokes, Rocko. Over the last few days I've had my shoulder broken by an ogre, someone attempt to assassinate me, wrecked my car, got jumped by a fae hit squad, and nearly got eaten by a bukavac."

"A buka-what?"

"That's what I said. Pisses me off when I nearly get eaten by a monster I don't even recognize, and suffice it to say that my patience has worn thin." I leaned on the desk, getting up in his swarthy, fat little face. "Now, I know you tipped off Maeve's killers when I showed up here the other day. You're working both sides, Rocko—and frankly I don't like being played."

"How'd you know I tipped them off?"

"Nobody knew I was driving Ed's truck that day, so it's doubtful I was followed. Besides, high fae don't drive automobiles—not if they can help it. Which puts the odds that Eliandres and Lucindras were tailing me that day at slim to none."

Rocko slammed his whiskey, then grabbed his cigar from

the ashtray. The cherry had gone to ash, so he grabbed a butane lighter from the desk and fired it back up. He puffed on the cigar a few times, gesturing at me with it as he blew smoke in the air above him.

"You're right, I did tip those two off. But only because the Queen requested it. Times like these, you don't go pissing your queen off—not when her patience is worn thin. You got a knack for getting her goat, you know that? I'm surprised she hasn't killed you yet, but what do I know? I'm just a lowly crook, trying to make a buck."

"And what about that hunter crew I ran down? I'd been working the murder cases for weeks and hadn't turned up a damned thing. How'd you make that connection?"

Rocko sniffed and flicked ash in the tray. "I hear things, druid. Ain't nothing that happens on the shady side of the world beneath that I don't know about. Word was, someone was looking to hire a crew to take out an ogre. It ain't like there's a ton of ogres running around town, you know. Wasn't hard to put two and two together and find out who took the job."

"You could have told me, instead of letting me do things the hard way."

He shrugged. "You'd quit the case. Wasn't until that ogre bit the dust that you got all high and mighty about tracking the killers down. I didn't see how I was obligated to give you more than a nudge. And that's what you got."

"You sure that's all of it? Cause if you're holding out on me..."

He grabbed the glass he'd poured for me, knocking it back. "That's all there is, all I know about it. Believe me, or don't. Fuck if I care."

I eyed him warily, looking for some tell or twitch that might indicate he was lying. But Rocko's face was a blank canvas, just as it'd been since I'd walked through his door. That alone told me he was hiding something more, and I intended to find out what. I turned to lock the door, just as my phone started buzzing in my pocket. I pulled it out—it was Bells.

Rocko's face was smug as he kicked his feet up on his desk. "You going to take that, or was there something else you wanted to discuss?"

I exhaled heavily through my nostrils. "This isn't over, Rocko. Not by a stretch."

His voice called out to me over the noise from the barroom out front. "I look forward to it, druid."

I almost turned around, but instead I headed out the rear entrance to the truck, answering the call on the way. "Yeah, Bells, what do you got?"

"You're not going to believe this, Colin. Hell, I can't believe it myself. The geek squad tried to find something in Carver's phone records, texts, and email accounts that would tell us who hired him, but they came up with squat. So, I had them run facial recognition on footage from every convenience store and Wal-Mart in town to see if Carver had purchased a burner recently."

"You guys can do that?"

"We've had access to the NSA's surveillance system for some time. Anyway, they got a hit at a store right there in Bastrop, not two miles from Carver's place. He bought a burner phone a week ago, and called a number that was encoded in the job posting on that dark website Rocko gave you."

"Shit, Bells, you're killing me here. Skip the details and tell me what they dug up."

"Long story short? It's Gunnarson, Colin. Commander-fucking-Gunnarson is the one who ordered the hit on Elmo."

———

NOW I REALLY WAS PISSED. I gripped the phone tight enough to crack the screen, seething over the revelation. "That prick—I should've known it was him!"

Belladonna's voice was steady on the other end of the line. "Now, Colin, settle down. We're still not entirely sure it was him. All we really know was that the person Carver called was at headquarters and in the vicinity of Gunnarson's ranch when they took the calls."

"That's pretty fucking suspicious, Bells. Who else could it have been?"

She hissed. "Shit, would you listen to me, before you go off half-cocked and start a war with the Circle? Gunnarson has dozens of people working for him—assistants, mage-hunter teams, research geeks, informants, you name it. It could have been anyone who had access to his place."

"Well, there's only one way to find out. Give me the address to his ranch. I'll head out there and dig around, see if I can come up with anything concrete that we can use against him."

Belladonna was silent for several seconds, then she sighed her reply. "Fine, but promise me you won't confront him directly. He's a lot tougher and more cunning that you might think. You don't get on the waiting list for a high council seat in the Circle without being a badass."

"I'll take that under advisement," I replied. "Text me the address and I'll update you if I find anything."

"If you do dig up any dirt on him, call me before you act on it. And just don't get your cute ginger ass killed, alright?"

"I definitely promise not to get myself killed. As for anything I might run into, I make no promises."

I hung up before Bells could respond, and I was already headed out of town on 290 West when she texted me his address. When I pulled it up on my maps app, it showed a large residence in the Hill Country, a posh area full of multi-million-dollar "ranch estates." Several local celebrities lived out that way, along with a few captains of industry.

I guess being a commander in the Cold Iron Circle pays well, I thought. *Or Gunnarson is on the take.*

I'd certainly find out once I got to his place. The drive was only thirty minutes or so, and soon my phone told me to turn down a narrow asphalt two-lane that led to the address Bells had given me. At first, I passed a few upper-middle-class developments—the kind with "acreage homesites" and McMansions set far enough back from the road so the rabble didn't bother the homeowners.

But the farther I drove, the fancier the homes got, until I was passing a custom stone and wrought iron entrance gate every quarter-mile or so. I finally neared the address indicated by the map, so I slowed down to check it out as I drove by. The gate was an enormous stone and iron affair, with a huge Texas star and "Bar G Ranch" in custom iron lettering and scrollwork above the automated gate. Beyond that, all I saw was a long, paved driveway that wound away into the distance.

"Damn, Gunnarson, either you won the lottery or you're

getting paid under the table," I muttered as I drove past the gate. About a quarter-mile down the road I cut the lights, then I cruised to what I thought was the corner of the property. I parked alongside the road, well into the rocky shoulder to avoid getting Ed's truck crunched by a passing car. I grabbed my stuff and locked it up, then crossed the road to get a closer look at Gunnarson's fence.

The fence around the ranch was more like a stockade, of the type used on hunting ranches all over central and south Texas to keep game and livestock from wandering off. It was eight feet tall and sturdily built with welded iron pipes and thick wire mesh, painted flat black so as to blend into the natural scenery. I'd seen fences like this lining the roads near exotic game ranches in the Hill Country, and I couldn't imagine what it had cost to build something like this around a multi-acre property like Gunnarson's place.

And that was hardly where the perimeter security ended. In much the same way that I'd warded the fence at the junkyard, Gunnarson had spelled his fence to keep most supernatural creatures out of his property. When I looked at the barrier in the magical spectrum, Norse runes lit up in pale blue light up and down the length of the property. In addition, he had alarm spells set up to alert him of anything coming over the fence, and I suspected he might have cameras set up further inside the estate.

Well, if I can't go over or around, then I'll go under it. I began to walk the fence line, looking for the tiny natural drainage ditch I'd noticed when I'd first driven by. About fifty yards back, I located the small rocky channel—a trench no more than twelve inches deep or so. It'd be plenty to allow me to sneak past.

The ditch had been crisscrossed with wire mesh and baling wire where it dipped under the fence, but years of rainwater washing through had rusted the metal and weakened any connections to the spells that warded the fence itself. I severed the spells connected to the makeshift barrier where it was attached to the fence, then snipped the wires until I'd made a large enough opening to slip inside.

Once I was in, I waited for several minutes just to see if I might have triggered an alarm that I hadn't spotted in my examination of the place's security. When no sirens sounded and nothing came after me, I decided the coast was clear. I headed further into the property, crawling on my belly and following the small dry creek so I might remain hidden from prying eyes and unseen surveillance devices.

Here goes nothing.

IT TOOK me some time to travel the quarter-mile distance from the road to the estate proper. Belly crawling might seem like a fairly rapid method of locomotion over short distances, but it was hell doing it over a rocky, dry stream bed, in the dark, while trying to stay silent and unseen. Suddenly, I wished I could shift into some sort of animal form, like a Native American skinwalker. If I could turn into a coyote or a fox, there'd be no need for all that uncomfortable crawling.

But when I shifted, I became a cross between Quasimodo and Bane. So I'd have to make do with sneaking like a normal human for now. Maybe later in my druid training, Finnegas could teach me how to take on an animal form. That made me wonder, if I were a shaman, what would my spirit animal be? A wolverine? A honey badger? An eagle?

Of course, if I got caught sneaking around Gunnarson's ranch, my spirit animal would be a turkey vulture. Those birds were like the rats of the sky in this part of Texas, and my corpse would end up in the bellies of a dozen of them if I bit the dust out here. Sure, Gunnarson would eventually get rid of my body, but I was pretty certain he'd leave me out to rot for a day or two, just on principle.

Finally, I crested a rise and Gunnarson's home came into view.

If you've ever seen one of those HGTV dream homes they give away each year, just so the lucky recipient can sell it to avoid paying the ginormous property tax bill, that's what Gunnarson's house looked like. It was a massive, sprawling affair made up of huge floor to ceiling windows, natural lime-stone walls, and plenty of exposed cedar. A huge L-shaped swimming pool wrapped around two sides of the place, and it had a neatly manicured lawn bordered by a stone terrace, with a crushed granite walkway that led around to the back.

To be honest, I sat there for a moment taking it all in before I sized the place up for potential security measures.

So, this is how the other half lives, huh? It was more like the one percent in this case. Whatever Gunnarson was into had to be dirty, because there was no way the Circle was paying him enough to afford these digs. From what I could tell based on the little Belladonna shared, working for the Circle was a lot like working for a government agency. You might make six-figures once you hit upper management, but no one was making CEO money.

As far as I could tell, there weren't any glaring features

that screamed security system, magical or otherwise. Without any schematics of the place or proper recon, I had to assume that most of the security measures had been added to the perimeter. I sincerely doubted that was the case, but until a fire-breathing dragon popped out of the ground, or I got chased by an army of animated topiary, I'd operate on the assumption that I was more or less safe.

Just for grins, I scanned the place in the magical spectrum. Nothing jumped out at me, so I kept creeping forward. I was about fifty feet from the main residence when I felt the hairs on my arms stand up.

"What the hell?" I muttered, just before the sky lit up and a lightning bolt flew from a weathervane that sat atop the house, straight at me where I lay in the creek bed. "Aw, fu—"

That was all I got out of my mouth before it hit me. I was fairly certain I blacked out for a few seconds, because the next thing I remembered was rolling around on the ground. Before I could recover, a team of six men and women wearing black fatigues and balaclavas came storming out from various hiding spots near the house. They were carrying funky-looking rifles, and the two people in the lead each shot me as they approached.

I looked down, and instead of bullet holes I had two tranquilizer darts sticking out of my chest. The effects of getting hit by that lightning bolt spell were wearing off, but I soon felt a distinct numbing sensation spread out from where the darts had hit, across my torso and out to my limbs. Within seconds, I was completely paralyzed.

Well shit, this is just great.

The guards had surrounded me, and they held position in a loose cordon around me, weapons at the ready. I soon heard someone crossing the lawn toward us, and a tall, lean man with a severe face and military crew cut came marching over to me.

Gunnarson barked commands at his security team in his Sam Elliott drawl. "Secure the prisoner, immediately! Do not fucking let him pull any of that druid bullshit on you. And keep him tranqed, or else that thing inside him will be crapping your bones out tonight. Shit barely worked on the ogre, so you can bet his other form is resistant. Am I understood?"

"Yes, sir!" the team replied in unison.

After they'd gagged me and locked my hands in some sort of medieval torture device that immobilized my fingers, Gunnarson tromped over and squatted down next to me.

"I knew it was only a matter of time before you came sniffing around. You're stupid, McCool, but once you get your teeth in something you hang on like a tick on a dog. That stubbornness is the only thing I admire about you."

TWENTY

He gestured at the landscape and architecture around us.
"You like it? Circle doesn't pay much, but you get the right
Council member on your side and the sky's the limit."

I glared at him, or at least I thought I was glaring. My face
was pretty numb, so I wasn't exactly sure whether I looked
pissed or slack-jawed. Hell, I couldn't even blink—whatever
crap they'd drugged me with, it was some powerful stuff.

"It's a selective paralytic," Gunnarson said, anticipating
my thoughts. "Something the lab geeks mixed up from manti-
core venom and a few modern pharmaceuticals. We keep it
on hand, just in case a mage-in-training loses their shit. Didn't
work too well on the ogre, though—thing put up a hell of
a fight."

I managed to move my eyes enough to glance at the
weathervane.

"You liked that, did you? That was my idea. We were just
going to dose you with the tranqs when you showed up, but
the trap Carver and his yahoos sprung on you worked so,

well, I figured the hell with it—why not have a little fun?" He spat tobacco juice off to the side before leaning in eye to eye. "I gotta admit, seeing you do the funky chicken all over my lawn, well—that was a rare treat."

He stood then, wiping his hands on his pants as he eyed me with a smug grin. "There'll be plenty of time later to chat, McCool, don't you worry. Right now, I'm going to have you locked up while I tie up a few loose ends. I think I'll start with your girlfriend and those keyboard jockeys she has wrapped around her finger down in Research. Then, I'll take care of that fat fuck you call your uncle. But not the old man —my benefactor on the Council will take care of him. As Reagan once said, 'I may be dumb, but I'm not stupid.'"

Gunnarson turned his back to bark a few commands to his people. I might have been immobilized, but I could still see magic, so I took the opportunity to scan him for artifacts, charms, and spells while he wasn't paying attention. He had some protection spells woven into an amulet around his neck, but most of his power was situated in the bracers around his wrists. Each of them practically pulsed with energy, and they gave off a low electric hum when I focused in on their magical signature.

Technomancy, I thought. *I am definitely looking forward to killing this asshole.*

Gunnarson signaled to the security team. "Lock him in the 'thrope pit."

Two burly members of the team grabbed me and tossed me into back of a nearby utility task vehicle. I tried to shout at Gunnarson—curse him, whatever. Hell, I even tried to grunt at him, but I was unable to do anything but get thrown around like a rag doll.

Worst-case scenarios flew through my mind as they drove the UTV behind the house and down a narrow concrete path. Soon, the trail ended at a nondescript metal outbuilding, and the security team dismounted and dragged me inside. One of them pressed a button inside a hidden panel on the wall, and a section of the concrete floor slid away to reveal a pit below.

They took my Craneskin Bag and all my gear and weapons, then dragged me to the edge and tossed me in. Unable to do more than flounder helplessly, I landed hard on my left side and back. Something snapped when I landed, but I couldn't be sure if it was a bone breaking or a rib popping out of place.

Before the lid closed on the pit, I looked around as best as I could, just in case they were going to leave me in the dark. The entire "room," if you could call it that, was no more than twelve feet cubed. The walls were lined with steel plates, as was the floor and the sliding ceiling overhead. Other than a tiny toilet pit in the corner, some small vents near the ceiling, and one bare light bulb, it was devoid of any furnishings.

As the lid slid back over the holding cell, I heard the members of Gunnarson's security team laughing and taking bets about who was going to kill Belladonna.

Fucking hell, but I needed to get out of there.

I knew it'd be hours before the drugs would completely wear off. Even then, with my hands bound and my mouth gagged, I was helpless as a baby and completely unable to do more than pace the room. And good luck getting any animal friends to free me inside a steel cube... not that they could chew through the metal devices around my hands.

My only hope of escaping in time to warn Bells and Ed

was letting my Hyde-side free. I knew it was a gamble, because once I let him out I had no idea whether I could put him back in his cage. But in that form I could beat or melt my way out—with the Eye's help, of course—and hopefully maintain enough of my faculties to get a message to my friends before it was too late.

I closed my eyes and slowed my breathing. Thankfully, paralyzation made it incredibly easy to enter the druid's trance. I soon fell into that still and peaceful place inside that allowed me to commune with all natural life-forms nearby... and, more importantly, Balor's Eye.

I focused on finding the Eye's presence, to the exclusion of all else. Time lost all meaning and measure as my consciousness floated in that ethereal realm. Seconds, minutes, or hours later, my efforts were rewarded by a familiar voice speaking inside my head.

-Hello, Colin. It appears we are trapped.-

You mean I'm trapped, Eye. You can travel to another dimension. Me? I'm stuck here inside this metal cube, unless I find a way to get out of here.

-I would remind you that the vessel that I reside within is now bound to your physical form. Displaced though I am, I cannot move myself through space and time. I can only shift from one dimension to another while remaining in the same overlapping position as I travel from dimension to dimension.-

That's fascinating, Eye, but what I really need is a way to get out of here. I've been bound, gagged, and drugged with a paralytic agent. And, Gunnarson's sending a team to kill my uncle and Belladonna at this very second.

-You're asking me to remove the block I placed inside your

brain that's preventing you from shifting into your Fomorian form.-

Exactly. Then we can burn our way out of here, and I can warn my friends.

-That is a dangerous proposition. Spending time in your Fomorian form is changing you, and that side of your personality is becoming more and more dominant each time you shift. If I allow you to change, the "you" that you are now might be completely replaced by that darker side of your person. And if that were to happen, you might never come back.-

I have to tell you, buddy, it's a risk I'm willing to take. Besides, can't you just zap me again if that happens? I shift, we melt our way out of here, and then you zap me. I wake up human again, and we're good.

-Not so, Colin. If I give you another aneurism, you could easily die, or suffer permanent brain damage.-

You mean, in addition to the brain damage that's keeping me from shifting?

-Yes.-

Right now, I don't really have much choice. Also, consider that the men and women who are keeping me here are extremely powerful, and they have access to magical resources that could allow them to pluck you out of my head. If that were to happen, there's no telling what evil purposes you might be put toward.

-True. But they also might use me to destroy the fae, which is my primary directive. I detect a 22.97% chance that the Cold Iron Circle would use me to obliterate the fae from the planet.-

Sounds like slim odds to me. And if you choose to help me escape?

-Based on your past negative experiences in dealing with the fae, as well as your current antipathy toward them, I calculate a 76.81% chance that you will set events into motion that will result in the eventual downfall of the fae who remain here on earth.-

Huh. Then I guess there's not much for you to consider.

-I will remove the mental block and repair the physical damage to your brain, allowing you to shift into your Fomorian form. Brace yourself—this will not be pleasant.-

It felt like a bomb went off inside my head. There was an intense pressure, followed by increasing pain that started behind my eyes and spread out to encompass my entire skull. My jaw clenched involuntarily, and I felt teeth crack. Despite being under the influence of a paralytic, every muscle in my body convulsed all at once. It was easily on my list of the Top Ten Most Painful Things Colin Has Ever Experienced.

Mercifully, it was over seconds later, and I heard the Eye's voice inside my head.

-Neurological repairs complete. You may shift into your Fomorian form at any time.-

Alright then... let's do this.

I WAS PREPARING to shift when I heard the whine of electric engines and the ceiling above began to roll away. Then I heard the most welcome sound possible... Belladonna's voice.

"Colin, thank God. Guys, tie that rope off over there so I can climb down."

An unfamiliar, nasally male voice echoed from overhead. "Not a clove hitch, you idiot. Use a figure eight."

A very young-sounding male voice responded. "A figure eight? Duh, we need to get out of here quickly without leaving any sign we were here. A clove hitch is clearly the best quick-release knot for this application."

"You guys are idiots," a third, older and deeper voice replied. "You use a bowline knot to secure a rope to a stationary object. Here, give it to me."

The three voices descended into bickering over who would tie the rope and which knot they'd use. Finally, Belladonna's command cut through the din.

"Just tie the fucking rope off so I can get down there and pull him out! I'll cut it when we leave, alright?"

"A simple and elegant solution," the deeper, older voice said.

"That's why she's in the field," nasally voice muttered.

"I'd plow her field, any day," the teenaged voice replied.

"Like you've ever had any," nasal voice said. "You wouldn't know what to do with her, even if you had the chance."

The older voice cut in, sotto voce. "Might I remind you two that her boyfriend can hear you—you know, the one they're calling 'God-Killer'? So, maybe you should cool it before he rips you in two and wears your intestines for a necklace."

I chuckled inwardly at the last remark. That was one I needed to keep in reserve for future use.

-It appears we are being rescued. Might I suggest a partial shift, if only to shake off the effects of the tranquilizer?-

Good idea.

I'd gained much greater control over my ability to shift forms during the time I'd spent trapped and starving in Maeve's underground portal chamber. Without any food to sustain me, I'd had to shift each day to heal myself. Yet every time I had, my body had consumed fat and muscle for energy to shift, which speeded up the wasting process considerably. For that reason, I'd learned how to only partially shift forms to conserve energy.

I triggered the change, stopping it when I'd completed about a quarter of the transformation. As soon as I shifted, the teenager began babbling, his voice rife with panic.

"Oh shit, oh shit, oh shit! He's already hulking out. He's going to kill me and make face paint out of my liver, I just know it! I am so fucked. Hide me, quick!"

As the yammering above continued, I began to regain control of my muscles, just enough to blink and stand. Belladonna was already scrambling down the side of the pit, and when she hit bottom she quickly closed the distance to give me a hug. She cut the gag away and held some sort of key fob device next to the manacles. I heard a beep and a click, and they fell off my hands.

"I thought you were dead," she whispered. "The nerd herd intercepted a message from Gunnarson telling his people that you'd been captured and to proceed with contingency plan oh-five-three. I had no idea what that meant, but I figured it couldn't be good, so I headed right over here."

I worked my jaw around and shook my hands, feeling the blood rush back into them. From deep in the back of my mind, I felt a murderous prodding—just the faintest urge to *rip-snap-maim-torture-kill...*

Belladonna snapped her fingers in front of my face. "Colin, are you alright?" She called up to her companions, two of whom were now standing at the pit's edge looking down at us.

I shook off the evil thoughts and focused on Belladonna's voice. "Yeah," I replied in a near-whisper. "Just a bit woozy, is all."

A black guy in faded jeans, purple Converse All-Stars, and a t-shirt that said "Fuck Lab Safety, I Want Superpowers" stared at me with interest. "Oh man, see that look in his eyes? I think Dex is right—McCool really *is* going to eat his liver."

A muscular, middle-aged Asian guy in wife beater, cargo shorts, flip-flops, and a Hawaiian shirt replied. "Oh yeah, Dex is definitely screwed."

The only response I heard from "Dex" was a high whine and rapid footsteps fading away, which made the other two researchers laugh hysterically.

Hawaiian shirt guy pointed with his thumb toward the exit. "You think we should go get him, Deets?"

Deets scrunched his face up and scratched his head. "Cameras are down and Belladonna pwned Gunnarson's entire security team." He waved a hand at what I assumed was Dex's retreating form. "Eh, let him sweat it 'til we leave."

Belladonna hung her head, massaging her temple with one hand. "Do I have to remind you guys that Gunnarson and the rest of his team could come back at any minute? Now, go get Dex before someone shows up and captures him."

Deets looked at his buddy. "She's right, Kien. Let's go find him before he gets lost."

The urge to hurt someone, anyone was getting stronger, so I shifted back into my fully human form. I still felt some after-effects from the drugs, but I was strong enough to move. As the thoughts faded and my mind cleared, I remembered the dire situation we were all in.

"Bells, give me your phone."

"What? Why?" she asked, handing me her mobile. I checked the time—Ed would be on his way to open the junk-yard soon.

"The last thing Gunnarson told me was that he was going to tie up some loose ends—namely you, the geek squad, and uncle Ed."

"Colin, we had no idea. I only brought the nerd herd along because they said they could bypass Gunnarson's security."

Ed's phone just went to voicemail, so I called Fallyn's cell.

"Colin, it's seven o'clock in the morning—this had better be..."

I cut her off. "No time to explain. Tell Samson to send the Pack to the junkyard, now. Ed's in trouble." I hung up before Fallyn could reply. "C'mon, Bells—we have to go, *now*."

———

WE LEFT no trace of our passing back at Gunnarson's. The geek squad had shut down all Gunnarson's surveillance when they'd broke in. Then, Belladonna had snuck up on a guard, knocked him out, and used his tranquilizer gun to take out all the rest before they knew what hit them. We left them where they fell, and Deets locked the place up tight, making it look like I'd disappeared or teleported out of there. At the very least, it would keep Gunnarson guessing.

Bells and the research team had "borrowed" a surveillance van from the Circle's motor pool. It was a Mercedes Sprinter that had been decked out with electronics, with a modified suspension and a souped up engine. Belladonna drove, flooring it the whole way, while Dex and Kien worked the communications array inside the van, to keep local law enforcement from pulling us over for speeding.

"They think we're Homeland—nobody's going to stop us," Kien said, giving me a sympathetic look as he handed me my gear.

I took it without comment, suiting up and steeling myself for come what may. Then, I called Finnegas. His phone went to voicemail, no surprise there, so I dialed Maureen's mobile and told her what was going on. She promised to find the old man and meet us at the junkyard.

Gunnarson's place was a forty-minute drive from the junkyard, but Bells did it in twenty-five. When we pulled up there were half a dozen Harleys in the lot, and Sledge and Trina were guarding the front gate. Their grim expressions told me everything that I didn't want to know.

"We're sorry kid," Sledge said as I jumped out of the van, his face awash in guilt. "We came as fast as we could, but we got here too late."

Trina, used to seeing all manner of tragedy in her day job, was much more stoic but no less sympathetic. "We hauled ass the whole way here, as soon as Fallyn got the call. I am so sorry."

I shook my head as I shouldered past them, unwilling to hear what I already knew. Fallyn walked out of the office, stopping me before I hit the front stoop.

"It's bad in there, Colin. You sure you want to—"

I pushed her aside. "Ed! Ed, you in there?" I shouted as I slammed the door to the office open.

Samson was kneeling beside Ed, wiping his hand with a bandanna. Ed lay behind the counter in a pool of blood, his body riddled with bullet wounds. The computer was missing, the register had been smashed, the cash drawer had been flung to the side. Loose change was scattered everywhere.

Samson stood aside as I approached. "He was almost gone when we got here. I held his hand and stayed with him as he died. They made it look like a robbery, but I smelled magic, deep and strong when I walked in—the kind you use to erase evidence. Circle magic."

Tears flowed freely down my cheeks as I walked over to Ed, squatting down to grab his hand. Of all the people who'd stepped in after Dad had died, Ed was the one who'd always been there for me. He'd drive all the way in from Austin to watch my games, he'd let me hang out for hours watching him work on cars, and he was the one who'd taught me how to fix just about anything.

Anything but this.

I hadn't really realized it, but Ed had been much more to me than an uncle. He'd been my surrogate dad.

"Ed... oh hell. I never thought—I mean, shit. Why didn't I see this coming?"

Samson placed a firm, warm hand on my shoulder. "If I

could take this away from you, I would. I've seen a lot of kin die since I got turned, and it doesn't get any easier over the years. I'm sorry, Colin."

I wiped my eyes and looked up at him. "Thanks for coming, Samson. I know there was nothing you could have done."

"I wish I'd been a few minutes faster, kid. I really, sincerely do."

I nodded. "You'd better go. I'm going to have to call the cops, and it would probably be best if you guys weren't here when they arrived."

Samson replied with a grunt. "Don't worry about us. If you need anything, you know who to call."

The grizzled old 'thrope left without another word, but none needed to be said. The implied message was, "Call us when you find who did this, because the Pack looks after their own." It was a small comfort.

What the hell am I going to tell Mom? Her only brother, dead. And it's my fucking fault.

Belladonna walked in the office as soon as Samson left. "Blaming yourself already, aren't you?"

I raised a hand, warning her off. "Bells, this isn't the time—"

She spun me around to face her, grabbing me by the shoulders and shaking me. "You listen to me, Colin. There will be time to mourn later, but right now we have to take care of Gunnarson. He *will* be coming after us—all of us—and if we don't go on the offensive right now, soon there'll be nowhere left for us to hide."

I took a deep breath, letting it out in shuddering gasps that gradually became steadier as I calmed myself by focusing on the task at hand. "You're right about almost everything, Bells. Now isn't the time to mourn, and we do need to go on the offensive. But there's one thing you're dead wrong about."

"Which is?"

"We're not the ones who need to find a place to hide. He is."

TWENTY-ONE

The Pack and nerd herd split before I called the police, and by the time they got there I'd used magic to sweep the parking lot free of tire tracks. It might look suspicious, but I figured it was better to let the police puzzle over it than to have them looking for a bunch of bikers instead of the real killers. Of course, they'd never catch the real killers, and this case would go unsolved—just like a half-dozen other famous murder cases in this town.

And that was fine by me, because justice could be served in more ways than one.

Bells and I told the cops that I'd stayed the night at her place, and when she'd dropped me off I'd found Ed in the office, dead. That story went over like a turd in a punchbowl at a debutante ball, so we spent the next several minutes being grilled and saying, "I don't know" over and over again.

Maureen showed up a half-hour after the cops got there, with Finnegas and Manny Borovitz in tow. Borovitz was the hotshot attorney who'd helped Hemi when he'd gotten pinned for a murder he didn't commit. He was sharp, well-connected, and respected by the cops, so once he got involved the cops left us alone and went about their investigation.

We allowed the police to process us for evidence, of course. Finnegas and Maureen surreptitiously used magic to clear us of all gunpowder residue, and neither of us had any blood on us so we passed that litmus test with flying colors. With a promise from Borovitz to bring us down to the station for further questioning, the cops left us to our own designs. Belladonna went to meet the geek squad to gather intel and figure out our next move, and I stayed so I could see to Ed's personal affairs.

I spent the rest of the morning speaking to Ed's employees, who'd been gathered outside the front gates speculating as to what happened. Everyone had loved Ed, and as it turned out he'd been a father to more people than just me. If you've never seen a bunch of hardened mechanics and heavy equipment operators cry inconsolably, trust me, it's not something you want to experience twice. Nobody asked about their jobs, or whether the junkyard would remain open. They were too gutted about Ed's death to think of themselves. It was a true testament to the man he'd been.

Breaking the news to Mom had been the worst. She'd cried and cried on the phone with me after I'd explained what had happened—the story we gave the cops, at least. Finnegas offered to stay with her while she was grieving. She believed he was an older relative on my dad's side—we'd called him "Uncle Finn." I knew his presence would help her during the grieving process, so I took him up on his offer. Besides, I knew if he was with Mom, she'd be absolutely safe.

As Finnegas was leaving, he grabbed me in a fierce hug,

squeezing me tight before releasing me and gripping me by the shoulders. The emotion he displayed surprised me, because Finnegas was not known for such displays of affection. He looked me dead in the eye, his grey-blue eyes wet and bright as he spoke.

"He was a good man, your uncle Ed. He took me in when I was at my lowest, helping me in small ways with kind gestures that most would overlook. Ed helped bring me back from the brink, you know. 'Finn,' he once told me, 'that boy needs you, clean and sober. I know you're going through a rough patch, but my nephew looks up to you like no one else. So, you stay here as long as you need to get back on your feet, because Colin's gone to a dark and lonely place, and he needs your help to find his way back again.'"

"I... I don't know what to say."

Finn squeezed my shoulder. "There's nothing *to* say at times like these. Nothing will make things any easier or help it all make sense. Just know that your uncle was a decent man, and he loved you a great deal. In another time he'd have made a fine warrior, someone who would fight by your side to the very end. I'm proud to have known him, and there are damned few I can say that about, even after all my time on this earth."

With that, Finnegas left, and then it was just me and the dogs. They'd been locked up in the main section of the yard when it had happened, and Rufus nearly cut his front paws to bits trying to get through the gate to help Ed. Every once in a while, Rufus would let out a mournful howl—but Roscoe just sat down at the office door and stayed there, as if waiting for Ed to appear by magic.

"Sorry, boy, but no amount of magic's going to bring him

back," I said as I patted his head gently. I puttered around the office after that, trying not to look at the blood while I put things back where they belonged. I soon realized that everything had blood on it, so I started sorting things and tossing what wasn't needed. Finally, I tackled the dark red stain where Ed's body had rested, mopping it up and scrubbing the floor as clean as I could get it.

With that grim task done, I suddenly found that I wanted to be anywhere but there. I walked out and sat on the curb in front of the junkyard, looking at the sign over the entrance that bore Ed's name. I glanced down at the smaller sign I'd taped to the gate to let people know we were "closed until further notice," and wiped a hand across my forehead.

"Fuck!" I screamed at the sky, clenching my fists and roaring in anger as a little of my Fomorian side seeped through. As it did, those nagging subconscious urges came back, telling me to *rend-tear-smash-gut-rip-destroy*. The impulse to hurt something—*anything*—nearly overwhelmed me until I managed to calm myself down.

It occurred to me that anger was a weakness right now, because if I went on a rampage I might never come back from the brink of madness—and Gunnarson would escape justice forever. So, in place of anger, I let a cool, calculating sense of righteous indignation sink down into my chest, turning my heart to ice so I could stay focused on what needed to be done.

I'm coming for you, Gunnarson. And when I find you, I'm going to make your whole world burn.

I SAT on the curb until the sun was low in the sky, then I got up and started walking aimlessly, working things out in my head. It was long after dark when Belladonna called. I considered letting it go to voicemail, fearful of losing her too. But I needed her help, and Bells had her own stake in this game.

"Yeah, I'm here."

Belladonna sounded a bit frantic. "Colin, where the hell are you? The nerd herd and I drove by the junkyard to pick you up, but it's all locked up and dark inside. *Ay carajo*, but you had me so scared—I thought Gunnarson and his goons got you."

"I had to get away from there, you know? So I took a walk."

"That's fine—tell me where you are so I can come pick you up."

I looked around, realizing I had no idea where I was. "Hang on a sec." I fired up the GPS and pulled up my maps app to get my position. "I'm on the East Side, near Oakwood Cemetery."

"You walked all the way over there? With Gunnarson and who knows who else on the hunt for us?"

"Better than staying at the junkyard. That's the first place anyone would look."

"Colin..." her voice trailed off, despite the obvious frustration she was feeling. "Just stay where you are, alright? We'll be there to get you in, say, twenty minutes."

"Meet me by the chapel. That's where I'll be."

I entered the graveyard at an unhurried pace, welcoming the silent company of the old gravestones and buried dead as I thought through my current situation. I'd always found graveyards to be conducive to silent reflection, which was just what I needed at the moment. And even though this had been a place of recent tragedy, it was still one of my favorite places in the city.

I took a short, shuddering breaths as I began to stroll the lanes, focusing on my surroundings until my breathing gradually became deeper and more relaxed. Smells of freshly mown grass and newly turned earth mixed with just the faintest underlying odor of decay, and rather than being turned off by it, I found it somehow soothing. Within minutes, my body calmed and relaxed, and I felt at least somewhat able to consider what might lie ahead.

As I strolled between headstones that were moss-marked and pitted by time, I thought back to the huge battle I'd fought here against the Dark Druid his undead army. Hemi and Guts the troll had fought at my side then, in a fierce battle that had nearly cost us our lives. The trolls lost several warriors that night, but thankfully no innocents had been killed. The Dark Druid might have been a dick, but he was at least a dick who followed predictable patterns of engagement.

Gunnarson, on the other hand, was a different animal—completely unpredictable and devoid of any moral compunctions against taking innocent lives. I knew he'd keep coming at me, hurting people I loved, until I gave up or made a mistake that got me killed. It was clear that I needed to face him, but did I really want to take on someone who was that powerful alone... especially now, with all the trouble I was having controlling my other half?

Before I took my next step, I needed to think through my other options. The most obvious choice was to take what I'd learned to Maeve and let her handle it. But that would be tantamount to asking for her help, and that was something I simply would not do.

I also thought about using the geek squad to alert the High Council at the Circle, but I was pretty sure that Gunnarson had already labeled Belladonna and the nerd herd as defectors. In fact, I wouldn't have been surprised if he was busy pinning the fae killings on them... and me. Plus, at least one person on the Council was dirty. So, that path was out.

An alternate route would be to get the vamps and the Pack involved. I knew both Samson and Luther would back my play. The problem was, that would be pitting them against the most powerful faction in the city, disturbing a peace that had lasted decades. Tensions were already running high, what with fae dropping like flies lately. The city's supernatural underworld was a powder keg, and all it needed was a spark to go off. Far be it from me to get either faction in a war with the Circle. I was responsible for enough deaths already.

That left me with one option, which was to either expose or eliminate Gunnarson myself.

Bells pulled up in the van a few minutes later, tires squealing. The side door slid open, and inside, Dex stared at me like a deer in headlights. I'd ignored him earlier, too worried about my uncle to pay him any mind. He looked to be about fifteen years old—a skinny, pimply kid dressed like a CPA in a white Ralph Lauren button-down, khakis, brown dress shoes, and a belt to match. He looked like he was about to shit a brick, and his voice cracked as he spoke.

"I'm sorry about your uncle, Mr. McCool. Please don't

hulk out and eat my liver." He wrung his hands nervously while Deets looked at him with contempt.

I pointed at Dex with my thumb as I climbed into the van. "Where in the fuck did you find this guy, at the local Kindercare?"

Kien grinned as he cast a glance at his friend. "Pretty much. Little prick was working on a PhD in information security at Texas when recruiting caught wind of him. They asked him if he wanted to hack the NSA's intel gathering program, and he said he already had. After he proved it they offered him six figures on the spot, along with the opportunity to complete his thesis while 'interning' at HQ." He picked a Skittle off his workstation keyboard and beaned the teen in the head with it. "And here I am, ten years in and still making five figures."

Dex looked hurt. "It's not my fault you never got an IT degree. I keep telling you, go back to school and it'll open up doors—but oh no, nobody listens to Dex."

"That's because you're fifteen fucking years old, dick," Deets said as he closed the door behind me.

Dex flipped Deets off, then his eyes settled on me again. "So, you're not going to kill me?"

"Nope. Belladonna is perfectly capable of feeding you your nut sack herself. Seriously, kid, if I thought you were a threat you'd already be dead."

"Uh, thanks?" he squeaked.

"Thank me after you find out what we're about to do." I slipped up to the front and took a seat next to Bells. "Are you ready to fuck some shit up?"

"Hell yes," she replied with an evil look in her eye. "Do we even have a plan?"

"Oh, I have a plan." I looked at the nerd herd in the back of the van. "These guys might not like it, but I most definitely have a plan."

"AND YOU'RE sure you can track his location from the back of this thing?" I asked as we sped down the highway.

"Sure as death and taxes," Deets replied. "So long as he's carrying his phone, we'll know where he is."

"I figured you Circle types would have untraceable phones or something," I remarked.

Kien shook his head. "They are, except that the Circle tracks all of their personnel via their communication devices. No one else can trace them, but we know where every operative is at all times. Even big shots like Gunnarson."

Dex raised his hand. "I wrote that program, by the way."

Kien's lip curled as he typed away at a laptop. "Yeah, yeah—you're the wonder boy, Dex. Now, go grab me a grape soda from the cooler. And don't lick the top!"

Dex made funny faces as he mocked Kien behind his back, but he did as he was told. I moved behind Kien and pointed at a pulsating dot on the screen.

"Is that him?"

"It's his phone, anyway," Kien replied, taking the soda from Dex and sniffing the top. His eyes narrowed. "You didn't lick this, did you?"

"Maybe I did, and maybe I didn't. Maybe I wiped my ass with it," Dex teased.

"Cleaner than his mouth," Belladonna quipped from up front.

"Oh, burn!" Deets declared. "Alright, I'm sending the notice out on the wire right now. As far as anyone will know, you were spotted at the junkyard five minutes ago alone. Gunnarson's team will converge there to take you out, giving us plenty of time to do what's needed at his place."

"Fucking one-percenter," Kien muttered. "I'm looking forward to watching you smash that place to dust."

"You aren't going to be anywhere near there when Gunnarson and his clowns show up," I said. "Stick to the plan—Bells and I can't take Gunnarson out while we're worried about keeping you three safe."

Belladonna turned her head around to yell at the nerd herd. "Did they take the bait, or not?"

Deets adjusted his headset, raising a finger in the air. "Hold for confirmation... yes, they're taking the bait. We are clear to go."

Bells punched it, the whine of the van's turbodiesel engine reaching epic proportions as she passed cars with abandon. "Alright then," she said over the engine noise. "ETA in twenty minutes, give or take. Dex, you'd better have that thing ready by the time we get there, or else I *will* feed you your nutsack."

Dex was now in the rear of the van, tinkering with a large electronic device. "Promises, promises," Dex muttered around the screwdriver in his mouth.

"What was that?" Bells yelled.

"I said it'll be ready, don't worry," the kid replied.

I moved to the back to squat down next to Dex. The kid was so wrapped up in his work, he practically ignored me. "What's the range on that thing, kid?"

"Maybe one-half mile, tops. It'll brick every electronic

device within that radius. Including your cell phone, so you'd best leave it with us. And don't call me kid."

I held up my Craneskin Bag. "Pocket dimension. It'll be safe."

"Neat. Now, would you get out of my light? I'm working here," Dex replied without pausing to look at me.

I did as he asked, taking a seat near Deets. "Man, he gets attitude when he works, doesn't he?"

Deets moved his hand like he was jerking off. "Dex gets mouthy, but he knows he's still my bitch—aren't you, Dex?" Dex flipped him off without sparing him a glance, and Deets laughed as he whispered to me behind his hand. "The little shit is good at what he does, and he knows it. Trust me, if he says it'll be ready, it'll be ready."

"Good to know," I said, turning forward in my seat and closing my eyes. I took several deep breaths, entering a light trance to calm my nerves.

It'd better be ready, I thought. *Because I don't know if I can beat Gunnarson without it.*

TWENTY-TWO

We got to Gunnarson's ranch in record time, with Kien and Bells switching out driving duties before we arrived. The nerd herd dropped us off down the road from Gunnarson's place, along with the device I'd had Dex cobble together earlier. Now, we just had to wait for Dex to nerf the security, then we'd take out the remaining guards and set our trap for Gunnarson.

Deets' voice came over the military-style radio earpieces we were wearing, courtesy of The Cold Iron Circle. "I see two guards on perimeter patrol, heading south toward your current position. They will reach you in thirty seconds."

"Copy that," Bells said. "On the move."

Belladonna had kept one of the fancy tranquilizer guns she'd stolen from the guards during our last visit. We took cover in thick foliage along the other side of the fence and waited for the patrol.

"Won't they be expecting an attack?" I asked.

"Nope," Bells whispered. "Deets has been feeding them false surveillance info. They think we bailed on you and headed to Dallas."

"Hmm. You think Gunnarson will buy it?"

The UTV drove toward us on the other side of the fence with two guards in the front seats. Bells waited for them to pass, then stood up and fired the tranq gun twice. Both men reacted, grasping at the darts before slumping down in the vehicle, which veered off and crashed into a tree.

"Oops," Bells said. "Come on, let's get moving in case someone heard that."

We ran for the fence, crunching through gravel and undergrowth. I disabled the magic wards, noting that the configuration had been upgraded considerably since my break-in. It still didn't give me much trouble. If there was one thing I was good at magic-wise, it was bypassing magical security measures. I temporarily shut the spells down in this section of fence, making sure to avoid tripping any alarms. Once we vaulted the fence, I turned them back on, and moments later we were headed toward the main residence.

Deets' voice crackled in our ears. "Three guards outside the house and one inside remain. First up, southeast corner."

"Got her," Bells whispered as the tranquilizer gun went off. The dart whizzed through the air, hitting her target squarely in the chest. Instead of falling down, however, the guard turned toward us and opened fire with a submachine gun.

"Damn it, she's wearing body armor!" Bells hissed as she discarded the tranquilizer gun.

"Well, I guess they know we're here now," I said as I returned fire with my silenced Glock.

Bells swung up the suppressed Kriss Vector that hung from her shoulder. It was technically a submachine gun, but the configuration she carried qualified it as a short-barreled rifle, accurate at medium range and perfect for taking out pesky Circle operatives. She brought the Kriss to her shoulder and squeezed the trigger twice, dropping the guard immediately.

Belladonna took off at a run toward the house, and I came hot on her heels. As we passed the body, I noted that my girl-friend had put a bullet in each of the guard's eyes.

Note to self—don't piss off Belladonna Becerra.

"Two more coming from either corner of the residence," Deets warned.

"They're mine," Bells said, raising her rifle and pointing it dead center at the house. As soon as one of the guards appeared on the right, she swung her weapon smoothly, popping off two more rounds. As the guard was falling to the ground she was already sighting in on the other corner of the house, moving smoothly in a crouch toward the residence. As that guard came around the corner, she dropped him with a single round to the head.

The radio crackled again. "One left inside the residence. We've cut comms, so you are free to engage."

Dex's voice came over the comm line. "Actually, we're talking to the idiot now. He thinks help is on the way. What a moron."

"Get off the comms, Dex!" Deets shouted in our ears. "Geez, how many times do I have to tell you that? Fucking amateur."

"Okay, so now I'm deaf in one ear," Belladonna said. "Thanks, guys."

"Sorry," they said in unison.

Silence followed, then the radio crackled again. "Do you want to know the position of the last guard?"

"No, Deets—I was just going to sit here and play with myself while you jokers figure out what radio discipline means."

Dex's voice echoed from the background over the radio. "That's so hot."

"Shut up, Dex. They can still hear you," Kien whispered loudly, also in the background.

Deets audibly sighed before responding. "Last tango is hiding in the galley area behind the kitchen island."

"Left side or right side?" Bells asked.

"Left—no, right, your right!" Deets replied.

"Copy that," Bells whispered. She popped up and fired two shots through the window.

"Tango down, all clear," Deets said over the radio. "And can I just say holy fucking shit that was so awesome!"

"Radio discipline guys, remember?" Bells replied as we rounded the corner and entered the house. "If you ever want to work field support, you're going to have to learn some professionalism."

"Hey, I'm being professional over here," Kien shouted in the background. "You don't hear me hopping on the radio to chat."

"No, Kien, you didn't," Bells purred. "And for that I will thank you later, personally." Bells clicked the mute button on her receiver as she looked at me. "I have to throw them a bone every now and again—keeps them on their toes."

"I'd be jealous if it wasn't all so damned funny," I said, clicking my receiver off as well.

Bells kept the button depressed as she replied. "I find that the occasional peck on the cheek, cleavage display, or bend and snap gets me pretty much anything I want where they're concerned."

"Okay, now I am jealous." I clicked my receiver back on. "Gentlemen, we are going to have a serious talk about boundaries when this mission is over."

Deets' voice came in over the radio. "Kien, you brownnoser! Now we're all in trouble. Way to go, man—way to fucking go."

I KNEW I'd be in deep trouble going up against Gunnarson without shifting into my Fomorian form. If he'd managed to take out Elmo with just a little help from Carver, that meant he had access to some serious technomagic. Even worse, I'd yet to see him in action. I was going in blind with no real intel, against an opponent who wielded magic powers that easily dwarfed my own.

Gunnarson also had military training, which meant he was familiar with standard firearms and weaponry. I could also assume that he had extensive hand-to-hand combat training, just as all Circle operatives did. I doubted he'd sink to using those skills if he could help it, since he'd probably get his rocks off by crushing me with spell craft. Unbeknownst to Gunnarson, though, my plan was to force him to face me without magic.

I clicked my comm receiver. "Comms check."

"You are coming in five by five, God-Killer," Deets replied.

"Um, don't call me that. Bells, are you in position?"

"Roger that. I'll start dropping bodies, just as soon as you give the signal," she replied.

I had taken up an observation point inside the house, alone. It had taken me some time to convince Belladonna that I needed her on overwatch more than I did on the ground. Bells was a hands-on kind of gal, which I admired, but I worried that Gunnarson would take any opportunity to make me flinch. All he'd have to do was skewer Bells like he had Elmo, and I'd lose my shit as well as this fight. It was a risk I wasn't willing to take.

"Deets, how far out are Gunnarson and company?" Dead silence. "Deets? Aw hell, are you really going to make me do this?" More silence. "Fine. 'Control'—how far out are they?"

Deets' voice buzzed in my earpiece. "God-Killer, this is Control. Tangos are three clicks out. I show ten bodies in three vehicles."

"Do you want me to eliminate them while they're in the vehicles?" Bells asked. "I can start paring down their numbers as they're coming up the drive."

I thought about it for a second before answering. "No, I want them all on the property. If anything, wait until they stop, then take out the engines in the vehicles."

"Unnecessary, but can do... God-Killer," Belladonna replied with a snicker.

"Har, har, very funny," I replied. "I'm going to kill you guys for pinning that on me, you know that?"

Dex's squeaky voice sounded in the background. "Tell him it wasn't my idea! Besides, we didn't come up with that nickname—the supes did."

"Enough!" I barked. "We'll discuss it when this is all over. Remember, everyone, if shit goes sideways I want you to haul ass. Is that clear?"

"I'm not going anywhere, druid boy," Bells growled.

I sighed. "That's what I figured. Deets—I mean, Control?"

"You don't have to tell us twice. Kien already has the van in gear. No offense, but if you go down we're headed for the Bahamas on the next flight out."

I heard Bells chuckle over the radio. Clearing my throat, I bit back a response that involved my plans for her, if we both made it through the next hour in once piece.

"Thanks for the vote of confidence, fellas. Radio silence from here on out until the shooting starts. McCool out."

I pulled my earpiece out and tore the throat mic off as well, setting them close by. Damned thing made me feel like I was choking—and besides, I didn't want anything metal on me when Gunnarson arrived. I took my pistol off as well as my belt, and tossed them in my Craneskin Bag. Then I changed out my jeans and t-shirt for a pair of board shorts and a rash guard. I had a loose pair of spandex Jockeys on underneath, just in case I had to shift. I hung the Bag over my shoulder last, unwilling to give up that one reliable advantage.

Once done, I sat down cross-legged on Gunnarson's expensive rug and went into a druid trance.

Eye, are you there?

-I am here, Colin.-

If I wig out, I want you to drop me like a hot rock.

-If I do that, you could die.-

Just do it. I don't want to put any innocent lives in danger if I can't hold my shit together.

-Understood.-

I came back to reality just as the throaty rumble of three V-8 engines came roaring toward the house. I stood and peeked out the blinds, watching from concealment as Gunnarson and his goon squad hopped out, guns ready and in full battle-rattle. They knew I was here, but they were still cocky enough to think they were invulnerable.

Or, rather, that Gunnarson's powers made them invulnerable.

"Bells, take them out."

I heard the crack of a suppressed high-power rifle, then watched as a rifle round flattened itself against an invisible barrier, right in front of Gunnarson's face. He grinned, then spread his arms wide while his team took cover behind the vehicles and building.

"Nice shooting, Becerra!" he yelled in his Texas drawl. "I think I'll kill you last."

Belladonna's voice squawked out of my discarded earpiece. "Well, it was worth a try."

Three more shots rang out as Belladonna's bullets punched neat holes in the hood of each vehicle. As the engines sputtered and died, Gunnarson's men returned fire— a distinct tactical mistake with Belladonna up-range behind a sniper scope. Three heads exploded in a cloud of spattered brains and bloody mist before they realized their error.

"Fuck, I didn't think she could shoot that good," one of the men said, earning him a scowl from his commander.

GUNNARSON REACTED THEN, raising his hands in the air and chanting in some ancient Germanic language that was strangely pleasing to the ear. As the sleeves on his BDU shirt slid down, I noticed a glint of steel and green LED lights at his wrists. The technomage brought his wrists together then, and a pulse of magical energy surged forth from his hands.

Belladonna's rifle cracked again, but the round hit an invisible wall a few feet away from the intended target—one of Gunnarson's goons who had leaned out from behind cover. Bells kept firing at different targets, but no matter where she aimed her bullets kept hitting an invisible shield. Her commanding officer kept his hands in the air, brow furrowed and sweat running down his face.

"She can't hit you now, you idiots," he barked over his shoulder. "Advance and lay down fire on her position! McCool is around here somewhere, and I can't take him out while I'm protecting you dipshits from his girlfriend."

The tac team cautiously eased out from behind cover, directing their gunfire where they'd last seen Belladonna's muzzle flashes. I knew she'd already changed position, but it still made me nervous as all hell. Gunnarson walked forward, advancing on the house with his tac team following as they fired at the hill where Bells had been.

I waited until the entire team was lined up across the front lawn, then I grabbed my comm device and gave the signal.

"Dex, hit it."

We'd hidden the electromagnetic pulse device on Gunnarson's roof, where it would have the most reach and do the most damage. I sensed rather than saw a tremendous pulse of energy explode out from above me, and watched as the LED lights on Gunnarson's bracers went dark. Moreover, every electronic device within one-half mile went dead, including the lights inside and outside the house, lights in houses off in the distance, and our communications devices.

Belladonna's rifle cracked several times in rapid succession, and Circle tac team members began dropping left and right. The rest ran for cover as Gunnarson's face blanched, his eyes going wide as he realized his primary technomagical devices had just been rendered useless. Then Gunnarson's surprise turned to anger, and if I read him properly, resolve. Nostrils flaring and teeth bared he reached behind his head, pulling on something that I couldn't see from my vantage point.

Suddenly, Gunnarson vanished. One minute he was there, then *poof*—he was gone. I blinked twice, just in case I'd missed something, but he was still gone. I quickly shifted my vision into the magical spectrum, but nothing registered—not even a fading vestige of the magic he'd been casting. It was as if he'd been vaporized, or teleported away to some distant location.

Despite Gunnarson's strange disappearing act, Belladonna kept firing at our enemies. And although the drive and front lawn had been littered with bodies, there were still a few tac team members returning fire from behind their vehicles.

So, Bells switched tactics. An incendiary round zipped through the now darkened sky, straight at one of the SUVs that Gunnarson's team had arrived in. The strontium and magnesium-laced bullet hit the truck's fuel tank, igniting it.

The truck exploded in a huge fireball, lighting up the night sky with a deafening roar. The explosion turned the remaining tac team members into person-shaped fireballs that flew through the air like flaming rag dolls. Each landed several yards away in random directions, void of movement except for the tongues of fire that licked at their clothing and gear.

All gunfire ceased, and I was left wondering what the hell had happened to Gunnarson. With comms down, I had no way to signal Belladonna to ask if she had spotted him anywhere near. Invisibility spells were incredibly difficult to cast, and considering his area of magical specialty, I doubted him capable of casting such magic. To be effective, "look away, go away" spells generally required that observers were not looking at the spell caster when the magic was triggered. So, I was fairly certain Gunnarson hadn't used that sort of magic, either.

Could he have teleported away? Possibly, but I hadn't seen any sort of portal appear, and the only magic user I'd ever known who was powerful enough to straight-up teleport was Maeve... and she was a full-on deity in the Celtic pantheon. No, there was something else going on here that I didn't fully understand.

I exited the house by the front door and headed out onto the lawn, where I intended to examine the spot where Gunnarson had been standing when he'd disappeared. There were minor depressions in the ground, bent blades of grass, and footprints that led from the direction he'd walked after he and his crew had pulled up. But aside from those traces of his passing, there was nothing to indicate he'd fled in another direction while hidden by magic.

Further examination in the magical spectrum yielded the same results.

"Gunnarson, you spineless bastard," I muttered. "Where the hell have you gone to?"

I felt a burning pain across my shoulders, and felt hot slick blood running down my back. I knew that sensation well —I'd been cut by a sharp blade. It wasn't a crippling wound, but a painful one. Now I really wished I'd worn some armor.

Gunnarson's voice rang out from the darkness, somewhere to my left. "I'm right here, McCool, right where I've been all along. Did you think those bracer's were the only trick I had up my sleeve?"

I reached into my Bag and drew my sword, determined to put up a fight. But there was nothing *to* fight, because Gunnarson was a ghost, a phantasm that I couldn't see, hear, or smell. Another cut appeared on my wrist, then one on my stomach, and a third on my brow. Several more wounds appeared in rapid succession—each shallow but clean, the type of cut you made when you wanted someone to suffer. Blood flowed freely into my eyes, forcing me to wipe it away to see.

Gunnarson's sword stung me a dozen times in the span of thirty seconds. Each time I felt another gash appear, I swung my own blade in response, only to hit empty air for my troubles. Soon, my hands were slick with my own blood. My arms felt heavy, my legs weak, my vision dark with warm, sticky wetness.

I was bleeding out, death by a thousand cuts.

For a moment, the attacks ceased. Then, I felt a stinging sensation across the backs of my thighs and collapsed to my knees, hamstrung. My hands grasped at the grass beneath me in a struggle to hold myself upright so I could fight back.

Yet I knew it would be in vain, because I was fighting against someone who, by every sense and skill I possessed, simply wasn't there.

TWENTY-THREE

"Really, McCool?" Gunnarson's voice dripped with the confidence one gains at the prospect of impending victory. "Are you willing to give up so easily? Your friend the ogre even put up a better fight than this."

I pushed myself up straighter, hands slipping beneath me on the blood-soaked grass. My eyes scanned the area around me through a crimson haze, hoping against hope that I might see something to give my opponent away, a shadow or flash of movement. But nothing appeared within the range of my now limited vision, not a single indication of Gunnarson's position.

"I fully intend to kill you, you know. That's a promise." My words rang hollow, empty of conviction in my current state.

Gunnarson cackled, his laughter echoing over the roar of the vehicles burning nearby. "Look at you, McCool. For all your vaunted skills and talents, all it takes is a sharp sword and a little magic to bring you down."

I slung blood out of my eyes, fighting to stay upright. Most people don't realize how crippling hamstringing a person can be, but it was one of the first strategies I'd learned as a swordsman. As Maureen explained it, the muscles on the backs of the thighs both flex the knee and extend the hip. When they're cut, it's nearly impossible to keep your torso vertical, much less stand or walk.

"I could shift right now to heal myself and crush you," I growled.

Gunnarson chuckled at my empty threat, his voice constantly changing position as he spoke. "Ah, but you won't. Not with your girlfriend close by, because you know I'd just slip away and leave that monster inside you to rip her to shreds. Just like you did to that poor girl you dated in high school. What was her name? Jenny? Janine?"

"Her name was Jesse, you son of a frost giant!" I knew he was a Norseman at heart, and while weak, it was the best insult I could come up with on the spot.

"So angry," he drawled. "Sounds like someone has some guilt to work through. Too bad you won't have a chance to deal with it, McCool, because your time's about up."

"Fuck you, Gunnarson! Kill me and Finnegas will come after you. You and I both know he could bring you and your boss down without breaking a sweat."

"Oh, I doubt it," my opponent responded, his voice coming from an entirely different direction. "The old man is past his prime. You might think he's immortal, but the truth is the human aging process can only be suspended for so long. Time has caught up to him, and despite that little show he put on for Maeve's court, he's no threat to us—well, at least not to my benefactor."

I was desperately trying to figure a way out of this mess. I knew Belladonna would be somewhere nearby, waiting for the chance to put a bullet in her commander. If I didn't take him out soon, she'd come charging in here to try and save me, then we'd both be dead. And if I shifted, it'd be the same story—only *I'd* be the one doing the killing.

After what had happened to Jesse, I simply would not take that risk. So, I stalled for time and dug for info while I figured out how to beat Gunnarson.

"What I don't understand is, why kill all those fae? They'd already lost access to most of their magic, so why start picking them off? It just doesn't make sense."

Gunnarson's voice was relaxed as he spoke, so sure was he of his victory. "I know you're stalling, but you're also bleeding to death, so I'll gladly take the time to explain. Besides, in a minute Becerra is going to come storming out of the woods, and then I'll get to kill you both."

"She's not that stupid, Gunnarson," I said loudly, hoping Bells would hear and be warned off. "She'll get some backup and come back to kill you."

"At which point I'll be long gone, and she knows it. No, she'll try to save you, you can count on that." He paused, clearing his throat. "Now, where the hell was I, before you interrupted? Oh yes, the fae...

"Here's what you don't know, McCool—you think you crippled them, but you're wrong. Those fuckers live a hell of a long time, much longer than we do. Even without an endless pool of magic to draw on, they're still a force to be reckoned with, and now they're pissed and desperate. It's just a matter of time before they gather their resources and attack us."

"I doubt that," I replied, lying through my teeth. The fact was, I'd considered that possibility already... but I wasn't going to give Gunnarson the satisfaction of knowing I agreed with him.

"Doubt all you want, Pollyanna, but it's coming. I guaran-fucking-tee it."

I glanced down to make sure I still had a grip on my sword, because my hands were going numb. If I had even the slightest chance to kill Gunnarson, I wanted to be ready.

"Let's assume what you say is true," I asked. "Why start a fight with the fae here?"

"Austin is the key because Maeve is their queen. Not just *a* queen, *the* queen. From what we can gather, she goes way back to the Tuatha, and we think she's the oldest of all the fae left here on earth. When she talks they all listen—every single court and remnant from here to Europe, wherever the Celtic gods once ruled."

I shook my head slowly, the blood loss making it hard to even keep my head up. "So, by taking Maeve out you'll send the fae into disarray, making them that much easier to destroy."

"Yep," he replied. "But first we had to remove their key magic wielders, which is what we've been doing all along. The only thing left to do now is kill Maeve, but with you involved we had to wait for you to screw the pooch. But thanks to this little party you've put on, my benefactor can assassinate Maeve and then I get to pin it all on you. Shit, this is like Christmas all over again."

"I still don't understand why you murdered lower-order fae," I whispered. "They were no danger to you."

"I just told you—weren't you listening? Let me spell it out

for you, McCool. You'd never know who the major players are among the fae just by looking at them. Take that girl from the trailer park. She was a full-blown clairvoyant, capable of tipping the queen off to our plans."

"She was just a kid!" I hissed.

"A kid? She was three times your age, McCool! Shit, but you're about as sharp as the leading edge on a bowling ball. I bet you still haven't figured out it was me that day at the junk-yard, asking after the ogre." Gunnarson paused to laugh softly. "No wonder Maeve was able to run you ragged for so long. Hell, knowing how dense you are almost takes the fun out of killing you. Almost."

I was starting to fade out, which I considered a better option than shifting and killing Belladonna. She'd run, of course, if she saw me go bug shit crazy—but that wouldn't guarantee her survival. I slowed my breathing and relaxed my mind as Gunnarson's voice droned on, until I began drifting in and out of lucidity. Finally, I slipped into a dreamlike state, one not unlike the druid trances I'd entered before.

Run, Bells. Please, run.

That was the last thought I had before I closed my eyes, for good.

THE WEIRD THING WAS, I was more or less used to being exsanguinated. After going through the shifter trials with Samson and the Pack, I'd become accustomed to being bled out in a similar fashion. The only difference was, back then it would trigger my change. But during that process I'd learned to suppress those urges, holding my Hyde-side back until the very last second when Samson would heal me—then we'd do it all over again.

Unfortunately, there wouldn't be any Pack healing magic saving me today. I'd chosen to die at the hands of a lesser man, in order to save a woman I loved. And I was okay with that.

Hiya, slugger.

Somehow, I'd expected this. It was Jesse, my first love and the woman I'd accidentally killed the first time I shifted. For some reason she hadn't moved on after her death, and she'd been following me and haunting me ever since. Not in a scary way, though—mostly she just showed up when I had a near-death experience, which was sadly a common occurrence of late.

"Jesse! Funny meeting you here. Why can't I see you this time?"

*Because you're not dead yet, silly. But let's not focus on that. Instead, tell me what you **can** see.*

"Well, this is pretty much like being in a druid trance, when I go deep like I've been doing lately. I can feel the grass beneath me, the insects and small animals in the earth, and the swallows and bats flying overhead."

Really? Now tell me something, slugger—what do they see?

I extended my senses out, entering each creature to take in what they saw, smelled, and felt.

"It's just insects and rodents digging for dirt and food down here. Up above the birds and bats sense each and every air current, and they're having a ball feasting on all the insects that have been drawn to the firelight."

And?

"And—oh, my. I am so freaking dense, but you're a genius."

Don't be so hard on yourself. I see all the good you're doing, and believe me, you're making a difference. You just need a little help sometimes, is all.

"Jesse, I still miss you. Even though I'm with someone else, I think about you every day."

I know. Now, go save your girlfriend, because she's about to get herself killed.

"Jesse, I—"

GO.

Jesse's voice faded off with that last command, an imperative that reminded me just what was at stake. I focused in again on what was happening around me back in the here and now.

Belladonna was running from the woods behind the house, crossing the lawn as she fired at random in the air above me. She was doing her damnedest to keep Gunnarson pinned down, but it wouldn't work because he was nowhere near where she was shooting. As soon as her guns ran dry, he'd step out from behind cover and kill us both.

Whatever magic Gunnarson was using, it allowed him to appear invisible and throw his voice as well. Whether it worked by bending light or by some other means, I wasn't sure. But what I did know was that he was still present, because the bats knew exactly where he was—they'd been picking him up on sonar the entire time.

Gunnarson was hiding behind a low wall near the driveway, just on the other side of me and opposite the direction from which Belladonna approached. Why he didn't just grab a rifle from one of the dead and pick her off was a mystery; I could only assume it would give him away. Or, he just wanted the pleasure of slitting Belladonna's throat instead.

I was only going to get one shot at this, so I had to make it count. Bells was sprinting toward us shooting like an extra in a Bruce Willis movie, and when her pistol clicked on an empty chamber Gunnarson would cut her down. But he'd have to come near me to do it.

I expanded my awareness, keeping watch on them both. Belladonna was still running and firing, changing out magazines on the move. Damn, but she carried a lot of spare ammo. Finally, she closed the distance and slid to a crouch beside me, dropping the gun and drawing a long knife in each hand.

"I won't let you touch him, you hear me?! You'll have to come through me to get him!" Her lips curled back and she snarled in a fierce display of teeth and fangs.

Fangs? I had to be hallucinating due to blood loss. *Focus, McCool!*

Gunnarson's voice echoed from somewhere off to the left. "I'll gladly cut you down to get to him, Becerra," he mocked. "I never did care for you anyway."

"Why, because I'm a woman?" she growled.

"No, because you have a conscience," he replied, this time throwing his voice so it came from the direction of the house.

Bells turned around, leaving her back exposed to his sneak attack. Through the bats' collective sonar, I sensed rather than saw him come out from behind the retention wall, strolling casually toward us with a longsword in his hand. I remained absolutely still, waiting for the right moment to make my move.

Come on, sword—strike true for me today.

Gunnarson reared back with his blade as he came into cutting range, obviously aiming to take Belladonna's head off in one clean stroke. At that instant the sword flared to life, burning with an intensity that I'd never witnessed prior to that moment. The heat and light bathed me in their glow, the sword's warmth filling me with strength. Even with my eyes closed the glare was blindingly bright, but that was okay—I didn't need eyes to see my enemy.

It's now or never, McCool. Time to make this cock-gobbling knob-jockey pay.

GUNNARSON SHIELDED his eyes from the light, and that gave me the opportunity I needed to strike. I rolled to my side and thrust upward, catching Gunnarson in the groin and driving the flaming blade up until the handle made contact. I felt almost no resistance until the hilt struck something solid, so I opened my eyes to see if I'd even hit my target at all.

The blade above the hilt had disappeared, all except for the tip, which blazed brightly a few feet above my hand. Hot, wet fluid ran down the sword's guard and handle, and the sour smell of piss mixed with the iron tang of blood filled my nostrils.

"How...?" Gunnarson croaked. "Siegfried's cloak... never failed its wearer. I pray for Hel to damn you, druid—"

He fell then, wrenching the sword from my grasp. As I lost my grip, the sword's flames extinguished immediately. I heard Gunnarson's body hit the ground, followed by his dying gasp. Whatever magic that had been concealing him faded, revealing his corpse as he bled out on his perfectly manicured lawn. While it must have been invisible before, I now saw that he wore a dark, hooded cloak, of a style not commonly seen in the modern era.

A real-life cloak of invisibility, I thought. *I'll be damned.*

Belladonna tackled me in a hug. "I thought you were dead, *cabrón!*" she shouted, showering me with kisses all over my face and neck.

"I will be if you don't stop this bleeding," I said. "And, Bells? Be sure to grab his cloak—that thing is way too powerful for the Circle to have."

She laughed, a soft tinkling sound that warmed me despite the cold I felt now that the sword's magic had faded. "*Joder, por qué no te callas, mi amor?*" she purred as she tweaked my nose.

"What does that mean?" I asked.

"It means shut the fuck up and let me worry about shit like that," she replied.

"Holy crap! That was awesome!" Deets yelled.

I turned my head just in time to see him and Dex sprinting across the lawn carrying a medical bag and flashlights. Bells directed them to assist her as she started an intravenous line and began bandaging my wounds.

"Dex, did you get it?" I asked as I propped myself up on my elbows.

"All of it, man. We got out of range of the EMP, then Kien hauled ass back here. The crazy fucker forced the gate open with the van so we could record the whole thing. I had the video and audio feeds broadcasting live to HQ, and uploaded copies and sent them to every operative and support technician in the organization."

I plopped back down, resting my head on the grass as I closed my eyes. "Then I forgive you for that comment you made about wanting to plow Bells." I cracked an eyelid to look at him. "But don't let it happen again."

Deets was wrapping gauze around my legs, and he tapped my knee to get my attention. "What I want to know is, how'd you know where to stab?"

I pointed in the air above us. "Bats. Tapped into their sonar using druid magic."

"That is so freaking cool!" Dex declared.

"Speaking of Kien, where's the van?" Bells asked.

"The wreckage is blocking the drive, and he said he didn't want to get stuck," Deets replied. "He's waiting for us halfway down the driveway."

Belladonna's voice was urgent as she spoke. "Guys, I think I hear sirens. We have to get the hell out of here before the authorities arrive."

About that time, I felt the distinct sensation of a magic portal opening nearby. I turned to look, reaching for a pistol that wasn't there. A swirling blue circle of light appeared in the air a few feet away, and Finnegas stepped out of it. His eyes looked cold, hard, and flinty as he began barking commands.

"You!" he said, pointing at Dex. "Tell your friend in the van to meet us at Éire Imports—and don't ask me for the address, because I know you can look it up on that bit of digital deviltry in your hand. Belladonna! You and this young man need to get Colin through that portal, now."

He turned and looked me right in the eyes. "And you— never mind, I'll have words with you later." He stormed off, casting spells left and right to cover up the mess we'd left, muttering under his breath all the while. "Damned crazy kid, has no idea the trouble he's caused, no telling what will happen now. Be lucky he doesn't start a war…"

With Finnegas busy immolating bodies and removing all traces of our presence, Belladonna and Deets got me on my feet. I draped an arm over each of their shoulders, leaning on them heavily as I limped to the portal. I heard the squeal of tires in the distance, just as Dex came jogging up next to us.

"Kien's headed to meet us at the old man's warehouse." His eyes got huge as he approached the portal. The teen pushed his hand through it experimentally, pulling it back out and then through again. "Oh wow, this is incredible! I mean, I've heard of magically-formed wormhole phenomena, but I never thought I'd get to see one up close."

"Believe me, this is nothing," Belladonna groaned as she struggled to support my weight. "Hang around Colin for a while and stuff like this becomes an everyday thing."

Finnegas' voice boomed at a magically-enhanced volume. "Quit jawing at each other and get through that portal—now!"

Dex yelped and jumped through the portal. Deets gulped audibly, so I tapped him on the shoulder and whispered in his ear.

"Don't let the pissed-off Gandalf act fool you—he's a big softie, once you get to know him."

Finn's voice echoed even louder behind us as we entered the portal. "Call me that again, young man, and I'll see to it that portal dumps you in the county lock-up!"

"See what I mean?" I said. "A total softie."

TWENTY-FOUR

The next day, I woke up on a cot inside the hidden training room behind the warehouse at Éire Imports. Finnegas had worked on me for hours the night before, and between his druid goop and the trance magic, I'd healed rapidly. Bells and the nerd herd had stuck around until they got an all clear from Circle headquarters—along with a command to report immediately, "or else."

So there I was, alone with my memories. I pushed myself up to a seated position, extending and flexing my legs experimentally to make sure they still functioned. My hamstrings were tight, but it was nothing a few weeks of stretching couldn't cure. I glanced around the place, wiping the sleep from my eyes as I took in the familiar sights and smells.

I was in a large room that was well-lit by sunlight coming in from skylights above. Thick martial arts mats covered most of the floor, and cord-wrapped pells and wooden training dummies lined the walls. At one end of the room, an archery butt sat gathering dust. It even had a few arrows sticking out of the bullseye from the last time Jesse had practiced, just before our final fateful mission.

I breathed deeply, hoping to catch the faintest whiff of her scent, but all I got was a hint of mold and dust—along with the underlying locker room smell that had permeated the mats after years of sweat and abuse. I sighed heavily and allowed my eyes to wander once more.

There were the punching bags we'd spent hours pummeling together after school, day in and day out. Over there were the wooden practice swords we'd beaten into splinters, sparring each other and practicing partnered fighting patterns until they were burned into our reflexes. And here was the cot where we'd lain together after practice, sweat-drenched from more than just our time on the mats.

Just when I thought I'd gotten over her, she'd show up again to remind me how much I still loved her... and how much her absence still hurt.

"You saw her again, didn't you?" It was Finnegas, leaning in the doorway with a steaming cup of coffee. "Sorry, I didn't mean to disturb—but I heard you stirring and I know what a pain in the ass you are without caffeine in the morning."

He approached me and handed me the mug. I took it without comment.

"How are the legs?" he asked, avoiding bringing attention to the fact that I hadn't answered his question.

"I've not tried standing yet, but they seem to be working fine." I glanced over at him, noting the dark circles under his eyes and the hollowness of his cheeks. "You look like shit. Did you really need to cast that portal spell?"

He sat down heavily on the cot next to me. "I did, as you well know. If the cops didn't get you then the Circle would have. And believe you me—they'd be trying to shut all five of you up for good, if those boys hadn't recorded and broadcasted the whole damned thing."

We sat in silence for a moment, me enjoying the coffee and Finnegas enjoying the rest. I looked at the target again, remembering how Jesse always bested me with a bow and arrow.

"I spoke with her last night while I was under. I'd have died if she hadn't helped, but this morning—" I let my words trail off, unwilling to finish the thought.

"You wish she hadn't shown up at all?" Finnegas asked. I nodded, pursing my lips and hanging my head as my eyes filled with tears. The old man placed a firm hand on my shoulder, squeezing it and patting my back.

"It never gets any easier, son. Not even after two thousand years do I feel the loss of loved ones any less than I did when I was your age. Death was common back then, you know, which was one of the reasons I apprenticed under The Dagda when he started our order."

I raised an eyebrow at that little nugget of information, but sipped my coffee and remained silent. Interrupting would only mean that I'd never get the rest of the story— and besides, I felt more like listening than talking at the moment.

"He didn't mention it, did he—that he was my teacher, and I, his first apprentice?" Finnegas stretched his legs out in front of him, joints cracking. "Well, he wouldn't. He's a crafty old bastard, that one."

"He said the same thing about you," I said softly.

Finnegas drew himself up, scratching his beard. "Hmm, yes, well—he always was a hypocrite, if a well-meaning one.

Damned fine teacher though, and the reason I still sit before you now."

"How so?"

"In order to get him to agree to teach me the ways of druidry, he made me promise to keep the knowledge alive— and he taught me how to cheat death. But I outsmarted him. The Dagda envisioned an army of druids, going forth to the four corners to work magic in his name. But after the rest of the druids died off, I kept the knowledge alive by teaching just one or two students at a time. Pissed the old trickster off good. Serves him right."

I considered how much Finnegas must have despised the Tuath Dé and his fellow druids, to allow the order to dwindle to nothing when he was supposed to be its keeper. It made me wonder why he chose to take on pupils, even now in his very old age.

"Finn, do you think the world is a better place without the druid order around?"

He frowned slightly, then his expression softened. "I think the world is a better place with the right druid in it," he said, tapping me with one gnarled finger on my breast. "Empathy, my boy, empathy for others and a desire to provide justice for the common folk. That's what they lacked. And that's why you will succeed where I failed. That is, so long as you allow me to pass on the fullness of my knowledge before I'm gone."

As I sat there with the old man, I realized what our relationship really meant to me. Finn was dying, there was no doubt about that, yet he gave no thought to expending magic he needed to extend his life in order to preserve mine. I'd held it against him that he'd deeply mourned the loss of a girl he'd thought of as his own daughter. Yet he'd forgiven me for being the one who'd taken her away from him.

And despite the fact that I'd rejected his tutelage before, he'd eagerly taken me back as his student, without showing a shred of hesitation or resentment. In light of that, I didn't think I'd ever have a friend or mentor as good as the one who sat next to me. That was a fact.

"I'd be honored, Finnegas the Seer. It would be my honor to have you pass on your knowledge to me."

He patted me on the shoulder again as he stood. "That's good, because as soon as you feel strong enough to stand, the bathroom in the lobby needs cleaning. Hop to it, oh worthy apprentice."

LATER, after I'd helped Finnegas clean and straighten the place up, I went out to the patio behind the warehouse to sit and think. It was an enclosed space—more like a garden, really, with a few chairs, lots of flowers, shrubs, a few tall trees for shade, and not much else. I'd often sat there as a teen, thinking about things or just letting my mind wander... and *wonder* at the strange turn my life had taken.

I had just sat down with a cup of coffee and a nice pastry when a large raven flew down and perched on the back of the chair next to me. It eyed me with curiosity, and I returned the favor. We stared at each other like that for a time, until I tore off a piece of my cherry turnover and tossed it over to him. The raven snatched it out of the air, choking it down before shaking his feathers out from head to tail.

Then, the damned thing opened its beak and spoke.

"Colin McCool, druid apprentice, god killer, shape shifter, curse bearer, traveler of realms distant and arcane, wielder of the Fomorian's eye, and slayer of the last of King Gunther's line... you are now summoned to attend a conclave of the High Council of the Cold Iron Circle, to be held at *squawk*—"

Finnegas had snuck up on us somehow, snatching the bird by the neck with both hands. The bird flapped its wings and made a ruckus for several seconds, until finally it decided it was caught and there was nothing to be done about it. Once it had settled down, Finn turned the bird around, staring it right in its eyes.

"Listen, and listen well, you pompous bunch of upstarts and amateurs. The meeting will be held on neutral ground, at the Toothshank clan's fight pits, on the shores of Lady Bird Lake. The local races and factions will all be in attendance and equally represented, and if you don't like it you can sod off. Midnight—be there if you want a say in how the factions choose to deal with your fuck up."

Finn whispered something in the bird's ear, then he released it into the sky.

"What did you whisper to the bird, there at the end?" I asked.

"Sideshow barkers and con artists, every last one of them," he ranted, shaking his fist at the raven as he watched it fly away. "Bah! I freed the raven from its service to those bastards, just as soon as it delivers my message. They have no right to indenture wild creatures like that. Bastards."

He spat on the ground, then he took the chair next to me, pulling out his tobacco pouch to roll one up. I waited until he had some nicotine in him before speaking.

"So, what the hell is a conclave?"

"It's an archaic way to say you're having a meeting. Only freemasons, Catholics, and those self-important pricks use it anymore, the morons."

I took a sip of my coffee, not at all interested in the pastry anymore. I suddenly wished I'd fed it all to the poor raven. "You know, I got the impression I was being called to sit trial."

Finnegas blew smoke from his nostrils. "They'd like you to think you were, but the truth is they don't have the authority. Those jackasses would love to intimidate you and cover this all up, but that's not going to happen. What we're going to do instead is shake things up a bit."

"Okay, so I'm not in trouble, so to speak. But the Circle wants me to think I am, so they can keep me quiet while they pretend that Gunnarson wasn't a murdering nutcase who killed a bunch of fae under orders from someone on their Council."

"Right."

"And we're going to meet these clowns on neutral ground to take away any advantage they might have, and you're going to invite Maeve, Samson, and Luther to stand witness to what goes on at this little powwow."

"Yup. They have a stake in what's about to happen, believe me."

"And just what exactly is about to happen?" I asked.

Finn puffed on his cigarette with a wild look in his eye. "Oh, never you mind. Just start calling your friends to tell them where to be, when, and why."

"Ahem... if you'll recall, Maeve and I aren't exactly chummy at the moment."

"Ah, don't worry about her. I'll make sure she gets the message." He took a long drag, pinching the butt in his lips as he rubbed his hands together. "Oh yes, this is going to be fun."

WHEN WE SHOWED up at the meeting, Chief Ookla and Guts were there at the Toothshank Tribe's little campground in full regalia, with their warriors stationed all around the place. Whether they were there to be an honor guard or as security, I wasn't really sure. Regardless, I was damned happy to see them there, because I knew who they'd stick up for if things got ugly. And let me tell you, the last thing you wanted was a couple dozen trolls coming at you with sharp pointy objects and bad intent.

Finnegas had made me dress somewhat formally for the occasion. I was wearing a pair of black jeans, a white dress shirt, and a new black military trench. I'd even polished up my Doc Martens, although I'd kept the iron spikes I had braided into the laces intact.

You think anybody wants a roundhouse kick to the face while I'm wearing these bad boys? Forget about it.

I nodded to Chief Ookla and Guts as we entered their sacred party park. It seemed like just yesterday that I'd fought Guts here, in a bareknuckle brawl to settle a dispute between the tribe and Maeve. The troll and I had bonded over that brutal and bloody exchange, and since then we'd had our share of fun together. The nod and wink he gave me in response helped settle my nerves a bit.

I followed Finnegas into the place, smiling at how he

wore jeans, cowboy boots, a black western shirt, and a straw cowboy hat with aplomb. Somehow, he managed to look intimidating as all hell in that get up. And if I didn't know better, I'd swear that the taxidermied rattlesnake head on his snakeskin hatband was alive and watching us all.

We rounded a small copse of trees as we approached the designated meeting place. The trolls had placed a bunch of carved wooden chairs around a huge bonfire, twelve of them in all. Since the Toothshank Tribe's little campsite was located on the outskirts of a public park, their shaman had cast a glamour over the whole thing to avoid prying eyes.

The Pack was in attendance, and Samson stood behind their faction's seat with Fallyn and Sledge backing him. It was likely that the rest of the wolves were close by, waiting in case trouble broke out. That also made me feel better about the situation. The sly old wolf gave me a nod and an almost imperceptible grin when he spotted me, then he went back to looking like a constipated Chuck Norris.

Luther showed up next, coalescing in a puff of shadow and smoke fully seated in the spot prepared for him. Two vampires appeared behind him, one of them being Mateo and the other some blonde chick I'd never seen before. Mateo looked much more serious this night than he had when we'd met, and he scanned the area with an almost casual disinterest that I knew was faked. The female vamp did the same, and I could tell they were on high alert, no matter how relaxed Luther appeared to be.

Maeve ported in at the same time the Council members did. She looked radiant as always, and was flanked on one side by the healer who'd helped us at the brothel when we rescued the trafficked children, and on the other by Eliandres. The faery queen moved with an understated grace as she took her seat, followed by eight hooded, faceless figures in dark robes, each taking their seat in unison with Maeve.

Finnegas walked up and took the final empty seat, and I stood behind him. Finn didn't need another person backing him, and everyone knew it. Besides, we were the only druids left besides that prick the *Fear Doirich*. And fuck that guy. We didn't want or need his help.

One of the nameless, faceless figures across the circle stood and spoke. "We, the High Council of the Cold Iron Circle, call this conclave to order, the purpose of which is to discuss the disposition of one Colin McCool, druid apprentice to Finnegas the Seer, who stands accused of crimes against a ranking member of the Circle."

Finn groaned loudly. "Oh, sit down, Andrew, and take off that fucking hood—you look ridiculous. Everyone here knows who you are anyway."

The hooded figure drew himself up, and his voice took on a dangerous tone. "I will not be spoken of in that way in an official meeting of—"

Finn raised a hand at Andrew. "Stop," was all he said, and it was like a curtain of stillness fell across the meeting place. Everyone remained frozen except for the other factions, including Maeve, Luther, Samson, and their entourages. Even the flames in the fire grew still, an elemental power yielding to the will of a master druid.

Finn stood up. "I'll allow you to speak in a minute, Andrew, but be advised that Colin isn't the one on trial here," he gestured in a broad sweep at the eight Council members who sat frozen across from us. "You are."

"Agreed," Maeve said. "One of you is guilty of conspiring

to assassinate me, as well as murdering several of my people. Oh yes, I received the same message your operatives did, broadcast by your own research technicians from Commander Gunnarson's front lawn. It's well known by all present that the Circle was at fault all along. Now, all that's left to determine is what to do with the lot of you."

"Queen Maeve hit the nail on the head," Samson said in a low, quiet voice. "The Pack has tried to stay neutral all this time, but we can't stand by while our allies," he nodded in Maeve's direction, "are slaughtered. The Pack demands justice, and we will have it before this night is through."

"As does the Coven," Luther added. "We stand with the Pack, and our *allies* the Fae, in demanding that justice be served and executed before dawn."

Maeve looked at Finnegas. "And what say the Druids?"

"About that," Finnegas replied. "I happen to have something in mind..."

EPILOGUE

The meeting lasted well into the night, with Maeve, Luther, Samson, and Finnegas discussing what to do about the corruption within the Circle's ranks, all while the High Council sat around frozen stiff. I later found out that spell had been a joint collaboration between Finnegas and Maeve, a trick they'd worked out beforehand in case the High Council tried to play dirty... which, of course, they had.

Two of the Council members had attempted to cast spells to influence Samson and Luther to speak against me. When Maeve caught wind of them she'd given Finn the signal, and the old man had dropped the hammer. Turns out that healer Maeve had brought along was also a high-level mage, head and shoulders above any of those Council jerks, so the combined might of the three of them had been sufficient to put the Circle leaders in their places.

Finn's proposal had been worked out long before the meeting as well, which was one of the reasons why Maeve had been trying so hard to keep me under her thumb. As it so happened, the four of them had been talking since the first few fae bodies had started turning up. At first, Maeve really had been concerned it was the Pack or the Coven making a move against her, but Finnegas had quickly put those fears to rest and got them all scheming together against the real threat —the Circle.

That fit Finnegas had thrown at Maeve's hadn't just been for show, though. He had been well and truly pissed at the shit she was trying to pull, what with him working behind the scenes to help save her people. The old man said that the fae were like predators in the animal kingdom, which was why a display of strength was often necessary to solidify an alliance. And Maeve had fallen right in line, once she knew that the Seer still had some juice left in him.

Man, but I had a lot to learn. And I'd need to learn it fast, too, because Finn's proposal was a doozy. His idea was to make me something called a Druid Justiciar, a sort of independent investigator and enforcer whose job it was to keep peace between the supernatural races and humans. Apparently, it was a position originally created by The Dagda—part of his grand plan to even the scales between humans and the major powers in the world beneath.

So basically, I'd be doing what I'd been doing all along, but in an official capacity and without all the meddling and string-pulling bullshit from Maeve. Being a justiciar meant I had authority to deal with members of all races—humans, fae, vampires, 'thropes, and *other*. And by "deal," that meant doing whatever was necessary to make sure another Gunnarson situation never happened again.

Sure, I'll step on some necks to keep the peace. Hell, count me in for overtime.

As for Belladonna and the geek squad, once word got out about what had happened, the Circle couldn't punish them or slap them with a gag order. Instead, they decided to turn them into heroes so they could trot them out whenever someone brought up Gunnarson's crimes. The nerd herd took increases in pay in lieu of promotions—Kien got his six-figure salary, by the way—and Belladonna told the High Council to go fuck themselves. She pretty much gave them a two-fisted resignation letter, written in sign language and delivered straight to their faces.

That's my girl.

Click never did show up to finish "paying" me for solving the case and killing those responsible. I didn't bother discussing our deal with Finnegas either, seeing as how the mere mention of Click's name set his teeth on edge. But if the fae ever did come around, I intended to ask him how Gunnarson's cloak worked, because I still hadn't discovered how to control its powers.

I thought it a strange coincidence that he'd referred to me as a "justiciar" back when this whole thing had started. That was yet another thing I intended to ask him about.

Ed's funeral was a sad affair, but it was also a testament to all the lives he'd touched. The church was standing room only, and the funeral procession was a half-mile long. I served as one of the pall-bearers, along with the senior employees from the junkyard. Finnegas said a few words, and Maureen sang a Celtic dirge that ran chills down my spine. Mom cried and cried—again, that was the hardest part of all.

As for the junkyard, Maureen showed up with Borovitz the day after our big meeting with the High Council. Apparently, Ed left his entire estate to me, including the junkyard and everything in it. Unsurprisingly, the junkyard was just barely making a profit, because Ed had overpaid his people and was constantly giving away money to help others out.

Borovitz said all Ed's assets were tied up in the place. He also said I could liquidate the junkyard and everything in it, and that I'd easily walk away with enough money to set me up for life. I declined, saying I'd rather be broke and making people happy than rich and putting people out of work.

And all that gold? Carver didn't have any heirs, at least none that Borovitz could find. The hunter had planned to leave it all to his crew, if you can believe that. As for me, I didn't want Carver's dirty money. Long story short, I had Borovitz pay for funeral arrangements for the murder victims who couldn't afford it, and I had him set up a foundation for the sex trafficking survivors with the rest.

Today was my last day alone in the junkyard. I planned to open it back up for business tomorrow.

I'd been putting things back in order with Maureen's help, and generally just saying my last goodbyes to Ed. His memories would always be there, of course, but I needed a few days to make those memories behave themselves... if you know what I mean.

Now, there was just one last order of business—Elmo. I'd asked Finnegas what his last gesture had meant, and the old man said he'd been making the sign for "friend."

Some friend I was, for letting him get killed. Damn it.

Anyway, I wanted to give him some sort of monument, something to remind those who'd known him of his final resting place. He deserved so much more than an unmarked grave in the junkyard, but it'd look weird if I placed a gravestone right there among the stacks.

So, I'd just been sitting here at his gravesite, me and Elmo's furry plush toy, trying to figure out how to best honor the one person in this sordid affair who'd gotten the rawest end of the deal.

I felt something move beside me.

Did I put batteries in that stupid doll?

Nope. I looked down, and there was my Craneskin Bag on its side, flap wide open. I reached over to close it, but before I could something rolled out. It was dark, round, and shiny, with a light brown cap and stem on one end.

The Dagda's acorn.

"Bag, are you trying to tell me something?" The Bag flipped itself closed and clammed up tight as a nun's knees. "Okay... I'll take that as a yes."

I held the acorn up to my eye, examining it and rubbing it between my fingers. As I did, the tree seed warmed to my touch, almost as if it had life inside of it that was trying to get out... or maybe that *wanted* to get out.

"Alright, little acorn. I can't think of a better monument to the life of such a gentle giant as Elmo. Let's put you in the ground, and give you the shot at life that he no longer has."

I knelt down, using my hunting knife to scoop dirt away— just a small divot of earth in the center of the aisle where we'd laid the ogre's body to rest. I went to place the acorn in the ground, then paused—was I missing something? On instinct, I held the acorn in my palm and spat on it. It was a strange and impulsive gesture, but it seemed proper in the moment.

I set the acorn in the ground and pushed the dirt back over the hole. I patted the dirt gently, not wanting to pack it so tight that the little acorn wouldn't grow. Then I stood, taking a step back to admire my handiwork.

"Ah, shit. How am I going to keep people from trampling it, once it starts to grow?" I racked my brains for ideas for several seconds, then the ground beneath my feet began to rumble and quake.

"What the f—?"

This concludes Book 5 in the Colin McCool Paranormal Suspense series, *Druid Justice*. But, the story continues in Book 6, *Druid Enforcer*!

Be sure to sign up for updates at my website, so you can be among the first to know when it releases:

MDMassey.com

Plus, you'll get two free ebooks, just for subscribing!

ABOUT THE AUTHOR

I write dark fantasy, paranormal suspense, and urban fantasy novels.

My first series, THEM, is a jaunt through a post-apocalyptic central Texas where the dead walk, and vampires, werewolves and other unsavory creatures roam the night. It has elements of the zompoc genre, dark fantasy, and military survival fiction.

On the other hand, my Colin McCool series falls squarely between urban fantasy and paranormal suspense. Colin's world is full of magic, mystery, and folklore come to life.

I currently live in the Hill Country near Austin, Texas, which is where much of my fiction is set. Most days you can find me in a local coffee shop or in my office working on my next book, or in my garage pummeling inanimate objects. If you'd like to find out more about my work and get a FREE book, visit my website at MDMassey.com.

facebook.com/mdmasseyauthor

twitter.com/mdmasseyauthor

instagram.com/authormdmassey

CPSIA information can be obtained
at www.ICGtesting.com
Printed in the USA
BVHW041732250520
580290BV00012B/290